RUMBIN GALLERIES

BOOTH TARKINGTON

RUMBIN GALLERIES

ILLUSTRATED BY RITCHIE COOPER

THE LITERARY GUILD OF AMERICA, INC.
New York   1937

To
BETTY TROTTER

ILLUSTRATIONS

RUMBIN GALLERIES

CHAPTER ONE

IN HUMAN AFFAIRS cause and effect often behave not like the inseparable twins science says they are but like two harebrains never even acquainted. Young Howard Cattlet's acting as an usher at a classmate's wedding settled his destiny not by means of a marvelous bridesmaid but because he was unable to borrow an usher's uniform and had to have one made.

Thus, just out of college in the deep midst of the Depression, he had a home, parents, two sisters, one brother, a "cutaway" and some other clothes; but no income. Seeking his fortune, he began to commute between his native Hackertown, New Jersey, and the city of New York, where he strove patiently to join the diminished army of the employed. Systematic, he began an orderly geographical combing of northern Manhattan in mid-June, and was dishearteningly down as far as Seventeenth Street by the end of the month. Anything but an electric, eye-to-eye, make-it-happen young man, he was large, slow-spoken, good-looking somewhat solemnly; and a solemn sort of thoroughness was a sturdy element in his character. Nothing less could have led him to include in his list an advertisement for an Art Dealer's Assistant.

On the morning of the first of July, he crossed over from West Seventeenth Street (where his offer to become a Night Watchman had been declined) and walked valiantly to the address of the Art Dealer on the eastern stretch of that same thoroughfare. Arrived at the shop, he found it to be upon the ground floor, and paused to learn what he could from its rather dusty exterior. There was a recessed half-glass door and a single display window; not a large one, yet imposing, even a little pompous, because of the gilt lettering it bore.

RUMBIN GALLERIES

CHEFS D'ŒUVRES   PEINTURES   SCULPTURES

OLD MASTERS   OBJETS D'ART   PERIOD FURNITURE

Inside the window were two candelabra—black bronze Venuses or Muses, or somebody, upholding gilt flowers from which rose the candles—and between the candelabra, upon a mound of green velvet, was a venerable murky landscape painting from which young Howard Cattlet got only the impression that he wouldn't like to own it. Already discouraged, he nevertheless doggedly stuck to his routine, opened the half-glass door and went in.

Within the oblong room he was aware of dark old-looking paintings upon brown walls, of old sofas in faded colors, of stools, tables and commodes in unfamiliar shapes; and beyond this daunting foreground he saw at the shadowy other end of the room two people—a fair-haired young woman at a desk and a thin, baggy-kneed man who spoke to her urgently.

She interrupted him. Her clear, light voice was but too audible to the young man near the door.

"Professor Ensill, your experience with the Amwilton Museum and on the Institute's art faculty would be valuable of course; but there isn't the slightest use for you to wait till Mr. Rumbin comes in. I mustn't hold out any false hopes to you, Professor Ensill. I'm sorry."

Professor Ensill's shoulders drooped. "Well, I'll keep on with that damn Orcas," Howard Cattlet heard him say. "I'd hoped for almost any kind of change—but all right." He turned from the desk, and, on his way out, set drearily a soiled grey felt hat upon his scholarly head. Before the door closed behind him, young Howard decided to depart also.

He was in motion toward the street when the young woman at the desk rose, came forward and spoke to him.

"May I show you something?"

"No," he said. "No, I believe not."

"No? Perhaps you came in answer to Mr. Rumbin's advertisement?"

"I—yes, I believe I—"

"Then why don't you—"

"Thank you," Howard said. "I wouldn't do."

To his astonishment she said thoughtfully, "I don't know," and for a strange moment the scrutiny he had from her intelligent grey eyes was appreciative. "I think I'll take your name."

He gave it, wistfully adding his address, then again moved toward the door; but she still detained him. "Wait here."

She went to a door at the rear of the shop, opened it, called "Mr. Rumbin!" and returned to her desk. A wide silhouette appeared in the doorway; she said, "Mr. Howard Cattlet, Hackertown, New Jersey," and applied herself to a typewriter.

Mr. Rumbin came forward, a middle-aged active fat man with a glowing eye. His features, not uncomely, were flexibly expressive, like an actor's, and just now, oddly, seemed anxious to be ingratiating. "Hackertown?" he said to the solemn applicant.

"Mr. Howard Cappits, you know Mr. and Mrs. Waldemar Hetzel that built the macknificent country residence looks like maybe a chateau outside Hackertown, anyways costs half a million dollars?"

"Hetzel? No, I—"

"Then you couldn't intaduce 'em to me," Mr. Rumbin said regretfully, a foreign accent of elusive origin becoming a little more noticeable in his speech. "Hanover Galleries sold 'em a Claude for hundut seventy-two t'ousand dollars. It's nice money; it's a crime." He sighed; then smiled almost affectionately. "Where was you before?" he asked.

"Before? Where was I?" However, comprehending that the question sought for his previous business experience, the young man explained that he hadn't any; but mentioned a possible qualification. In his Junior year he had attended a course of lectures on the Fundamentals of Aesthetics and had passed the examination. He hadn't passed it prominently, he thought right to add; but still he had passed.

Mr. Rumbin, though looking at him attentively, listened with indifference; and, when the applicant produced a written approval of his morals from the Rector of St. Mark's, Hackertown, gave it but an absent glance and returned it.

"Listen," Mr. Rumbin said. "You got a cutaway suit?"

"A what?" Howard said. "Yes, I have. I've only had it on once."

"You got a useful face, too," Mr. Rumbin observed, frank in meditation. "You don't show nothing on it. Like you ain't got no feelings. Like maybe you got high educated brains, too, or not; nobody would be surprised which." Suddenly he smiled beamingly, glanced back toward the girl at the typewriter. "Putty good. Oddawise Georchie wouldn't kept you for me to look at. I take you."

"What? You say—"

"On prohibition," Mr. Rumbin added quickly. "On prohibition the first couple weeks. After that, if I commence liking you, it's permanent. Twelve dollars a week. Make it fourteen."

"Fourteen?" Dazed, Howard seemed to perceive that his wedding garment, supplemented slightly by his face, was perhaps launching him upon a career. "Fourteen? When would you—when do I—when—"

"When you commence, Mr. Howard Cappits? To-day, now; it's got to be some time, ain't it?" Mr. Rumbin became confidential. "Fourteen a week payable mont'ly not in adwance. It's awful good; it's splendid. You got everything to learn there is. Besides the cutaway, you got to have some overalls."

"Overalls?"

"Howard," Mr. Rumbin said, "part of the work from beings my assistant, it's maybe some like a janitor. Sometimes you'll be using the floor-mop; you get to wash the windows, too, and I'm going to teach you how to dust *objets d'art*—it's puttikler. To-day, though, immediately I got to teach you something elst quick. Come to the stock room; I show you." Then, followed dumbly, the astounding man walked to the rear of the shop, but paused for a moment near the desk. "I intaduce you to Georchie; but don't *you* call her Georchie—her name's my sec'tary Miss Georchina Horne. When I ain't here she's the same as me. Got me, Howard?"

Miss Georgina Horne gave Howard a nod that didn't interrupt her typing. Howard murmured, and then said more distinctly, "Yes, sir."

" 'Sir'," Mr. Rumbin repeated, pleased again. " 'Sir', that's nice. Calling me 'sir' natchal I won't got to keep hollering at you for not doing it like that Bennie-feller I had last mont'." He spoke to Miss Horne. "He's got the cutaway, Georchie. At the elevenst hour you picked one with. It's like a Providence!"

He passed through the doorway that had admitted him only a few decisive minutes previously, and the owner of the cutaway went with him into a cluttered and confusing room. A few wide shelves occupied two of the walls; and, upon these shelves, framed pictures stood, not leaning against one another but separated by fixed uprights of wood. Against the third wall other pictures leaned, too large for the shelves; the middle part of the floor was crowded with old chairs and sofas, and close to the fourth wall stood cabinets, chests, console tables, commodes and an iron safe.

Mr. Rumbin put a fond, fat hand upon a panel of one of the cabinets. "Locked," he said. "Some day if I commence liking you, I show you. Ivories, porcelains, little Renaissance bronzes maybe. Ha!" He patted the black metal door of the safe. "Treasures! Some day maybe." The glow of his eyes became a glisten. "Maybe a couple pieces Limoges enamel. Maybe even one Byzantine enamel on gold —Saint Luke, size of a playing-card, Elevenst Century maybe. Maybe a couple little Got'ic Crozier Heads, so-called. Maybe a Fourteent' Century Pyx. Who I sell 'em to?" Abruptly he became somber. "Where's a real collector not dead that ain't lost his money or elst some pig dealer ain't already got him?" He sighed; then brightened and said briskly, "We commence! You got to learn a program. We start it with the Follower of Domenikos Theotocopoulos."

"Sir?" The course in the Fundamentals of Aes-

thetics wasn't helping Howard much; he didn't
know what Mr. Rumbin had been talking about or
was talking about now. "Sir?"

"Domenikos Theotocopoulos, it's El Greco's right
name," Mr. Rumbin explained kindly, completing his
listener's incomprehension. " 'El Greco', that only
means 'The Greek', Domenikos Theotocopoulos
beings a Greekish feller; so it's like somebody can't
pronounce your own name and calls you 'The
Hackertowner'. El Greco beings he's a painter with
his own style, all peculiar, natchly he had Followers.
Here, I show you." He took a picture from a shelf,
set it against a chair in the light, and asked, "How
you like it?"

Howard hopelessly thought it was terrible. What
he saw seemed the likeness of a gigantic sentimental
bearded person with a minute head. Clad in a robe
of twisted blue tin, he walked barefooted among
either rocks or clouds of lead foil. Howard wondered if the job depended upon his liking such a picture; but he couldn't lie flagrantly.

"I don't, sir."

"Right!" the surprising Rumbin said. "In odda
worts, this fine splendid picture of mine, we wouldn't
say it's a painting by El Greco himself nor by El
Greco's son and some oddas, because El Greco's son
you often can't hardly tell from El Greco himself,

only he's more so; but this picture you maybe could. That's why it comes first on the program. Got it?"

"Not—not yet, sir," Howard admitted. "I'm afraid I don't understand what you mean by the program."

"No? Sit down. I'll—" Mr. Rumbin interrupted himself. "Not in that chair! It's *Régence* needle-point; it's real. Here, we sit on this *Louis Treize* sofa; it ain't." Then, as they sat together upon the sofa, he spoke suavely. "I got just time to teach you the A P C of the alphabet. In art how you hendle a program it's your heart and pants. Oddawise give up hoping you'll ever get the ideel client."

"Client, sir? You mean—"

"Client!" Mr. Rumbin said emphatically. "In art it ain't customers, it's clients. Listen intelligencely. What a dealer needs, it's ideel clients. Ideel clients, the kind that won't trust no odda dealer, there ain't many. Some the piggest dealers ever was didn't had but two. Me? Give me only one that's ideel enough and I move up to Fifty-seven' Street! I got one coming this afternoon that might be; it's a chance. Got it?"

"Well, I—I—"

"If she gets made into a picture collector, it's all!" Mr. Rumbin became so confidential he spoke in little more than a whisper. "Six up to nine millions her husband the last seven years took in. Just found out she oughts to collect art. Some odda dealer'll get her if I ain't quick. You see, Howie?"

"I—more or less, sir. I—"

"Right!" Rumbin said. "Now we come to what's a program. Howie, it's uniwersal if you got a important article you want somebody to buy, only a bum would right away show him this article. If he likes skyscrapers and you want to sell him the Empire State Building, you wouldn't say nothing about it until after you got him discouraged showing him t'ree-story buildings and a couple car-barns maybe. Then you spring the Empire State, just before you got him too tired out to be excited. That's a program. It's execkly what we do in the galleries this afternoon."

"The Galleries?" Howard asked. "Where—"

"The Galleries it's the whole place; but in puttikler it's too a room from a door across the shop. When the client comes, I take her in the galleries; but you are waiting here. When you hear the buzzer, you pick up the Follower of Domenikos Theotocopoulos, bring it into the galleries, put it on a easel, stand looking at it just natchal till I tell you go beck and bring the next."

"The next, sir?"

Mr. Rumbin jumped up, replaced the Follower of

Domenikos Theotocopoulos upon its shelf. "Listen,
I got a feeling it's the most important day in my
life! Here, one next to the odda, it's fixed in order
the program, these special fife pictures you bring in
the galleries one at a time. After that you don't do
nothing at all, because it ain't any of these fife is the
one I got to sell her. That's my great Clouet; and it
I'm going to bring in myself. All you do is carry pictures. Got it?"

"Yes, sir, I—I think I—"

"Right!" Mr. Rumbin said abruptly. "Go put on
the cutaway suit."

"Sir? But it's out at—"

"Hackertown, New Chersey," Mr. Rumbin said.
"Be beck execkly half past two o'clock in it."

"I doubt if—" young Howard began; then he had
an important second thought and said, "Yes, sir."

CHAPTER TWO

HOWARD CATTLET's doubt had been of the time allowed; but by moving more rapidly than was usual with him he made it sufficient and re-entered Rumbin Galleries at almost the precise moment named. His employer, whose shining broad face showed excitement, approved of him.

"Pyootiful!" Mr. Rumbin exclaimed, and turned to Miss Georgina Horne. She was delicately passing a small feather duster over the landscape in the display window. "Georchie," Mr. Rumbin asked dramatically, "Georchie, you see it?"

Howard, slightly offended, wasn't sure whether "it" applied to himself or to his brave apparel; then discovered that something more elaborate than either was intended. Miss Horne nodded seriously at Mr. Rumbin and said, "It'll do."

"Do?" the dealer cried. "It's double a hundut per cent perfect! Me in only a nice sack suit but with a cutaway to order around—it's a picture!" Between thumb and forefinger he took a fold of his new assistant's sleeve, examined the texture. "Fine! Listen, Howie, I ain't going to ring no buzzer for you. After I got her in the galleries, I commence the program myself with my great Dutch lentscape from the window here; then next I open the door and call to Georchie. 'Miss Horne,' I'll say, 'send me the Head Assistant with the Follower of Domenikos Theotocopoulos.' Got it, Howie? It's more connoisseur than a buzzer and like there's more of you than just you. Get beck in the stock room so she don't see you right first when she comes in."

"Yes, sir." Then, on his way to the rear of the shop, Howard heard Mr. Rumbin speaking further, though in a lowered voice, to the grey-eyed secretary.

"That puttikler dumb look he's got when you talk to him it's good, too; it's aristocratic."

Howard, reddening somewhat, went into the stock room, closed the door and sat down on the *Louis Treize* sofa that wasn't. He stared at the strange furniture and at the racks of paintings, which he suspected of being even queerer than the furniture. The Follower of What's-His-Name certainly was. "Doman—" he said aloud. "Domanigo—Follower of Domanigo Tea—" He didn't believe he'd ever be able to remember all of El Greco's real name. Maybe, though, he could learn to be a good Assistant Art Dealer without having to know how to pronounce everything distinctly. "Domanigo Teacupply," he murmured, and thought that coughing in the middle of such names might help. He tried it, wasn't satisfied, gave up, and sat apprehensive—just waiting.

Miss Horne opened the door. "It'll be easy," she said, comprehending the apprehension, though his expression was merely stolid. "Just watch Mr. Rumbin carefully and be natural. Mrs. Hollins is here. You're to take the El Greco into the galleries."

Howard rose. "El Greco? He said it was a Follower of—"

"It's changed," Miss Horne informed him, not smiling. "It's the same picture. Take it in."

He took the painting from the shelf; then paused. He'd begun to like Miss Horne's appearance and had an impulse to talk to her. "Suppose the—the client asks me a question about one of the pictures—"

"Mr. Rumbin'll answer it," Miss Horne said. "When you've put the picture on the easel don't stand between it and Mrs. Hollins. Go ahead."

He obeyed, carried the picture out of the stock room, across the shop and into the "galleries". In the center of the rather small room, a lady sat in a velvet chair, looking peevishly at the murky brown landscape, which was upon an easel at a little distance before her. She was fragile, restless-looking, thinly pretty, and what she wore was of a delicate prettiness, too; a dress of ivorine silk, a hat of cream and old rose—colors that were echoed in the frail rose-and-ivory wrap drooping from the back of her chair. Mr. Rumbin had placed an ash-tray upon a little table beside her, for her cigarette, and he stood deferentially, though with an enthusiastic facial expression, at a little distance to the right of the displayed picture. He seemed unaware of his assistant's entrance.

"Not two people in a million," he was saying, "not two people in t'ree million would right away said like you, Mrs. Kingsford J. Hollins, this great Seventeent' Century Dutch School Italian lentscape it's too brown, it's too dark. In some people it's a instinck to be a connoisseur; it's born! Mrs. Kingsford J. Hollins, I congratulate you!"

"Oh, I don't know," Mrs. Hollins said. "I only know I know that picture's too brown and it's too dark."

"Too brown and too dark is right! Look!" The dealer made a gracefully negligent gesture toward his new employee. "Look, it's a young Herr Doktor from the Uniwersity, the Galleries' Head Assistant. Even he ain't never noticed it's too brownish dark.

Me? It shows I could be twenty-fife years a art dealer and still got something to learn. It's mirackalous!"

He removed the landscape, set it against a wall; and Howard, inwardly upset by the doctor's degree just conferred upon him, placed the Follower upon the easel.

"There!" Mr. Rumbin cried. "My great El Greco. You like?"

"Murder, no!" Mrs. Hollins said. "I should say not!"

Mr. Rumbin's enthusiasm for her was unbounded. He appealed to Howard passionately. "Didn't I told you yesterday right after I got the privilege she announces me she'll come to Rumbin Galleries, didn't I told you then right away I got beck she's a collector? Simply, it's proved!" More calmly, he addressed the client. "You're right it ain't no positive El Greco, Mrs. Kingsford J. Hollins. More it's like a Follower Of. If I had Mrs. Kingsford J. Hollins's eye for collecting I wouldn't been no art dealer; I'd be a Museum Director." He spoke again to Howard. "Bring my great Diaz flower piece."

"Wait. I don't like pictures of flowers," Mrs. Hollins said discontentedly. "Have you got anything by Leonardo da Vinci?"

"By who?" Mr. Rumbin's ample voice was suddenly small; he seemed enfeebled. "Who?"

"Leonardo da Vinci," Mrs. Hollins repeated. "I like that Mona Lisa of his immensely. Haven't you—"

"Frangkly, no." Mr. Rumbin, swallowing, convalesced after shock. "Frangkly speaking, I ain't never carried no Leonardos. Leonardos they're more less scarce; some people think there ain't almost any." Completing his recovery, he beamed upon her again. "It's good taste, though. Vonderful taste!" He spoke hurriedly to the Head Assistant. "Leaf out that next picture, the flowers."

"Yes, sir." Howard intelligently returned to the stock room, came back to the galleries bringing the third picture of the program, not the second. He placed it upon the easel from which Mr. Rumbin had removed the Follower Of. The new offering was an aged wooden panel with a surface of pigments once violent but now dulled into a dingy harmony.

"Adoration of the Magi by a Pupil of the Master of the Holy Kinship of Cologne." Standing beside the easel, Rumbin moved his right thumb in exquisite curves as though using it to repaint the ancient picture. "Them Madonna's robes! Sweetness! Them beards on the Wise Men! Majesty! Macknificent Flemish influenced prim—"

"Not as a gift!" Mrs. Hollins said. "You must think I'm crazy." She looked at a diamond-bordered wrist watch. "Listen. Kingsford J. and I're going on a three weeks motor trip to-morrow; I can't sit around here all day."

The new assistant, beginning to understand "programs" a little, was certain that this one had gone too far in discouraging the client and that she'd passed the precise degree of fatigue after which she could be made to get excited. He had not yet learned that his employer was himself an artist.

"Mrs. Kingsford J. Hollins," Rumbin said, in a low and breathless voice, "it makes me feel senseless. Simply, it shows a *grande dame* can be also a connoisseur. One look and you reckanized a Flemish influenced primitive ain't tasteful in your apartment. Ah, but wait!" He became dramatically commanding. "Bring my great Rosa Bonheur!"

"Yes, sir," Howard said, and turned to go; but, behind Mrs. Hollins's chair, Rumbin strode to him, whispered fiercely.

"*Ask Georchie!*"

Instantly the dealer turned smiling to his client. Howard went out to the shop and approached Miss Horne. "I think he must be mixing up the program. He told me to bring his great Rosa Bonheur."

"It's the side of a house; you'll need help," she said. "Come on."

She led the way into the stock room, and there

went to an enormous picture, the largest of those that leaned, backs outward, against the wall. Coincidentally there began to stir within Howard Cattlet, as he followed the competent young figure, a new and pleasurable feeling. It seemed to him that he might become warmly interested in his new calling on its own account. An art dealer's life, he perceived, could be absorbing.

"What's he want to show her this one for?" he asked. "She's beginning to be pretty sore; why doesn't he spring the one he really wants her to buy?"

"He's still preparing her mind for that climax." Miss Horne took a soft cloth from a shelf and applied it carefully to the edges of the big picture's frame. "He knows of course she'll say this Rosa Bonheur is preposterously too large; that's just what he wants her to say. Then, after that, he'll suddenly show her the Clouet, the portrait of a handsome Valois gentleman in jewels and velvet—a lovely small size and a really beautiful picture, too."

"Clouet? He was French, wasn't he?"

"Flemish and French," Miss Horne said, continuing to wipe the great gilt frame. "Of course there aren't more than ten or eleven fairly certain Clouets—the French Revolution wiped out so many records and pictures, too, you see—but likely enough one of the Clouets painted Mr. Rumbin's Clouet."

"One of them? One of the—"

"Yes, or one of the shop-staff of one of the Clouets. Of course, though, it just might be a Sixteenth Century police portrait."

"Sixteenth Cen—" Howard looked at the shelves laden with baffling and oppressive pictures. "Police what?"

"They didn't have photographs in those days," she explained. "Pretty often they sent around copies of portraits of somebody who was wanted or escaped. Then take all the copies they gave their friends, and naturally you hear a good many small French portraits being called Clouet or Corneille de Lyon or—"

"Corneille—Corneille de who?" He looked at her humbly. "Do you have to know all these things about every picture in the world? How does anybody ever learn such a business?"

She gave him a glance in which there may have been some compassion; then was brisk. "You'll pick up a good deal from Mr. Rumbin—if you stay. We'd better be getting ahead with the Rosa Bonheur; he's had about as much time as he wants for talking between. I'll only go as far with you as the door to the galleries."

One at each end of the heavy picture, they lifted

it, carried it from the stock room and across the shop.
Miss Horne proved to be one of those surprising
girls who don't look very strong but are; she was
also capably executive. Near the door of the galleries
she whispered, "Stop here!" and the two stood still.
Mr. Rumbin could be heard speaking appetizingly
of paintings of animals—of Paulus Potter's im-
mortal Bull, of superb cows by Troyon, of Monti-
celli's jewelled fowls, of splendid goats by Salvatore
Rosa. Other sonorous names rolled out from the
unctuous voice; and Howard Cattlet, beginning to be
fascinated, wished he knew something about them.
Also, he hoped they were impressing Mrs. Hollins,
and thus, almost unconsciously, the young man had
the first symptoms of a loyal apprenticeship.

Miss Georgina Horne coughed rather loudly; her
employer interrupted himself.

"Ah! She arrive', my great Rosa Bonheur!"

He came hurrying forth, took Miss Horne's place;
and then, as he and his assistant brought their
burden into the galleries and placed it before Mrs.
Hollins, reproached him gayly. "Ah, these young
Herr Doktors! *Never* should you lift a such picture alone! Why didn't you call Schmidt or Raoul to
help you?"

"Sir?"

"Never mind," Rumbin said hastily. "She's too pig

to go on the easel, set her down on the floor; we each holt her up at a corner. There! Mrs. Kingsford J. Hollins, the greatest of all animal painters, Rosa Bonheur! You seen her works in the Louvre, in the Metropolitan. I ask you as a connoisseur, which? Them or this, which?" He used his free thumb as if repainting again. "This left ear of this horse! That little passage there! Organization! Seven horses— four great grand foreground horses putty near life size, and t'ree behind in the beckground—altogedda seven horses. Action! Movement! Power! Simply, it's majesty!"

Howard looked at Mrs. Hollins expectantly, awaiting her denunciation of the seven horses; but, to his astonishment, her mood of bored annoyance seemed to change. She stopped smoking.

"Listen!" she said. "Why didn't you show this one to me in the first place? I got an uncle used to have horses like that on his stock farm. I always did like horses. Yessir; that's a right good picture." Her appreciation increased; she nodded decisively. "I'll take that one," she said.

"Madame?" Mr. Rumbin stared at her, chopfallen. "You say—you say you wish to acquire this great pig Rosa Bonheur?"

"I'll take it," she said, rising. "I'll take it if you can find a nice place for it in my apartment. Send it up this afternoon." She turned to Howard amiably. "Doctor Um, do you mind telling my chauffeur to bring up the car?"

Howard went out to the street and found a glossy cream-colored touring-car already before the door. He spoke to the chauffeur, who descended and stood by. Mrs. Hollins came from the shop. Mr. Rumbin accompanied her, voluble upon the lifelong joy she'd have in her great Rosa Bonheur and the honor her visit had done him. Bowing from where his waist should have been, he kissed her gloved hand, bowed her into the car and bowed thrice again as it moved away. Then, with a stricken face, he rapidly preceded his assistant into the shop.

"Georchie!" he cried hoarsely to Miss Horne, who was replacing the Italianate Dutch landscape in the window. "Georchie, complete hell she knocked out of the program! The Clouet she never even seen, buys the Rosa Bonheur, never asks the price, I'm ruined!"

CHAPTER THREE

THIS LAMENT of Mr. Rumbin's, one sustained out-cry, he uttered as he strode tragically through the shop, and the last and loudest of it, "I'm ruined!" was heard from within the galleries, where he seemed to wish to seclude himself with his anguish. To the new assistant, art dealing appeared to be a con-founding business. Here was the very largest pic-ture in the place sold—and the fortunate dealer expressing agony in a Latin manner! Howard again sought enlightenment from the serious, grey-eyed secretary.

"What on earth's he mean? How's he—"

" 'Ruined' ?" she said sadly. "It might be. It's a long time since we've made a sale. He really hasn't had any client at all and he'd set all his hopes on getting her down here to-day; he was pretty sure it was his last chance. It's a pity. He's an extraordi-nary man and lovely to work for. I'm afraid you

ought to know, Mr. Cattlet, because maybe you'd
better not count on—on—"

"On my wages?"

"Yes. He mightn't be able—"

"Yours, too?" Howard asked. For a moment the
two young people looked at each other in com-
radely concern; he had a sympathetic inspiration.
"You haven't had yours for a long time, have you,
Miss Horne?" Then, as she didn't reply, he protested, "But since he's just sold that big picture, why
on earth—"

"It's because—"

She got no further; Mr. Rumbin, looking as haggard as a heartily healthy fat man can, came striding vehemently from the galleries. "Try to sell her
a white mice; no, she buys a elephant! Buys a work
of art because she had a uncle with a stock farm!
Menacheries I could sell. Old Masters? No! I'm a
animals seller!"

"Don't give up," Georgina said. "Mr. Rumbin, it
isn't certain—"

"Certain? It ain't certain I'm benkrupt, either; it
just looks like it!" The dealer sank into a chair,
wiped his forehead. "In the first place, how would I
make a price? Year Eighteen eighty-eight a Rosa Bonheur sold twenty-one t'ousand dollars Christie's.
Nineteen twenty-eight it sells again, the same picture

identical, at Christie's, forty-six guineas; it's maybe
two hundut t'irty dollars. Ask anybody rich under ten
t'ousand dollars for a picture that size, they think it's
no good. If I ask Mrs. Kingsford J. Hollins twenty
t'ousand dollars, somebody comes in, tells her, 'I seen
a Rosa Bonheur good as yours, two hundut t'irty
dollars.' Right away she sues me!"

"No, she wouldn't," Miss Horne said. "She
wouldn't want her husband to know she'd been that
foolish."

"Georchie, I'm a art dealer, not a bleckmailer
—not yet I ain't. To-morrow who knows! Yet all
the time, what's the use talking the price of a mountain that starts her screeching, 'Take it beck out!'
soon as it's inside her apartment where I would got
to hire a architect to block up windows to—"

"Mr. Rumbin, you don't *know* there isn't wall
space. You haven't seen Mrs. Hollins's apartment.
Aren't you even going to try?"

"Try? Am I going to try?" A change almost
startling took place within and upon Mr. Rumbin;
he rose, grimly Napoleonic. "Them seven horses goes
into Mrs. Kingsford J. Hollins's apartment! The
price it's t'irteen t'ousand eight hundut fifty, sue me
or not. Georchie, get me Schwankel's truck on the
'phone. Howie, put on your hat; me and you ride in
the truck with the Rosa Bonheur. It safes a taxi and

teaches you hendling pictures. I create Mrs. Kingsford J. Hollins into my ideel client if it kills her!"

. . . One item of this desperate declaration the
apprentice found warranted. After getting the Rosa
Bonheur into and out of the freight elevator at the
Park Avenue apartment building, and moved from
one to another of Mr. and Mrs. Hollins's costly
rooms, Howard Cattlet indeed had learned something about the handling of pictures. The more skill
he acquired, however, the less hopeful dared he be
that Miss Horne's arrears of salary might be paid
(he put this first) and that he could establish himself firmly as an Art Dealer's Assistant.

It was his chief who snuffed out the last glimmer.
The two were left alone together by Mr. Hollins's
valet, who had accompanied them throughout most
of the laborious tour. Mr. Rumbin descended from
a stepladder, a tape-measure dangling from his flaccid hand.

"It's over!" He spoke in a husky whisper. "The
last chance—and she'd stick out nine inches across
them window-curtains!" His voice grew somewhat
louder and much bitterer. "The both drawing-rooms,
the reception-room, the music-room, dining-room
and Mr. Hollins's damn den—if it ain't a door it's a
window, and if it ain't a window it's a fireplace too

narrow, and if it ain't a fireplace it's a alcove stops it. Look! Decorated by Moultons; I'd know 'em anywhere—reds, whites, silvers, choc'lates, overstuffed brocades, new golds, silver-gilt French 'phones, bleck marble shiny Egypt cats—it oughts to be against the law! What Moultons must stuck 'em, anyways a hundut t'ousand, I know their prices, they're hogs, it's criminal!" He drooped again, smiled piteously. "Howie, I might commenced liking you some time. The cutaway worked good, too. I'm sorry you ain't going to have no chob with me. I'm finish'. It's a receiver."

Howard had an innocently barbarous bright idea. "Mr. Rumbin, why couldn't you trim off part of this picture and—"

"Orcas would; he's a wandal." The dealer shook his head. "No, any way you try to cut this picture down it leafs part of a horse. Even a chauffeur would get upset to look at it."

Thus the end seemed to have come definitely. Master and apprentice stood silent, sharing calamity and listening to approaching voices.

Mrs. Hollins came in, accompanied by a bored little girl of thirteen, recognizably her daughter; and Howard despondently observed that the mother had changed her clothes but not her colors and that the daughter's garments were similar in tint. Mrs. Hol-

lins at Rumbin Galleries had worn a silk dress, cream
or old ivory, with a hat and wrap in which the same
color was patterned with tones of rose. Hatless, she
now wore a rose chiffon dress with creamy lace; and
the little girl had on a skirt of palest tan, pink socks,
light tan slippers and a tan blouse embroidered in
rose. The young assistant hadn't much of an eye for
ladies' dress and he was gloomy; but the irrelevant
thought came into his mind that Mrs. Hollins's taste
must run pretty strongly to these two colors.

"Well, Mr. Rumbin," she asked brightly, "have
you found a nice place for my horse picture to go?"

"You don't get it!" Again Howard was startled
by a change in his employer. Stooped in despair but
a moment ago, the dealer stood erect; his voice was
commanding, his look imperious and stern. "Mrs.
Kingsford J. Hollins, you are a connoisseur and I
am a connoisseur. I wouldn't sell you my Rosa Bonheur for a hundut t'ousand dollars!"

"What? What's the matter?"

"Matter? What ain't?" Rumbin's sternness increased to a passionate severity. "How long you had
this apartment, all hot reds, cold whites, hot
choc'lates, cold silvers, hots next to colds, hot over-
stuffings, gilt 'phones, marble cats? How long?"

"What?" She was annoyed but puzzled. "About a
year. What's that got to do with—"

"A year!" Rumbin seemed to swell with a noble
fury. "A year and already you are sick of it! I know
it. What connoisseur such as you could endure this
rhodomontado of colors? I don't ask who you let
decorate or what you got charged; but if it was t'irty
t'ousand dollars it was a murder! For execkly half
that much in t'ree weeks I would make this apartment so pyootiful it would look like connoisseurs and
angels dreamed it and Mrs. Kingsford J. Hollins
lived in it. Fifteen t'ousand dollars, make it eighteen
t'ousand, t'ree weeks while you're away, and it's a
heaven!"

"Nonsense! If you aren't going to hang up that
picture—"

"The Rosa Bonheur?" he cried. "Never! I sell
people what they *oughts* to have; Rosa Bonheur you
shall not. Pictures come after, not before. What you
shall have, it's this apartment all over—every room,
all, all the whole of it—in just shades of two colors
and no more."

She frowned. "What two colors?"

"Rose! Rose and ivory!" he shouted. "Old rose
and old ivory. Walls, curtains, draperies, carpets,
everything! No reds, no whites. Just rose and ivory,
Mrs. Kingsford J. Hollins, rose and ivory!"

Mrs. Hollins's lips parted; her startled eyes grew
large. Like a magician, Rumbin, glaring, held her

fixed gaze with his, while the little girl, boredom suddenly gone, jumped up and down.

"Mamma, it sounds perfectly dee-vine!" she squealed. "Mamma, all we got to do I'll tell Papa it'll get you nervous again if he don't like it. Mamma, let's do it!"

"Listen," Mrs. Hollins said. "I believe it'd be right pretty. Kingsford J.'s just come in and gone to his den. Yessir, I believe I'll go tell him. It sounds good. Come on, Lulu; we'll spring it on him."

"Yay, Mamma!" The little girl, screaming with pleasure, ran out of the room and her mother followed.

Rumbin called after them. "Rose and ivory! All in tones of rose and ivory exceptings Mr. Hollins's den. He likes it; it stays. All the rest rose and ivory. All finish' done complete when you get beck from your t'ree weeks motor trip you start on to-morrow. Rose and ivory!"

He strode to a glossy oval table, picked up an instrument of silver-gilt and placed himself in communication with Rumbin Galleries. "Georchie, to-morrow morning I get me t'ree weeks more lease life again from the benk. Call up them inside house painters, Bort and Zolex, tell 'em be six o'clock this afternoon at the Galleries. Get me Frank the carpenter six-t'irty. Call up Orcas; tell him I maybe got a use for his Beauvais sofa and his six rose-and-cream *petit point* chairs, holt 'em, I see him to-morrow. The Rosa Bonheur it's out for good; forget it. I got a deal eighteen t'ousand dollars costs me twenty-fife, I lose seven. If it comes off t'ree weeks from now, Georchie, we move to Fifty-sevent' Street. If it don't your celery's maybe not and I'm sick in chail!"

CHAPTER FOUR

HOWARD CATTLET, listening, comprehended that he was still—though only by a hair—an Art Dealer's Assistant. He perceived also that the Rosa Bonheur was a dead issue; that his employer, penniless, intended to redecorate Mr. and Mrs. Hollins's apartment in rose and ivory at a cost to himself of twenty-five thousand dollars, for which he would receive eighteen thousand—and at this point the young man's mind seemed to be failing him. Mr. Rumbin, tense, made no explanation as they returned with the seven horses in Schwankel's truck to Seventeenth Street; nor did Miss Georgina Horne enlighten Howard at the Galleries, either then or later.

She couldn't, because she didn't know.

"There are times," she said, "when Mr. Rumbin hardly dares to let *himself* know what he's up to. He never does like questions much, anyhow; and we must just remember he's a remarkable man." She paused, then added conscientiously, "That is, I mean if you feel you'd like to stay—and can take the chance?"

Howard did wish to stay, would take the chance, and told her so. His unmentioned thought was that, even at the worst, three weeks of intimate association with old paintings, *objets d'art* and Miss Horne would add much to his knowledge; but here he erred. Mr. Rumbin moved as the whirlwind; his employees whirled with him, and, beginning next morning (in overalls) Howard was kept too furiously busy to learn anything except how to hurry unnaturally. During the whole of the vital period his association with Miss Horne was fragmentary, flitting and never anything like intimate.

He had an intimate association with Schwankel's truckmen, however, moving the furniture, carpets, rugs, curtains and ornamental clutter of the absent Hollins family out of their apartment and into a storage warehouse until not a trace of Moultons was left, except in Mr. Hollins's damn den. Also, he brought to Park Avenue momentous truckloads from Rumbin Galleries, and crates from auction rooms wherein Rumbin had plainly been plunging. Most of the time the assistant was kept at the apartment where, among jostling workmen, he measured floors, ran errands, mixed buckets of paint and carried them up stepladders to a fevered chief turned painter and working passionately to obtain exquisite accuracies in color.

Mr. Rumbin had begun to look like a thin fat man. On the last morning of the Hollins family's absence, he came into the Galleries pallid, having worked at the apartment all night, alone.

"We take my great Clouet in a taxi, Georchie," he said. "You get a sandwich in your left hand for lunch and dinner. You come, too, to-day. She wires me from Glouchester they're home eight o'clock this evening. Up to date, twenty-seven t'ousand eight hundut forty-one dollars, sixty-two cents, and noon comes the second drawing-room's carpet eighteen hundut fifty. Hurry, Georchie!"

Thus the assistant, unrolling a beautifully faded Aubusson rug, had the pleasure of seeing morning sunlight momentarily gild the fair head of the secretary as she came into the apartment and passed a window in the corridor. Until late in the afternoon he had only glimpses of her, mostly through doorways; then Mr. Rumbin sent him to help her hang the Clouet above the narrow mantel in the reception-room, and they were alone together.

"Even I can see it's a grand little thing," he said from the stepladder, in allusion to the glowing small picture she lifted to him. "It goes in for the eighteen thousand, too, does it? Either he's crazy or I am!"

Georgina was pale. "Even at auction this Clouet ought to bring four to seven thousand dollars. He's put the Largillière Duchess over the mantel in the first drawing-room and the Francis Cotes Lady Blount over the mantel in the second, with the English Eighteenth Century furniture. He's got the Troyon in the dining-room, and Thomas Sully's Madame Malibran in the music-room. They're by far his five best pictures. Besides that, he's brought up here most of the best *objets d'art* and every bit of the furniture that's really good! He'd already borrowed over the limit on everything he owns, long before this began. Now he owes over twenty-nine thousand dollars more!" She took from a box two slim statuettes of faintly gleaming, almost black bronze, and placed them upon the marble mantelshelf. "With their patine, these look beautiful here against the ivory wall. Italian Renaissance is pleasant with a Clouet. These dear little bronzes are probably by Francesco de St. Agata. I do wonder—"

"Wonder what?"

Georgina seemed to struggle with the pressure of her loyalty; then she burst out, "I've guessed his idea —I mean I'm afraid I have. It's just too—well, people do lose their minds and still go about talking rationally and—"

"Georchie!"

Rumbin summoned her to him in the broad hallway and set her upon a task there. He came into the reception-room, had the Clouet lifted an inch, then gave Howard the key to the locked-up Galleries and sent him all the way to Seventeenth Street for a tiny patch-box, *églomisé* mounted on ivory, that had been overlooked.

When the young man returned, the workmen were gone and Mrs. Hollins's staff of servants had begun to come back to the apartment and stare; but Rumbin and Georgina were still busy.

Rumbin stopped at last. "I can't do no more; I can't tell what I'm doing. If I got them crystal chandeliers and crystal sconces cleaned enough, I don't know. It's o'clock seven-twenty. Georchie, in them boxes on the hall Directoire consoles, it's four dozen pale pinky roses, four dozen pale yellow; you place 'em. Howie, I borrowed from the butler one the guest-rooms; the suit-cases they're in there—we go put on our tuxedo dinner theatre suits. If we get drownt, anyhow we go under dressed up!"

In the process of dressing, however, even this consolation seemed not to console. He sat sagged upon the bed, spoke hollowly from the inside of the shirt he drew over his head. "Howie, what's a art dealer's life?"

"Sir?"

"It's a eggony!" Mr. Rumbin's head emerged; he began with feeble fingers to insert small gold studs in the shirt. "It's a eggony of always struckling to create the ideel. Clients got to be made; they ain't born. Howie—"

"Sir?"

"I used to have NRA on the show window, Howie," Rumbin said. "It meant Not Running Any. Comes to-morrow I put up some more letters, different. I make it 'Rumbin Galleries, S.I.G.'"

"S.I.G., sir? What—"

"Socked In the Jaw," Rumbin explained. "Howie, you and Georchie come see me sometimes when the U.S. Government sends me to Leavenworse." He rose, completed his change of clothing, looked drearily in a mirror, and then, shifting his gaze to his assistant, showed a little interest. "Listen, Howie, when Hollinses come, you stand around looking at 'em just like that—the way you're looking at me now. Keep looking at Hollinses that way, like you know you're more fash'nable than them but wouldn't say so to their faces. That cold solemn look you got, it's good; it's a pig effect."

Howard grew red, spoke impulsively. "I don't feel cold, Mr. Rumbin. I—I wish I could do something. I don't understand at all; but I—I do wish I—"

"No, don't break it," Mr. Rumbin said sadly. "Just keep the face looking natchal; it's good. Come on; let's go get arrested."

Returned to the drawing-rooms, fine vistas through the suite seemed to please him mournfully, not making him more hopeful. "Space," he said. "Looks anyhow twice as large as Moultons done it. Space and coolness, no hot tones—all cool tones of rose—some ivories a little warmed, for richness; it's rich but yet cool. Georchie, you got just the right spots palish roses. Flowers lifts a place to life. It's all pyootiful; but does that make it heppen?" There was a sound of little bells, servants hurried through the hallway, and Mr. Rumbin crumpled; yet even in despair was practical. "Georchie, keep in the beckground; you look like you been working. My Lort, I got not the muscles of a kitten!"

With rolling eyes he sent one panic-stricken glance about the great place he'd so completely changed; then, upon the instant, he stood smiling, his abdomen distended, his gaze beaming, his whole person bold, confident and sleek. Indulgently, sure of praise, he waved both hands in wide and gracious gestures.

"Welcome home!" he cried. "Welcome home to all rose and ivory, Mr. and Mrs. Kingsford J. Hollins and little Miss Lulu. Look what a home you got NOW! Welcome home!"

Mr. and Mrs. Kingsford J. Hollins and little Miss Lulu paused in the open, wide doorway, facing Mr. Rumbin. Mr. Hollins, a small, dried, grey man with icy nose-glasses and a tooth-brush moustache, looked annoyed. Mrs. Hollins and little Miss Lulu stared into the room, gazed up and down the hall and through all vistas visible to them. Their eyes widened and widened; then both began to scream softly.

"Beautiful!" Mrs. Hollins cried.

"Perfectly dee-vine!" little Lulu shouted.

They came in, exclaiming rapturously. Then they began to flutter from room to room, making outcries. "Perfectly gorgeous!" "Look at this heavenly sofa!" "Oh, the lovely, lovely picture!" "Oh, look at this one, too, Mamma!" They were heard calling to each other from the farthest rooms. "Heavenly!" "Dee-vine!" "Grand!" "Oh, scrumptious!"

Mrs. Hollins, radiant, preceded by her whooping child, swept back to Rumbin. "Mr. Rumbin, I never dreamed anything could be so beautiful! It's worth all that horrible boresome trip we've been on. It's a dream!"

Lulu was already calling from the reception-room, "Mamma, come look! Here's something we missed. It's a man with lovely jewelry on. It's gray-and!"

Mrs. Hollins flew jubilantly to the summons; but Mr. Rumbin's expression, as he looked after her, became almost theatrically solicitous. He shook his head, made lamentant sounds. *"Ts, ts, ts!"* With an air of deepest concern he approached Mrs. Hollins's husband. "Mr. Kingsford J. Hollins, please, please! Please don't let your wife get so excited!"

"What?" Mr. Hollins said crossly. "I'm doggone glad she's tickled, myself. What's the matter?"

"It's going to break her heart," Mr. Rumbin said in a low, deeply troubled voice. "She didn't let me time to explain. When she finds out—but you know her nerfs yourself, Mr. Kingsford J. Hollins. She's delicate; and such a disappointment could send her moaning in bed. She thinks she owns all these pictures, all these *objets d'art,* all the furniture, all the antique—"

"What! What you mean she doesn't own 'em? She said you said eighteen thousand dollars for—"

"Certainly," Rumbin agreed benignly. "Eighteen t'ousand dollars for the apartment, Mr. Hollins— the pyootiful old-ivory walls, white-ivory ceilings, the rose curtains—Eighteent' Century French brocade—rose carpets, rose rugs—four Aubusson, Mr. Hollins—and you got antique crystal chandeliers, crystal sconces, all macknificent. Of course it couldn't include no paintings, no Old Masters, no Renaissance bronzes, no pieces Chinese ivory, no Eighteent' Century furniture, no details like snuff-boxes, patch-boxes, Riccio inkstends. I put all these pyootiful masterpieces in here for this one evening just to make it a bright welcome home for her, so she gets a treat looking at 'em a little, Mr. Kingsford J.—"

Mr. Hollins said *"What!"* so insultedly that two listeners across the room, affecting interest in an old silver vase filled with roses, looked at each other miserably. "What! Just for this evening? You mean you intend to move all this stuff out to-morrow?"

"But all your Moultons I move beck in of course, Mr. Hollins." Mr. Rumbin's solicitude increased poignantly. "Please! Please, Mr. Kingsford J. Hollins, run stop your wife from getting used to thinking she owns all these pyootiful things. Tell her she's got her lovely rose and ivory apartment but of course not no Clouet nor Troyon nor—Listen! She's hollering louder over the Clouet! You got to think of yourself, Mr. Kingsford J. Hollins, too, because what'll her nerfs be the longer you put off telling her? She'll be sick and reproaching you for not—"

"See here!" Mr. Hollins's expression was concentratedly bitter. "What's your figure?"

"My figure? My figure for—"

"For the whole damn jamboree! What's it got to cost me? Here, damn it, come out to my den where there's some damn paper and ink."

"Monseigneur!" Mr. Rumbin bowed as pro-

foundly as ancestors of his had bowed to their en-
snared princes. "Certainly, Mr. Kingsword J. Hollins," he said, and his voice, beginning with the bass-
viol, ended with the flute. "It's a pleasure!"

Then, as he followed the crossest millionaire in the
United States out through the doorway, he looked
back over his shoulder at two excited young people
who'd given up pretending not to listen. He slowed
his step and paused; Mr. Hollins could be heard
stamping down the corridor. Mr. Rumbin rolled
shining round eyes in that direction, thus by a purely
ocular gesture designating whom he meant by the
one symbolic and prophetic word he triumphantly
whispered.

"Ideel!"

Another thought detained him yet another moment. "Don't wait no longer, Georchie and Howie.
You're both raised ten anyhow—ten weekly, payable
weekly. You're permanent, Howie. I commenced
liking you."

CHAPTER FIVE

YOUNG HOWARD had already commenced liking Mr.
Rumbin, and, during the warm weeks of summer
after the night of the great stroke that was the salva-
tion of Rumbin Galleries, he liked him better and
better. The more he saw of him, in fact, the more
agreeable he found it to work for such an employer
and the more interesting he thought the business.

Naturally, since Howard was just out of college,
the business puzzled him; but he sought earnestly to
comprehend its eccentricities. Sometimes these dazed
him, and so did Mr. Rumbin. The young man had
just begun to understand, for instance, the importance of creating Mrs. Kingsford J. Hollins into
an ideal client, when Rumbin, turning lightning cal-
culator, had tossed Mrs. Hollins aside in favor of
her husband. Rather timidly Howard asked Miss
Georgina Horne to enlighten him upon this point.

"Why, don't you see?" Miss Horne said. "Mrs.

Hollins is a flibbertigibbet; got a mind like a flea—about that size, always hopping and you can't ever tell where it'll hop to. Mr. Rumbin saw he could never make a collector out of a woman like that; but there was a splendid chance of doing something with Mr. Hollins, because there he was already buying a number of pretty good pictures along with the rest of the fine things Mr. Rumbin had put in the apartment. Every collector has to make a beginning, and there was Mr. Hollins with a beginning already made. You catch collecting much as you catch some nice disease; Mr. Rumbin only had to make Mr. Hollins understand the bug had bitten him. It certainly had. Look at those three pictures Mr. Rumbin's sold him since our miraculous night at the Hollins' apartment! Mr. Hollins is behaving very much indeed like an ideal client."

Howard had perceived, though wonderingly, that it was possible for an art dealer's business to go on existing with but a single client. (He was learning never to use the word "customer".) Moreover, this was the slack season, as he knew, and, in the course of a whole week, not more than a dozen people perhaps would wander into the shop to look at the "antiques", usually without buying anything; but Miss Horne informed him that things were often much the same even at brisker times of the year. As for the paintings, the staple of Mr. Rumbin's trade, prospective clients came only by appointment to see these, and sometimes weeks might pass without any such appointment at all. Howard thought that probably some of his recently graduated classmates were finding business life peculiar, if they'd been lucky enough; but he was certain his own was queerer than anything into which the rest might be trying to worm their way.

At times his employer took great pains to shed light upon the business; but at others he didn't. Mr. Rumbin was at once the most copiously voluble and completely secretive man Howard had ever met. Miss Horne did the bookkeeping for Rumbin Galleries and sometimes worked long over ledgers; but the really important part of the business was obviously all in a section of Mr. Rumbin's head that he kept locked up. Miss Horne was more helpful. She suggested books for Howard's reading, and more than once, when he made bold to ask her, went with him to the Metropolitan Museum and other public galleries, on Sundays, talking informatively of the pictures; but there were times when the novice felt himself a misfit in his present calling.

He spoke gloomily to Miss Horne, one autumn morning. "I'm learning to be a good janitor," he said, concluding operations with a dust pan and a floor mop. "But the minute Mr. Rumbin lets me out of these overalls I'm lost. What art reading I get a chance to do goes right out my other ear. I wonder Mr. Rumbin doesn't fire me."

"No." Miss Horne was passing a soft feather duster over an old painting that stood before her on a chair; but she gave the discouraged assistant a twinkling brief side glance from nice grey eyes. "Large serious young gentlemen may be a little slow sometimes; but they inspire trustfulness, Mr. Cattlet. That's useful. Mr. Rumbin knows very well that nobody would dream anything shady could ever be put over with your connivance."

Howard's color heightened, not because he took this as a tribute. "I see. You merely mean I'm dumb-looking."

"I do not!" she protested, and had more color herself. "I only meant—"

"Never mind," he said. "I'm surprised, though. I didn't think Mr. Rumbin'd ever do anything at all shady."

"Certainly he wouldn't!" Georgina Horne returned loyally. "He's absolutely straight about whatever he sells his clients; he'd be foolish if he weren't. I meant you inspire confidence and that sometimes clients are nervous because they realize they know too little about old pictures. For that matter, though,

when almost any picture's several hundred years old,
even the experts can get to quarreling over it."

"I believe you!" the young man in overalls exclaimed. He looked at the aged painting she was
softly dusting—partly-robed small figures on the
edge of a dim river that was set into a bluish dark
landscape under a stormy sky. "How could anybody
tell who painted that, for instance?"

Miss Horne laughed. "Look at the tablet." She
moved aside so that Howard could read the name
upon the short strip of thin gilt wood affixed to the
base of the frame.

"Poussin," he said, meditating. "Poussin. Let's
see if I can remember. Seventeenth Century French.
Nicolas Poussin contemporary of Claude Gellée
called Lorrain. Velásquez, Rembrandt, Frans Hals,
Vermeer, Rubens, Van Dyck, Claude le Lorrain and
Nicolas Poussin all alive at the same time. Some
modern French critics put Nicolas Poussin at the top,
the most important of all. That must be a horribly
expensive picture, Miss Horne."

"Mr. Rumbin never tells me his prices beforehand," Miss Horne said, and added, "He thoroughly
knows what he's about, though, when he's handling
old French pictures."

She took the painting to the display window, set it
upon a mound of green velvet and let the upper part

of the frame rest against an iron support, so that the
canvas, a little tilted back, faced the street. Then she
turned to go to her desk at the rear of the shop;
but paused upon hearing an exclamation from Howard.

"Golly! Somebody's looking at it!"

An unusual thing had happened; a passer-by had
stopped to gaze into Rumbin Galleries' display
window.

The interested person was tall, slim and swarthily
handsome, though Howard Cattlet thought his
Chaplin-Hitler moustache, mauve silk muffler and
the rake of his hatbrim a little conspicuous.

"He's a dealer," Georgina Horne said, frowning
slightly. "It's Mr. Orcas. I don't see what interests
him in a Poussin; he's not supposed to know much
about French painters, new or old."

Mr. Orcas, however, opened the door and came
in.

"So our fat friend's got hold of a Poussin, has
he?" he said gayly to Miss Horne. "Well, well, well!
He must be flush! No wonder—since he's been selling
pictures to such a plutocrat as Kingsford J. Hollins,
Esquire!"

"I think Mr. Rumbin's in the stock room if you
wish to see him, Mr. Orcas."

"No, no." Mr. Orcas gracefully waved a pair of

flat, never-worn suede gloves. "Not on business; I'm trotting right along." He picked up from a Louis XV marquetry table a small casket of silver-gilt. "I just happened to see this little coffer through the window and thought for a moment it might be a German piece, Gothic." He laughed. "Baroque! Better get my eyes examined, what?" He put down the casket and walked to the door. "Day, day!" he said, passing out to East Seventeenth Street. "Dearest love to our fat friend!"

He closed the door behind him gently; nevertheless, the action seemed to open another door at the rear of the shop as by some instantaneous mechanism. Mr. Rumbin, bright-eyed, came forth from the stock room rapidly.

"Didn't I heard the woice o' that damn Orcas?"

"Yes; just stayed a minute," the secretary said. "Talked about the Poussin. Then pretended he'd mistaken the little baroque coffer for Gothic through the window; picked it up and looked at it."

"He did?" Mr. Rumbin put his right forefinger upon the tip of his nose, kept it there for a moment —one of his gestures to signify penetrative thought. "That's execkly his bum excuse for coming inside. What elst did Orcas—"

"He knows you've got Mr. Kingsford J. Hollins for a client," Georgina said. "He—"

"Counts nothing," Mr. Rumbin interrupted. "Proves he ain't got no lead to him, elst he wouldn't spoken about him." He turned to his assistant, who was replacing the mop and dust pan in a cupboard. "Howie, you see it ain't only the first step getting once holt of a client, because that's comparative easy compared to chasing odda dealers off from him. Now show me you're anyways some learning the business, Howie. Make me a guess really why Orcas comes in."

"Sir?"

"Take it easy, Howie," Mr. Rumbin said benevolently. "Putty soon comes to you the meaning of what I'm asking you."

"Well, sir—since you've told me nobody clever ever lets you see what he's really interested in, Mr. Orcas couldn't be interested in the Poussin because that was the first thing he mentioned."

"Wrong!" Mr. Rumbin exclaimed. "Most cases, yes; but not if it's Orcas. He thinks if he mentions the Poussin I'll think he ain't thinking about it on account he does mention it to keep me from thinking he's thinking about it, so I won't."

"Sir?"

"Take it easy, Howie," Mr. Rumbin said again. "Afterwhiles it comes to you. It's good, because not chumping at everything you don't never over-chump yourself." He smiled, nodded and spoke aside to Miss Horne, though without lowering his voice enough to be inaudible to Howard. "It's good for anodda reason too, Georchie, also. If the boy gets too bright and his face's expressions gets to showing it, he might lose that aristocratic don't-know look that's the most useful thing he's got, togedda with his clothing." Then he addressed both of his employees. "Orcas is crazy after French pictures; don't know nothing about 'em. Wait a couple days, he'll call me up and try to trade me for the Poussin maybe a Lawrence portrait that'll turn out to be a Harlow. Got me, Howie?"

"Sir? You mean because Harlow was an imitator of Lawrence—"

"Listen hard!" Rumbin said. "Trading pictures —look out! You get a Tintoretto; no, it's a Tintoretto the son, not Jacopo Robusti but Domenico. If it's a Velásquez it's a Mazo; if it's a Wan Dyke it's a Lely—even the Louvre's got a Wan Dyke that's a Lely. If it's a Lely it's a Wissing or a Hayls or a Beale or a Soest. If it's a Blakelock or a Corot or a Jean François Millet or a Cézanne it's a forchery from a forchery factory. If it's a Bellini it comes from pupils; if it's a Rembrandt it ain't one, and if it's a Giorgione it twice as much ain't. What's the answer?"

"Sir?"

"Eye!" Rumbin said. "You got to have a Eye. Cultiwate Eye, Howie. Got me?"

"Sir? You mean because so many pictures are copies or—"

"Listen some more intelligencely," Rumbin said. "You don't got to get the idea in the whole worlt there ain't no aut'entic pictures. Stands to reason there's got to be some, even if maybe not accordings to the experts. Don't try for it now, Howie. It comes to you later. Go put on your cutaway suit. We got business."

"Yes, sir." Howard retired to the stock room, and Miss Horne looked at her employer inquiringly.

"Mr. Hollins is coming this morning?" she asked.

"No, not Mr. Kingsford J. Hollins; it's his business partner, Mr. Milton Wilby. Mr. Milton Wilby, he lives since he got born in a nice old house from off Gramercy Park just a little piece distance. Promises Mr. Hollins and me he walks around here this morning, stops in, I can show him some paintings. Mr. Milton Wilby looks good, Georchie."

"Are you going to try to sell him the Poussin?"

"No," Rumbin said decisively. "One them foreground figures it's a almost nude. Pagan subject, and Mr. Hollins tells me Mr. and Mrs. Milton Wilby they're very strict old-fashion' American rich people.

Mr. Milton Wilby he's over seventy years old; teaches Sunday-school since before he was twenty-one. Best I try on him subjects from religion; but on the odda hand Mr. Kinksford J. Hollins tells me Mr. Milton Wilby don't like no primitives. Well, outside primitives, I got my early Nineteent' Century French Academic Bathsheba Viewed by David."

"I wouldn't." Miss Horne shook her head. "You say Mr. Wilby wouldn't want a nude, and Bathsheba—"

"Yes, so she is," Rumbin admitted. "You're always right, Georchie. Well, we got one odda religious subject. That Follower of Boucher picture, *La Femme de Potiphar*—" He paused, frowning. "Yet it's kind of a nude, too, though."

" 'Kind of'? Even more than Bathsheba, Mr. Rumbin."

"Yes, so she is, Georchie. Nuder and Frencher, too. Wouldn't do any for old-fashion' American rich people."

"Mr. Rumbin, aren't you going to show him any portraits or landscapes?"

"A portrait, yes; that's what I got to sell Mr. Wilby. Lentscapes Mr. Hollins tells me Mr. Wilby don't like much, too; so I show him some first, to get him a little tired, yet not disgusted at me like the way Bathsheba or the *Femme de Potiphar* would maybe make him. Then I shoot him a portrait. Which one you say, Georchie?"

"Early American, I think, Mr. Rumbin. For instance—"

"Wait. I got it!" he interrupted. "Reverend Joel Feeney of Connecticut by John Wesley Jarvis. Jarvis he's a putty good early Nineteent' Century American painter; might get me a good pleasant price from Mr. Milton Wilby." Mr. Rumbin looked at his watch. "Time to show Howie which pictures he's got to carry into the galleries for the program. Keep a look out through the show window for Mr. Milton Wilby, Georchie. Send him nice glences out from your eyes if he comes before I'm beck to let him in. It all helps, Georchie."

CHAPTER SIX

Miss HORNE laughed; so did Mr. Rumbin. He returned to the stock room and she sat down at her desk; but now and then obediently looked up from her work to gaze toward the street. Thus she happened to be looking when an obviously conservative elderly couple—a withered grey gentleman and a plump silver-haired lady—paused upon the sidewalk to glance up at the gilt lettering on the window. Georgina Horne comprehended that Mr. Milton Wilby had brought his wife with him to look at pictures; but the nice glances out from Georgina's eyes were not called upon. Mr. Rumbin just at that moment emerged from the stock room and he instantly hurried forward to admit the visitors himself.

Opening the door, he bowed again and again, spoke volubly of the honor being done him; all with-

out thawing the coating of austere wealthy reserve
that seemed to encase Mr. and Mrs. Wilby heredi-
tarily. Both, pausing just inside the door, looked
about the shop.

"I've never been in a place like this before," Mrs.
Wilby said. "Very odd things." She addressed Rumbin guardedly. "Mr. Hollins has talked my husband
into looking at some of your pictures; but the only
place for one in our house is over our living-room
fireplace, and we already have a beautiful picture
there. It's not loud, like most oil paintings, and's
by a very fine artist. Perhaps you've heard of it. It's
called Ducks on a Pond."

"Ducks?" Mr. Rumbin said in a small voice, and
with a smile in which there appeared to be nothing
except deference. "Ducks." He seemed to ponder.
"Ducks on a Pond. French maybe?"

"No," Mrs. Wilby answered stiffly. "It is not. It
was left me by my aunt, Mrs. George Penner
Thompson, and she told me herself the artist was
from Rhode Island."

"Ah, Rhode Island!" Mr. Rumbin exclaimed with
enthusiasm. "American School! Splendid!" He
bowed again. "May I ask you courteously step in the
galleries? There you seat yourselfs down comfortable while we show you some pyootiful, not loud,
American School pictures."

He led the way to the door of the room he thus spaciously called the galleries; stood aside for Mr. and Mrs. Wilby to enter, and then, as he followed them, spoke loudly to Georgina. "Miss Horne, please send wort to Mr. Cattlet, our Head Assistant, Mr. and Mrs. Milton Wilby's kindly waiting to see some American School masterpieces."

Georgina, however, didn't need to summon the Head Assistant, so-called. The door of the stock room was open and Howard Cattlet, impressively dressed, came forth carrying a brightly varnished large painting of the Hudson River Near Nyack At Sunset. He looked wistfully at Georgina Horne; but already her head was again bent over her desk, and he, too, just then at least, had no nice glances out from her eyes. Disappointed, he went on, passed into the galleries and closed the door. For three quarters of an hour, indeed, Georgina's devotion to duty was so complete that finally Howard ventured to speak to her about it.

"Couldn't you ever look up at all?" he asked humbly. "This is the seventh picture I've carried right past you."

At that, she did just glance at him. "How's it going?"

"It's not," he answered. "This is the one he wants to sell 'em—Portrait of Reverend Joel Feeney by John Wesley Jarvis. If Mr. Wilby half likes it, Mrs. Wilby won't—keeps talking about her Ducks on a Pond. Mr. Rumbin's a good sport; but it seems to me they've pretty near got him down."

Howard wasn't far off the truth here. A little later, when the party of four came out of the galleries and into the shop, Georgina saw that her chief's sensitive broad brow was bedewed. He breathed heavily, too; though still gallantly maintaining a confident aspect.

"Ah, but you ain't seen just two t'ree per cent our great pictures, Mr. and Mrs. Milton Wilby!" he said. "Give me only couple days to think. I find something you couldn't stop yourselfs from putting over your mantelpiece, Mr. and Mrs. Milton Wilby. Frangkly speaking, though, I wish you would think over acquiring my great Reverend Joel Feeney by—"

"No, indeed," Mrs. Wilby said with emphasis, as she and her husband walked toward the outer door. "It may have been a clergyman, as you say, Mr. Rumbin; but it certainly has a dissipated mouth. We couldn't think of having a picture with a mouth like that in our home."

"No, we couldn't." Mr. Wilby spoke judicially. "Besides that, it isn't only my partner, Mr. Hollins, that I've consulted about acquiring a picture. Our married granddaughter's brother-in-law, Professor

"This Is the Seventh Picture I've Carried Right Past You"

Egbert Watson of Ludlow University, advises me
that if we have any picture at all it should be by an
Outstanding Master. My own taste would be for a
more Outstanding Master than any we've seen here
to-day—ah—such a Master's portrait of a beautiful
and noble woman perhaps."

"A picture in the home should be appropriate, Mr.
Rumbin," Mrs. Wilby added, not approvingly. "In
such a home as ours it should be an inspiration
every time either I or one of the family looks at
it."

"Yes," her husband said. "Ah—some Outstanding
Master's portrait of a beautiful woman of pure and
spiritual life and—"

"Execkly!" Mr. Rumbin agreed, beaming upon
them. "I got the idea execkly." He opened the front
door reluctantly, as Mrs. Wilby extended her hand
to the latch. "We got a just such a picture, all
spirichul; only just right now this minute it's out a
couple days. Give me just until T'ursday—" His
voice, as he followed the visitors out upon the sidewalk, was lost to the ears of his secretary and his
assistant within the shop.

"Who'd Mr. Wilby say his married granddaughter's brother-in-law is?" Georgina asked. "Didn't he
say it's Professor Egbert Watson of Ludlow University?"

"Why?" Howard said. "Who's he?"

"Nothing. It's just something to remember."

Mr. Rumbin returned, drooping, and closed the door. "Georchie," he said, "how about that fency head, Cleopatra by Etty, we got out getting ironed from blisters at Paré's? It's finish' T'ursday and it don't got to stay Cleopatra on the tablet. On the tablet she could be Saint Cecilia just as easy as Cleopatra; she's got putty much almost a pure kind of a face, and Mr. Wilby tells me let him know if I find one that—"

"No!" Georgina said. "That Cleopatra's more than a head and it shows the asp, too. Besides, William Etty won't be an outstanding enough Master for Mr. Wilby. He means somebody like Murillo or Guido Reni."

"What a worlt!" Mr. Rumbin passed a handkerchief over his forehead. "Such a strain them people puts me in! Won't look at no Madonnas but got right away quick to have a noble pure spirichul woman by a Outstanding Master or somebody elst'll sell 'em one! Queen Mary of London wisiting a Nursing Home by Michelangelo Buonarroti or Jan Vermeer they want? Listen, Howie, go chump in the river; don't learn to be no art dealer!"

Howard was sympathetic. "But after all, Mr. Rumbin, people do buy pictures sometimes."

"Acquire," Mr. Rumbin said wearily. "Acquire, Howie."

"Sir?"

"You said 'buy' again, Howie. It wouldn't hurt none just between Georchie and me and you sometimes, exceptings it gets you in the habit so maybe you'd say it again before a client. 'Buying' ain't delicate; it sounds like owning Art would be only a question how much money, whereby at the same time, on tops of that, 'acquiring' sounds hundut times more important money than what 'buying' does. Understand me, Howie?"

"I think so. I—"

"Listen! Something fifty cents or hundut dollars you could buy, I don't say no; but over a t'ousand it's acquired. Take clients. Take Mr. Kingsford J. Hollins, for exemple. He don't show Mr. and Mrs. Milton Wilby his paintings and just rough tell 'em he buys 'em! No, he tells 'em he acquires 'em from Rumbin Galleries. Does good. Upsets Wilbys they ain't got nothing home they acquired their own selfs. You don't acquire no Rhode Island Ducks on a Pond. That's what commences 'em thinking." He sighed; wiped his forehead again. "Well, get dissipated old Reverend Joel Feeney and them odda pictures beck in the stock room, Howie; I got to get myself commenced thinking where's a spirichul

woman Mr. and Mrs. Milton Wilby's going to acquire from me."

"Yes, sir."

Howard went to his task, and later was assigned to
another that kept him busy until lunch time, when he
went out to a cafeteria. On his return he found
Georgina Horne alone in the shop, finishing a sandwich.

"Something's going on," she informed him. "Mr.
Orcas didn't wait long to call up Mr. Rumbin; he
must be eager. They had a very long telephone talk
—I'm sure it was about the Poussin—and then Mr.
Rumbin agreed to meet him at lunch, and went out. I
suppose you might as well help me get some dust off
the pictures."

Helping Miss Horne in the delicate task of removing dust from many old paintings was precisely
Howard Cattlet's conception of the happy side of an
Art Dealer's Assistant's life. Mr. Rumbin did not
return; hours passed and nobody at all came into the
shop. The young man had a golden afternoon dusting pictures—an afternoon he knew he'd always remember, if only because of the different ways the
slowly fading light from outdoors intermittently
haloed Georgina's fair head against the dimmed
colors of old canvases and panels. Not that he called
her "Georgina"; she was his superior, both in posi-

tion and in salary, and he was sensitively almost as
formal with her when they were alone together as
when Mr. Rumbin was present. A day might come,
though, he'd begun to hope, when he could respect-
ably stop addressing her as "Miss Horne". Mr.
Rumbin's disposition was generous, and, if ever the
Galleries should prosper enough to expand, there
might be other employees. It was possible that in time
Howard might become less of a janitor and more of
an assistant—perhaps even in fact, as already sometimes in name, a Head Assistant.

"Miss Horne," he said, late in the afternoon when
there was no more dust left on anything, "Mr. Rumbin's always dreaming of moving up to Fifty-seventh
Street. Do you think he'll ever get enough business
to do it?"

She looked dubious. "He's been out of debt, I
think, ever since we did over the Hollins' apartment,
and being out of debt's a good deal for any business
these days; but I'm afraid it won't take Rumbin Galleries to Fifty-seventh Street, Mr. Cattlet." She
glanced at her watch and was surprised. "It's almost
six o'clock and I'd forgot you're a commuter. You'll
have to hurry for your train, Mr. Cattlet." He protested; but she over-ruled him. "No, positively! I'm
going to wait for Mr. Rumbin. No; I mean positively! Good night, Mr. Cattlet."

"Well—good night," he said plaintively, and, submitting to her authoritativeness, departed.

In the morning, again in overalls, he'd finished dry-mopping the shop floor when she came in at nine o'clock and astonished him by asking, "Did you think thieves had broken in during the night?"

"Thieves? No; the door was locked when I opened it. What—"

"You haven't missed anything?" She laughed gayly. "Look at the show window." He looked and beheld not the Poussin but the Reverend Joel Feeney occupying the mound of green velvet there. "Mr. Rumbin didn't get back till after eight o'clock last night," Georgina explained. "Looked as if he'd been put through a wringer. He and Orcas had been at each other all that time and had drunk five and a half pots of coffee. He only stayed long enough to wrap up the Poussin and rushed off in a taxi to Orcas's shop —to tempt him more with the actual sight of it. He said he was working on a trade that would land him the biggest deal of his life. It's exciting, isn't it?"

Howard, agreeing, thought that excitement was becoming to her; and, excited himself, again began to dream of Fifty-seventh Street, a Head Assistantship and calling her Georgina. The arrival of Mr. Rumbin, moreover, at ten, in a condition of exalta-

tion was electrifying. He burst into the shop, shouting.

"I got it! Georchie, it's the day of my life, I got
her! . . . Howie, come quick; she's in a taxi. I'm so
trembling I'm scared to bring her, I might drop her!
Quick, Howie, you got to carry her!"

CHAPTER SEVEN

HE RAN BACK to the taxi and helped his assistant to draw forth from it a picture wrapped in thick paper. "Keep staying," Rumbin said to the driver, and fluttered after Howard Cattlet, who carried the picture into the shop. "Careful, Howie! . . . Holt the door open for him, Georchie! . . . Keep on going, Howie; we put her on the easel in the galleries where's the best light! . . . Open the galleries door for him, Georchie. Take the paper from off her, Georchie; you got the best hands. There! Now on the easel. Easy, she's my heart's blood and last socks! So! Look what you see, Georchie and Howie! Look!"

Thus, in the excellent light of the galleries, the three stood gazing upon the prize triumphant Rumbin had taken from Orcas after Homeric wrestlings; and for the first time in his life Howard Cattlet stood spellbound before a picture. What carried him away was not the mere fact that the painting was the por-

trait of a daintily lovely woman; he was enchanted
by ineffable harmonies in blues and silvers and greys,
and by other harmonies, linear, so exquisite as almost
to make the picture musically audible, like some old
lyric not sung but played with masterful lightness
upon a violin.

The portrait was a half-length. A lady in a shim-
mering blue dress stood leaning against a draped
short column; one of her hands was almost lost in
shadow; the other drooped from the column like a
long pale flower. Upon her rhythmically curled hair
she wore a sweeping dark hat, with one splendid
gleam of blue satin ribbon among dim plumes. The
lovely pensive face was ethereal and its complexion
of an unearthly delicacy in a light that never was on
sea or land—a light wherein the background seemed
to float misty foliage and vague distances.

"I never saw anything like it," Howard Cattlet
said in a low voice. "Gainsborough. Thomas Gainsborough!"

Mr. Rumbin, hilarious, slapped him on the back.
"Just only and merely nobody exceptings Thomas
Gainsborough! Aha! Howie knows because he reads
the tablet on the frame—Portrait of a Lady, Seventeen hundut twenty-seven, Thomas Gainsborough,
Seventeen hundut eighty-eight, when Thomas Gainsborough got born and then aftaworts died. Outstand-

ing Master enough for Mr. Milton Wilby, what?
Pyootiful noble spirichul woman, what? Can't you
say nothing at all, Georchie?"

"It's lovely," Georgina said slowly. "I can't help
thinking I've seen it before. It's odd how evenly the
crackle goes all over it."

"Odd? No! Splendid!" Rumbin cried. "Where's
any old picture don't show cracks? Feeling you seen
it before somewheres, it's good, too, the same as
when you first hear a orchestra play what you like
the most, you think you somewheres did heard it
long ago. Ain't it so, Georchie?"

"Yes, but—"

"Nicer still," Rumbin cried, "thinking about
Thomas Gainsborough and music togedda it's right,
because he painted musical and always plays instruments himself, always buys instruments when he can.
My Lort, all yesterday and half the night that damn
Orcas fights to make me trade even for my Poussin,
whereby if I'd ever let him think I was secret willing,
he'd grebbed for t'ousands dollars besides—and all
the time was I perspiring he'd see I *got* to get holt
this Gainsborough from him or bust into a stroke
appalexy? Georchie, can't you let out even one holler
when Rumbin Galleries acquires a such painting?"

"Where'd Mr. Orcas say he got it?"

"Say?" Rumbin laughed loudly. "And she knows

Orcas! Natchly he says it comes from old English family that won't let nobody know they're selling. Sometimes it's true, though, even when Orcas says it! My Lort, what's it matter? Look at the picture; it says enough! Georchie, wrap it up quick again in them papers. Mr. Milton Wilby don't go down to Wilby and Hollins exceptings in afternoons a while."

"You're going to show it to him this morning, Mr. Rumbin?"

"Quick's a flesh! By now he's had time to get through his breakfast, ain't he? Wrap it up, Georchie, wrap it up!"

She did as he bade her; but remained preoccupied. "You don't want to take a little time over it, Mr. Rumbin? Professor Egbert Watson of the Art Department of Ludlow University is some sort of connection of the Wilbys by marriage and of course he'll see—"

Rumbin interrupted her loudly. "Didn't Wilbys tell me so how many times yesterday? What'll Professor Egbert Watson do when he lays his eyes on this picture, Georchie? He takes one look and screeches from choy, writes a article he discovers a new such important Gainsborough in United States of America whereby the Blue Boy ain't nothing beside it." The dealer turned jovially to his assistant and pupil. "Which Blue Boy I speak of now, Howie?"

"Which, sir? Oh, murder!" Howard was distressed. "I'll never learn this business! Are there two Blue Boys, sir?"

"It's claimed so; but one's only a copy, maybe by Hoppner, Howie. Gainsborough's it's the one Gainsborough painted, but not because Sir Joshua Reynolds says you can't use that much that kind of blue that way. Don't belief all them stories, Howie; it takes all your brains to belief what the Duc de Westminster few years ago sells it for to American collector. Highest price ever paid for any picture up to then exceptings maybe one Raphael—eight hundut t'ousand dollars, Howie."

"Sir?"

"Eight hundut t'ousand for a Gainsborough, Howie. Keep that hollering at you in your brains and lift my great Gainsborough up again, Howie. Take it out to the taxi. You can't go, you're in your overalls; I get somebody at Wilbys help me in with it if I'm still trembling. Easy! You're carrying your own adwance in celery, Howie; you might get it. Walk sweet, Howie!"

Howie walked sweet; and, even when the taxicab had disappeared eagerly round the next corner, he still felt some of the radiance the cab carried away, shrouded, within it. Thus, coming back into the shop in a state of glowing hope, "Georgina," he began impulsively. "Georgina——" Then he apologized. "I'm sorry. I mustn't call you that."

"Mustn't you?" Mr. Rumbin's secretary was on her knees before a French Regency commode. "It doesn't seem fatal—so far."

"No; but I shouldn't. I'm afraid what Mr. Rumbin said about the price of Gainsborough's Blue Boy's got me exhilarated. Was that correct—eight hundred thousand dollars?"

"I've often heard so." She rummaged within the commode and spoke absent-mindedly. "Of course that took up the price of all other Gainsboroughs; but don't get the idea Mr. Rumbin expects this Portrait of a Lady to——"

"But mightn't he——"

"Fifty-seventh Street?" Georgina asked skeptically. "There are Gainsboroughs and Gainsboroughs, also Depressions, and I think Mr. Rumbin's trying to make a quick sale for quick cash. I imagine he'd be pleased with a very small fraction of what the Blue Boy brought."

"Very small? An eighth or a tenth, maybe?"

"A fortieth or a fiftieth more likely."

"A fortieth?" Howard was dashed but remained fairly buoyant. "Twenty thousand dollars? After all, that's quite a lot, Georg—Miss Horne."

"Yes; so it is," she murmured; whereupon, as she

seemed busy with the commode and also with her own thoughts, Howard retired to remove his overalls.

He was cheerful, whistled as he hung up the overalls in a cubicle off the stock room, whistled as he washed his hands and face in a basin there, whistled still as he brushed his hair, and, after that, as he thoroughly brushed both the business clothes he wore and the "cutaway suit" kept in the cubicle for occasions his employer thought momentous. Then, hoping that by this time Georgina might be less preoccupied, he looked into the shop and saw that she was more so.

She had just placed two thick stacks of photogravures before her upon a table. "Come here, please," she said, aware of him with the side of her eye. "Mr. Rumbin never lets me get any books because you can't hire him to look at 'em himself; but I knew we had these reproductions somewhere. I've had the dickens of a time to find them." She pushed one of the stacks toward Howard. "Those are Gainsborough's portraits. Look through them and let me know if you come across anything that strikes you as familiar. This other stack's Reynolds; I'll look through it."

"Yes, Miss Horne." He began to turn over the photogravures. "Is—is something bothering you?"

"Yes. Mr. Rumbin doesn't know the English School half as well as he thinks he does, and I do wish he hadn't been in such a whirl to sell that picture to Mr. Wilby. Didn't give me a chance to get my breath."

"But, Miss Horne, that picture's one of the very most beautiful—"

"Yes, it is," she said. "The trouble is, it out-Gainsboroughs Gainsborough."

"What!" Howard cried. "Why, how could—"

"I'll try to tell you, Mr. Cattlet. The old painters used to call a paint-brush a 'pencil'; and Gainsborough often used his as if it really were a pencil—the lightest, most delicate touch in the world. Sometimes he made hurrying little zig-zag wiggles with it, especially when he was painting lace and the light on drapery. That picture had too many of those wiggles and showed too many other Gainsborough strokes —as if they were anxious to make you notice 'em. The design didn't hold things together, either—not enough all of a piece. I don't like it."

"No?" Howard stared at her. "But that painting was certainly an old one. You said yourself it was cracked all over and—"

"Yes!" She laughed angrily. "Put a little glue in varnish, spread it over any picture, let it dry hard; then roll the canvas up and afterwards unroll it and

you'll have a grand map of cracks to rub soot into or
maybe just smoke up with a lamp and then clean a
little. Go on looking through that stack of Gainsboroughs, please, Mr. Cattlet."

"Yes, Miss Horne." He resumed his task, but
looked up again as he heard her utter an exclamation. "What is it?"

She was frowning at one of the Reynolds photogravures; she whispered something to herself and
set it aside from the others. "Go on looking, please,
Mr. Cattlet. It's pretty queer, I'm afraid."

"Is it?" He turned over the sheets before him
more rapidly; then paused and bent to look closely.
"Here's one that seems—it's really very like her—at
least the face is—but she hasn't any hat on and the
figure's all different. She's sitting down, under a
tree with a dog beside her, and yet it does seem to
me—"

"Let me!" Georgina took the sheet from his hand,
gave it one fierce look and ran to the telephone. Her
fingers plunged through the pages of the ponderous
telephone book, darted thence to the dial; she got
Mr. Milton Wilby's house and then the listener she
wanted.

"Mr. Rumbin!" she cried. "Don't sell that picture!"

Howard, aghast, heard from within the instrument

palpitations the significance of which he couldn't determine. Georgina, too, was baffled by them.

"What, Mr. Rumbin? What do you mean, a baby? I didn't say anything about a baby! . . . Mr. Rumbin, I'm telling you not to sell that Gainsb— What do you mean, 'good-by'?" . . . Stricken, she turned to Howard. "He's rung off!"

"What?"

She set the instrument down and jumped up. "I think he's crazy! He wouldn't listen, began talking about a baby when I was trying to tell him— Look!" She strode to the table where she'd left the photogravures. "Look at that Reynolds portrait!"

"What on earth's Sir Joshua Reynolds got to do with it?" Howard asked—then found part of the answer for himself. "Why—why, there's something about this Reynolds portrait, too, that's like Mr. Rumbin's Gainsborough. It isn't the face—the face is entirely different—"

"Yes," Georgina agreed bitterly. "Entirely!" She placed the two photogravures side by side. "There they are! Portrait of Mrs. Robinson by Thomas Gainsborough. Portrait of the Countess of Donoughmore by Sir Joshua Reynolds. The picture I've just been trying to stop Mr. Rumbin from selling has the Gainsborough portrait's face upon the Reynolds portrait's body and clothes!"

"But—but what for? Why—"

"Why would a dealer in stolen goods take a known diamond out of a ring and set it in a brooch? This forger's done just that with the face. Then, besides, he put in a Gainsborough hat from some other portrait and a typical Gainsborough landscape background from somewhere else, and counterfeited Gainsborough's brush-work and palette over the whole canvas, Reynolds figure and all. Then he rolled it up and crackled it—and that's what Mr. Rumbin got from Orcas for his Poussin!"

"Counterfeit! Miss Horne, you mustn't let him sell that picture to Mr. Wilby!"

"Didn't I try to stop him? Try yourself!"

"I will!" Howard ran to the telephone, got Mr. Milton Wilby's house, and, after a delay, the information that Mr. Rumbin had departed.

CHAPTER EIGHT

THE FACT that Mr. Rumbin had left as hurriedly as he courteously could, and had continued to hurry, was made evident, moreover, by Mr. Rumbin himself. He arrived almost immediately, and, for the second time that morning, shouting.

"Georchie! Don't do such things to me! Wasn't I talking in the 'phone with Mr. and Mrs. Wilby standing all around me and the 'phone hollering at me 'Don't sell that picture!' Didn't I got to holler to drownt it out, telling Mr. and Mrs. Milton Wilby it's my Cousin 'Melia wants to congratulate me I'm a uncle on account my sister Magda's just got a baby she's going to name for me, whereby I never had no Cousin 'Melia, far from it no sister Magda, nor her no baby?"

"Where's the picture?" Georgina cried. "Don't say it's sold!"

"Sold? What was I doing there?" Mr. Rumbin's

gestures increased in eloquence. "Didn't Mr. and Mrs. Milton Wilby both screeched from choy soon as they seen a such pyootiful painting? Ain't Gainsborough so outstanding they can make their friends look up to 'em sore they been acquiring him? Ain't it a pyootiful pure spirichul woman their family gets inspired by, even she says herself nicer'n them Ducks? Went crazy over it, swallered the price like nothing, wrote me a cheque I already got in my pocket all the time I'm hollering in the 'phone thanks for congratulations on Magda's baby good-by! Georchie, don't no more do such things to me!"

Georgina brought the two photogravures and held them out to him. He took them, looked at them coldly. "What's these?"

"Keep—keep on looking," she said compassionately.

"So? Well, I see this one it's the same lady's face. Anodda Gainsborough portrait of her sitting down and without no hat; that can be. This Reynolds, though—it looks—it looks kind of—" His plump hands began to be tremulous. "My Lort! . . . Georchie, it looks bad." He collapsed, dropped into a chair, and the two fatal photogravures slid from his lap to the floor. "That damn Orcas!"

"That's what you'll tell Mr. Wilby," Georgina said quickly. "You'll tell him that Orcas—"

"Tell Wilbys Orcas traded me a forchery; so here's the cheque, I take the picture beck?" Mr. Rumbin's voice was a feeble falsetto. "When this minute I told 'em it reaches me from a old English family that won't let nobody know they're selling? So *quick* I'm a liar? Just as quick they run tell Mr. Kingsford J. Hollins I'm one; I lose the only client I got. On the odda hand, I leaf this damn Orcas picture hanging up over Wilbys' mantelpiece in place them damn Ducks, and how soon comes in their married damn grand-daughter's brodda-in-law, Professor Egbert Watson from Ludlow's Uniwersity, he's a expert, takes one look, says I sold 'em a forchery, they sue me, I'm ruined! Each way is it a worse pickle?"

Georgina began to reproach herself. "It's my fault. I oughtn't to have been foozled an instant. I'm stupider than even the forger; and he was so dumb he took the face from a Gainsborough that everybody knows is in the Wallace Collection in—"

"Everybody does?" Rumbin said pitifully. "It leafs out me. What can I do, Georchie?"

"Get it back," she said. "Get it back before Professor Egbert Watson sees it. Then it'll be too late. Get it back!"

"How, Georchie? Can I walk in Mr. and Mrs. Milton Wilby's, tell 'em, 'Listen, please, here's your cheque beck; takes me ten minutes to get wised I sold

you a counterfeit portrait from old English family I
says they're so proud nobody knows who they are
and you swallered it? Can I walk beck there tell
Wilbys that, when even I can't walk on account my
lecks can't support me no more'n two pieces spa-
ghetti? Even if a taxi gets me there, can I go in
people's house walking on the floor like a snake?"

"You've got to, Mr. Rumbin, just as quickly as you
can! It's worse than any mere loss of money because
your reputation—"

"You're telling me?" Rumbin rocked himself,
rubbed plump damp cheeks with plump damp hands.
"I must and I can't! I got to and I got not to! What
do I do with me?"

"But after all, sir," Howard Cattlet said, a little
timidly, and picked up the fallen photogravures. "I
don't see that it'd be so impossible. You'd just go in
and say—"

"Yes, Howie? I say? What do I say about the old
English family that—"

"You wouldn't mention them at all," Howard said
dashingly. "You'd just go in and say, 'Mr. Wilby,
I'm sorry, but I sold you that portrait of Perdita
Robinson in good faith and I—"

"Who?" Rumbin interrupted. "Who I say I sold
'em?"

"Perdita Robinson. 'Perdita' is engraved in parenthesis under 'Portrait of Mrs. Robinson' on the photogravure; so it's certainly she. You'd just say, 'I'm sorry, Mr. Wilby, but—' "

"Who?" Mr. Rumbin looked up at his assistant haggardly. "What's it say 'Perdita', too, for?"

"Because Mrs. Robinson played 'Perdita' in 'A Winter's Tale', Mr. Rumbin. She was an actress, you know, when the Prince of Wales—"

"Who? Go on some more, Howie. What elst?"

"Well, of course, it's history that Mrs. Robinson and the Prince of Wales were called 'Perdita' and 'Prince Florizel'."

"Mrs. Robinson?" Rumbin said. "She's married?"

"Yes, she—"

"Wait," Rumbin said. Strength seemed to be returning into his legs. He rose, staring at his young assistant. "Howie," he said, "maybe it turns out useful you're broad educated. Go get on your cutaway coat and west, leaf on your ordinary pants; they won't notice 'em. You got to go quick beck with me to Mr. and Mrs. Milton Wilby's; I need your looks. On the way you tell me more. Hurry, Howie!"

"Yes, sir."

Howie hurried, was kept hurrying; and, from the moment he left the shop with his employer, was also kept talking. Mr. Rumbin's legs, meanwhile, completed their recovery. Whatever qualms still disturbed his insides when he and his tall assistant entered Mr. and Mrs. Wilby's old-fashioned house, his manner was again supple, distinguished and ingratiating.

Mr. and Mrs. Wilby, in the living-room, received Mr. Rumbin and his assistant almost affably.

"Aha! Still enchoying your great Gainsborough!" Rumbin said, waving his hand benignly toward the painting over the fireplace. "How pyootiful she looks! Mr. and Mrs. Milton Wilby, the reason I'm beck so quick I got a piece good news for you."

"Good news?" Mr. Wilby said. "That's pleasant, Mr. Rumbin."

The smiling Rumbin was effusive. "It's owings to my Head Assistant, my young Herr Doktor, here, from the Uniwersity. See, he's modest; yet it's him found it all out. Mr. and Mrs. Milton Wilby, I congratulate you! Your picture ain't simple no Portrait of a Lady nobody knows who. Instead, you got a lady that's out from history."

"Indeed?" Mr. Wilby said. "History?"

"Actress," Rumbin announced, beaming. "Pyootiful actress!"

"Actress?" Mrs. Wilby said, not gratified. "An actress?"

"Pig hit!" Rumbin informed her warmly. "That's what first gets the Prince of Wales so excited in the audience his papa the King has to pay fife t'ousand pounds to get beck letters what he writes to her, it oddawise ruins him, gets public. Not this lately Prince of Wales, Mrs. Milton Wilby; it's his great-grandma's uncle Georche."

"George?" Mr. Wilby said. "Which George?"

"King Georche the Fourt'. But after he skips out from her, Mr. and Mrs. Milton Wilby, she's always a grand noble spirichul woman like in the picture such what you wanted. Of course, though, before then you got to admit she's lively—like maybe Emperor Augustus's daughter Choolia what he had to keep locked up, or Lola Montez or Lucrezia Borgia or Empress Catherine when they're sometimes maybe a little wild. She—"

"Who?" Mr. and Mrs. Wilby were both staring at the picture over the mantelpiece; but Mr. Wilby turned incredulously to Rumbin. "Who did you say—"

"Oh, but only a very short time," Mr. Rumbin said reassuringly. "Only a couple years she's kind of gay—royal favorite, like Du Barry, La Vallière, Madame Montespan. Only durings whiles this Mrs. Robinson and Georche Fourt' is called 'Florizel' and 'Perdita' she—"

"What!" Mr. Wilby exclaimed. "Mr. Rumbin, are we to understand you've sold us a portrait of

Perdita Robinson, George the Fourth's light o'
love!"

"Aha, they know her! Light o' love's right!"
Rumbin cried, and patted Howard Cattlet's shoulder. "It ain't just you that's got all the history knowledge, my young Herr Doktor. See! Mr. and Mrs.
Wilby's excited they acquired the portrait even before
they knowed who it is. See! They're heppy!"

Mr. and Mrs. Wilby didn't look happy; they
looked uncomfortable, especially Mr. Wilby.

"Milton," Mrs. Wilby said, "I think you'll recall
that as soon as I saw this picture I said I was anything but sure it had a good face. I told you it had a
loose look around its mouth. I told you—"

"I don't remember anything of the kind," Mr.
Wilby said. "I heard you say—"

"Yes, maybe afterwards," she interrupted, "but
not at first. Whether you heard me or not, the very
first thing I said—"

"Excuse, please!" Mr. Rumbin, serious, took the
liberty of intervening. "Mr. and Mrs. Milton Wilby,
you ain't complete satisfied with this pyootiful portrait?"

"Satisfied?" Mr. Wilby turned to him somberly.
"What's that matter? We've bought it and we've
paid for it."

"No, sir!" Mr. Rumbin looked hurt and proud; it

might be said he looked noble, too. He took a billfold from his pocket, removed a cheque from it and
with a magnificent curving gesture laid the slip of
bluish paper upon the mantelpiece. *"Not* bought and
not paid for, Mr. Milton Wilby! Some day I hope
you acquire from Rumbin Galleries anodda picture;
but not this one, Mr. Milton Wilby. Rumbin wouldn't
accept a million dollars—not even two—if his clients
ain't satisfied! There lays your cheque; Perdita Robinson comes beck to Rumbin Galleries. Go stand on
the front steps catch a taxicab, my young Herr
Doktor."

His young Herr Doktor, reddening as usual when
this unearned degree was conferred upon him, went
willingly upon the errand, got the cab and gave himself up to a confused admiration of his employer.
Mr. Rumbin himself helped the admiration along as
they drove away from Mr. and Mrs. Wilby's, with
the lovely portrait tilted before them, facing them
abominably. Rumbin, flaccid, wiped his brow.

"Such a relieft!" he groaned. "Yet maybe it ain't
a strain to take t'ousands and t'ousands dollars out
from your pocket, push it beck to somebody you just
got it away from that don't need it! What feelings I
could have if I'd let me! No, I got to use philosophy,
Howie; I got to keep remembering I didn't had that
cheque long enough to get strong attached to it."

Then he seemed to brighten. "It's pig, though; it's pig. You should always remember you seen something to-day, Howie, you could never forget—how a dealer stands up by a mantelpiece, loses money like water protecting his clients. It's a lion picture, Howie. Ain't it?"

"Sir? Yes, sir."

"Yes, Howie." Mr. Rumbin brightened more, his eyes glowed; he was himself again. "Went over strong with Mr. and Mrs. Milton Wilby! They're grateful; makes two friends for Rumbin Galleries. So it's all good, no harm done. No loss; we're only just beck where we was before."

"Are—are we, sir?" Howard looked at the beautiful but odious counterfeit before them, thought of the Poussin landscape for which it had been exchanged, and once more found himself unable to follow the workings of Mr. Rumbin's mind. "You—you say we're back just where we were before, Mr. Rumbin?"

"Yes, only nicer, Howie; everything elst beings equal, but now I got a pig start on making Mr. Milton Wilby into a art collector, so it's better!"

CHAPTER NINE

HOWARD'S CONFUSION became even greater than his admiration; he put both before Georgina Horne at the first possible moment. Mr. Rumbin, after warmly describing his mantelpiece performance to Georgina, carried the mongrel portrait to the stock room himself, humming *Donna e Mobile* as he went.

"You're right he's wonderful, Miss Horne," Howard said. "He's got me thinking I'm crazy again, though. What about his Poussin? Wouldn't you think the first thing he'd do would be to telephone that crook of an Orcas?"

Georgina, too, was perplexed; but had a partly enlightening thought. "After all, there were two Poussins. Of course the great one was Nicolas Poussin; but he had a pupil whose real name was Gaspard Dughet, and he was called Poussin, too. Gaspard's paintings aren't so highly thought of nowadays as they were once; but still they're worth immensely more than that miserable counterfeit, and it certainly is strange Mr. Rumbin isn't trying to—"

"Two Poussins?" Howard said despairingly. *"Two Poussins!"*

That day he learned even more about Poussins. Returning late in the afternoon from an errand upon which he had been sent by his employer, he was just about to enter the half-glass front door of Rumbin Galleries when it seemed to him that he heard a distant uproar. He paused for a moment, wondering if the sound came from the street or from an upper part of the building; then he opened the door, and his ears instantly received a passionate impact. Georgina, pale, stood before him in the shop, alone.

"Mr. Orcas has brought the Poussin back," she said. "He came in screaming for his 'Gainsborough' and they've been in the stock room going on like that for over half an hour. Listen!"

The two young people, open-mouthed, both listened. In the stock room, neither Mr. Rumbin nor Mr. Orcas listened. Mr. Rumbin was using all the power of a voice that was a big one when he chose to make it so; Mr. Orcas's was higher in pitch and also more frenzied. He came forth, voluble, and so stimulated by excitement that almost effortlessly he carried with him his hybrid portrait of Perdita Robinson, wrapped in paper. Noisily he went through the shop, out of the front door and strode away upon East Seventeenth Street, where, although he was then alone, he still spoke aloud of Rumbin.

In the shop there was silence; then, after a time, Mr. Rumbin could be heard humming *Donna e Mobile*. He came to the open door of the stock room, and spoke casually.

"Georchie, we leave Reverend Joel Feeney of Connecticut in the window; I only stuck my Poussin there a while so's maybe Orcas comes by and sees it. We got to order a new tablet for our Poussin, Georchie. I ain't never been complete satisfied it's a aut'entic Gaspard Dughet, usual called Poussin. Gaspard had pupils—Onofrio, Vincentio and Jacques De Rooster."

"Who?" Georgina asked. "Who, Mr. Rumbin?"

"Rooster, Georchie. Jacques De Rooster. He was one the best pupils of Gaspard, usual called Poussin, Jacques De Rooster was. Our Poussin looks more like it's kind of maybe a De Rooster; but maybe it ain't. So anyways order me a tablet says up top 'Poussin' and just below 'Follower Of'. 'T's all, Georchie."

He retired.

"Howard," Miss Horne said, "please begin calling me 'Georgina'. Two people can't go on working for such a man and stay formal!"

Howard said, "Oh, Georgina!" so gratefully that

she went back to her desk; while he stood where he was, thinking how singularly heaven had favored him in making him an Art Dealer's Assistant.

For the moment he'd forgotten all about Mr. Rumbin, to whose interesting behavior he owed the privilege just accorded him; but, a few days later, calmed by workaday routine and intervening slumbers, his mind dwelt again upon the puzzle of his employer's recent conduct. He saw that when these two dealers, stout Mr. Rumbin and sleek Mr. Orcas, set to bargaining, the issue was dog-eat-dog, and that Mr. Rumbin had known he could get his Poussin back if he wanted it, and why.

Meanwhile, however, Mr. Rumbin had begun to bring about another disturbance of the young man's mental equilibrium, a puzzlement by no means agreeable. The dealer's expression was often a frowning one; he became fretful about small things, peckish with his assistant. Something serious seemed to be going wrong with a gay and generous disposition; the friendly manner was becoming a crusty one. The assistant, previously often praised beyond his merits, was now as frequently reproached without good cause. Mr. Rumbin found fault with everything.

Howard spoke ruefully of this uncomfortable change in manner. "I'm almost sure something besides me's the matter with him, Georgina," he said.

"Don't you think maybe he's had his blood pressure taken or something?"

"No; it's business worry."

"What?" Howard was surprised. "But he got out of that trouble with Mr. Milton Wilby all right and said he didn't lose by it; even hoped to make Mr. Wilby into a collector. Then, besides, there's always Mr. Hollins and—"

"No," Georgina said. "The trouble is he's been getting anxious about Mr. Hollins."

"What? Isn't Mr. Hollins's health—" The young man cut short his inquiry. Mr. Rumbin, returning from an uptown excursion, had paused upon the pavement outside and was looking moodily through the display window. He delayed but a moment, however; then came into the shop.

"Cattlet!" he said, thereby somewhat hurting his assistant's feelings.

"Sir?"

"Cattlet, what's supposed to be the use me putting in the window two sweet little terra-cotta statuettes, pagan times, might be Tanagra, you can't tell, and also Adoration of the Magi, tempera painting on plaster that's on linen on panel, School of Bernardo Daddi, with wine-color' Wenetian welfet behind 'em, if nobody can't see through the glass? Cattlet, when last you washed the window?"

"This morning, Mr. Rumbin."

The stout dealer sat down, careless that the delicate Adam chair upon which he sank might be endangered by his weight. "Maybe so," he said. "Maybe it's washed and don't look like it. Everything I look at looks wrong on account I'm having bad experiences and just had anodda. What a worlt!"

Georgina Horne spoke cheeringly. "See this French *poudreuse,* Mr. Rumbin. Mr. Cattlet's been very skilful; he's got the veneer swelling down just by rubbing it with that preservative polish you invented."

"One bump off a *poudreuse* keeps a art dealer in business?" her employer asked plaintively. "Couple hours ago Forty-nint' Street, didn't old busted-down Charlie Ensill come chasing me, sells me bad news I had to pay him ten dollars for, elst he wouldn't tell it? Ensill you can't trust him if he's sober; but's always complete reliable if he's drinking. And such a breath he had; macknificent!"

"Ensill?" Georgina said. "Not poor old Professor Ensill that worked so long for Mr. Orcas?"

"Same, but forget saying 'professor', Georchie. It's a insult to such pants and shoes he had on." Rumbin sighed. "Vonderful feller, too! Art classes teacher, museum curator, loves good painting, yet always slipping to the basement till now he even got

fired from Orcas and's only a art scout, picks up bum
pictures for nothing, spies on sales, peddles dealers
information. Georchie, Ensill sees Mr. Kingsford J.
Hollins going in Hanover Galleries last Friday; sees
his limousine just leafing there yesterday afternoon!
Looks like Hanover Galleries sells him a painting
important money." Mr. Rumbin turned querulously
upon his assistant, who was polishing the *poudreuse*
Miss Horne had mentioned. "Cattlet, you're supposed learning art business. In my place what would
you done?"

"Sir? You mean if this Ensill told me he'd seen my
best client at another dealer's?"

"What elst you think's my meaning, Cattlet, when
I just says that's what my meaning is? Such a intel-
lex!"

"I'm sorry, sir," the assistant said with frigidity.

"Sorry? Yes, you ain't! Listen to your woice,
Cattlet. Look how spiteful you're standing. Does that
help me keep odda dealers from getting holt Mr.
Kingsford J. Hollins, Cattlet?"

"No, sir."

"Then don't do it, Cattlet. What's useless, don't
do." Howard, red, resumed his rubbing of the
poudreuse; and the dealer's tone again became plaintive. "Georchie, no more Mr. Hollins don't want no
little out-o'-fashion Barbizons, no Coteses, no School

of Clouets, no Followers Of, not even a Sully, best I got holt of."

"Not even Barbizons, Mr. Rumbin?"

Rumbin shook his head. "Early Corot maybe—French dealers' propaganda's got early ones fash'-nable now—but not Rousseau, not Daubigny, not Diaz. No, Georchie, it's simple the old story—a collector commences timid; then he gets to art-talking; putty soon he wants only Holbein, Titian, Watteau; gets worst, wants a Giorgione or a Jan Vermeer—like wisiting Washington he won't shake hands with nobody exceptings the United States President. Understand me, Cattlet?"

"Certainly I do."

"I bet you don't, Cattlet! Listen how pettish he says it!" Mr. Rumbin spoke tartly; then his chin descended upon his winged white collar. "What's worst, Georchie, Mr. Hollins he's been getting himself strong acquainted with his business partner's granddaughter's brodda-in-law, Professor Egbert Watson from Ludlow's Uniwersity that wrote them books on English Painting and Rubens and Wan Dyck in England. What a life does a dealer lead that's yet got only one client and *he* goes and gets himself intimate with a art expert!"

"But it might even be useful," Georgina said. "We've got some really good pictures, even if they aren't fashionable and don't bear the few very greatest names, and so Professor Watson might like—"

"No, Georchie. Can't nobody influence Professor Egbert Watson, oddawise maybe could be coaxed to slide in a few poison hints on Mr. Hollins in regards Hanover Galleries." Mr. Rumbin sighed again. "Well, I done the best I could. Ensill's up at Mr. Hollins's apartment trying to get in, Georchie."

"What!" She was astonished. "You sent—"

"Georchie, where's a suspiciouser financial man than Mr. Kingsford J. Hollins? Just when he's disloyal to us, maybe already got a picture from Hanover Galleries, don't his brain chump right away to I'm spying on him if I go, myself?" Mr. Rumbin brightened a little. "Listen now, Georchie and Howie; catch the elegantness of it. I took Ensill in Schorr's, bought him pants, shoes, hat, nice blue-speckled bleck tie. Suppose he gets in, spies round, sees a picture from Hanover Galleries, what a adwantage! See it, Howie?"

"I'm afraid not, Mr. Rumbin."

"No? Suppose Ensill reports me Mr. Hollins acquires Hanover Galleries' Holbein, next time I see Mr. Hollins I don't let him know I knows it; I commence talking quick about how many Bellinis, Giorgiones—and Holbeins especial—is doubtful pictures; it's too bad. Conshenshus, too, on account of all the

bum Holbeins, Hanover Galleries' Holbein of
the bum is the bummest." Mr. Rumbin's head sank
again. "Yet if Mr. Hollins did bought it, oh, what a
smack I'm taking against the nose!"

Georgina was puzzled. "Mr. Rumbin, I can't
imagine anybody like Ensill's getting an appointment
to see Mr. Hollins."

"No," Rumbin said. "Ensill couldn't, himself. No
inwention. A four-year-old schoolgirl could keep Ensill out of her house. Yet how simple! Mr. Hollins
he's home now for lunch. Me, I tell Ensill ring the
bell, tell the butler tell Mr. Kingsford J. Hollins he
wants to buy one of his pictures any price he asks.
He's got to have it immediate."

"What!"

"Certainly, Georchie. Any collector would anyways got to *look* at anybody says *that,* wouldn't
he?"

"Yes," Georgina said. "But Mr. Hollins is a business man and suppose he'd say he *would* sell one of
his—"

"No, it's safe, Georchie. That Beechey portrait of
Eighteent'-Century Sir Frederick Hollings I sold
Mr. Hollins last mont', he's got English lawyers in-
westigating if it's a ancestor. Ensill don't say which
picture he buys until after he gets in. Then, all the
time looking round, he says he's a Beechey collector

and it's Sir Frederick Hollings he's got to own. Will Mr. Hollins sell it, Georchie?"

"No, I suppose—"

" 'Suppose'? Mr. Hollins might sell the mink off Mrs. Hollins's beck but not Sir Frederick Hollings that maybe turns out commenced the Hollins family! So Ensill acts disappointed—a such macknificent Beechey, too! Kills two birts with one club—Hollins thinks a hundut times more of his Beechey from Rumbin Galleries and Ensill finds out has he got that bum Holbein or maybe some odda new picture that breaks my heart!" Stern again, Mr. Rumbin spoke harshly to his assistant. "Cattlet! Rubbing furniture forever, have I got no nerfs? Here I'm sitting waiting bad news and you keep me watching boils on antiques! Must always a cat's tongue be licking my eyes' balls? Rub somewheres elst, Cattlet!"

"I beg your pardon!" the assistant said with dignity, and retired to the stock room behind the shop.

CHAPTER TEN

THERE, working upon a catalogue of the Galleries'
paintings, he heard erelong a husky voice muttering
hurriedly and Mr. Rumbin moaning in response. The
husky person was obviously the "art scout", ex-
Professor Ensill, making his report; and Howard
had a sentimental curiosity about him. Remembering
that eventful first morning in Rumbin Galleries, the
young assistant thought he'd like to have another look
at the luckless man who'd preceded him as an applicant; and he ventured presently to create an errand
for himself that took him to Miss Horne's desk in
the rear of the shop. He was in time to see a stooped
figure silhouetted in departure by the opening and
closing of the outer door.

The silhouette was repeated, however, as the scout
reopened the door and looked in. The husky voice
called to Mr. Rumbin, who was retiring from the

front part of the shop. "Forgot to mention it. I'm
on the trail of a really great picture. If I get hold of
it I'll—"

"No!" Rumbin looked back over his shoulder and
shouted fiercely. "Snake-in-the-grass, I don't want it!
Stay away!"

"All right," Ensill called, withdrawing. "If I get
hold of it I'll bring it in."

"Nuisance-maker!" Rumbin grumbled, on his way
to the desk. "Always wants to bring me some picture
because it's good painting; don't care who's it by.
Can I sell pictures of Nobody by Nobody? To who?"
He sank into a chair beside the desk and groaned.
"Georchie, what he tells me, it's bad!"

"Bad? I couldn't hear distinctly; but I thought I
heard him say Mr. Hollins hadn't bought—"

"No, not yet; but he sees Ensill knows pictures,
talks to him. Georchie, Mr. Hollins besides Hanover
Galleries, he's been at Morie's, Thompson Hickok's,
Enberzner's. Asks Ensill serious about Morie's ugly
old lady's portrait by Ingres. Says he don't like no
ugly old ladies much but he hears Ingres is a great
Outstanding Master; asks him is he? What'd Ensill
answer him?"

"I suppose he could have said it was a matter of
opinion or—"

"Didn't! Bites the hands that feeds him! That

Ingres it's a such fine picture Ensill confesses me he
can't help telling Hollins any collector'd be congratulated! He's right, too; but anyways there's a feller
to be spending money on for shoes, speckled ties,
striped pants, Ensill! My Lort, how sure pops a
client in some odda dealer's hands if you can't keep
him near busted yourself! How can I stop him buying
that Ingres, Georchie?"

"But haven't we anything at all in stock that Mr.
Hollins might—"

"With a outstanding name? Georchie, we own now
not even a Schreyer bleck-whiskers, curly-gunstock
Arab sitting horsebeck on a white horse! No; I got
nothing in the worlt but my second cousin's letter he
writes me about that Watteau." The worried dealer
glanced sorely at his assistant. "Cattlet, should I
send you representing Rumbin Galleries to New Orleans?"

"Sir?"

"Listen, Cattlet. Metropolitan pays seventy-fife
t'ousand dollars for a Watteau, newspapers says. Suppose you're offered one; you can reckanize a aut'entic
Watteau from a Watteau wort' a dollar forty-nine,
can't you, Cattlet?"

"I'm afraid not," Howard said stiffly; and returned
to his cataloguing in the stock room. He'd been working there, resentfully, for only a few minutes, how-

ever, when Mr. Rumbin came in and spoke hurriedly but humbly.

"You're sitting mad at me, Howie," he said. "When my business looked altogedda busted I acted nicer. Now I got up a little, if it don't look good I get so excited either I commit suicide or commence cussing somebody. It can't be Georchie; she's a lady, so it's tough, I'm sorry, but it has to be you, Howie. I got to go quick get on a train, no help for it; don't nurse no bad feelings on me while I'm away, Howie."

"Indeed no, sir!" the young man said heartily, as they shook hands. "It's New Orleans you're going to, Mr. Rumbin?"

"Yes. Georchie she's your boss in charge everything same as me. I'm hurrying for time; good-by, Howie."

"Good luck, sir; good-by."

Howard asked nothing better than that Georgina Horne should be in sole command of him; and, when he'd heard Mr. Rumbin leaving the shop, he came out cheerfully from the stock room. She sat at her desk, looking serious. "You'll be telling me everything I do for quite a little time, won't you, Georgina?" Howard inquired hopefully. "Mr. Rumbin's gone on pretty important business, hasn't he?"

"Important? It's worse than that," she told him,

and explained the vital errand upon which their harried employer had departed for the South.

Mr. Rumbin had a second cousin who was a small antiquity dealer in New Orleans, she said; and the cousin had discovered what he believed to be a great treasure of art—an old painting, dim under more than a century's dirt but undoubtedly a *Fête Galante* by Antoine Watteau. The family who owned the picture had no suspicion that it was a Watteau; nevertheless, the second cousin had offered eighty dollars for it in vain. He was convinced that three or four hundred would be amply persuasive, and, unable to produce such sums himself, he had written to Mr. Rumbin of the immense opportunity. Mr. Rumbin, desperate for a Great Master immediately with which to tempt the disloyal Hollins, had suddenly decided to be on his way.

"Poor man!" Georgina said. "I know he's had to begin worrying over money again, Howard; yet he left me two hundred dollars to run the shop with—in case he's detained by bargaining with the family that don't know they own the Watteau!" She laughed sympathetically. "Said he'd wire me the instant he buys it; but either I don't know him or I'll hear from him before then."

She did. The next afternoon there came a "day letter", despatched from Atlanta en route.

PHONE HIM CAREFUL NOT SAYING WHERE I AM
SAYING ME ACQUIRING GREATEST WORK OUTSTAND-
ING MASTER NOT WHO CASE I DONT STOP SAY MUSEUM
MASTERPIECE LOUVRE WOULD GO CRAZY OVER FIT
FOR ROYAL COLLECTIONS STOP TALK ATTRACTIVE US-
ING ALL WILES TILL HE SCARED PROMISES YOU
NOT BUY ANYTHING TILL HE SEES

RUMBIN

"A little staggering," Georgina said. "I don't know
where to get any wiles—let alone trying to work
them by telephone on the grimmest dried-up old millionaire in New York!"

"You don't need to get any," Howard told her
earnestly; but failed of her full attention. She was
already at the telephone; and the listener near her
presently wondered how even a dried-up millionaire
could be so insensitive to beauty that such a voice
would have to argue with him.

"Yes, I know, Mr. Hollins," Georgina said. "But
mightn't you be sorry afterward if you . . . No, our
picture's so important Mr. Rumbin feels the name of
the master who painted it can't be mentioned yet; but
I can tell you this much—the subject's lovely and,
after all, that counts. Pretty often even works by the
greatest masters are unpleasant to live with on account of the subject's being disagreeable—a cross-
looking old woman, for instance. . . ." She laughed

prettily. "Yes; but I fear we dealers try that on collectors rather often, Mr. Hollins—making them
afraid somebody else'll snap up the picture . . . Oh,
but he did try to telephone you himself before he left;
he couldn't get you, Mr. Hol . . . Yes, I know
you're a busy man; but couldn't you at least . . . Is
that the best we can count on? . . . Well, if it is
. . . Good-by."

She turned to Howard. "They've got him excited
about the Ingres; Mr. Rumbin'll have to get here with
the Watteau pretty fast. Mr. Hollins did promise
not to do anything final without first calling me up,
and I'll have to wire Mr. Rumbin that's the best I
could do with him."

She sent her telegram, and late the next day received a response composed by Mr. Rumbin in New
Orleans in the morning.

HOLD HIM HOLD HIM HOLD HIM STOP SELF NOT
SEEN YET STOP FAMILY GONE GRANDPA FUNERAL
BATON ROUGE LOCKED UP TOO MANY NEIGHBORS
CHILDREN DANGEROUS BUT COUSIN POSITIVE STOP
GRANDPA FUNERAL TOMORROW NO WAY TO HURRY IT
STOP USE MORE WILES PROMISE ANYTHING HOLD HIM
HOLD HIM HOLD HIM

                                        RUMBIN

CHAPTER ELEVEN

GEORGINA TRANSLATED a passage for the perplexed
Howard. "He means that he and the second cousin
couldn't break into the locked-up house where the
Watteau is because there were too many neighbors'
children around." Then she laughed at the young
man's horrified expression. "No, not to steal the
picture—even in his present state of mind he'd hardly
risk that! Just to look at it and see if it's as good as
the second cousin thinks it is."

"How'll he know?" Howard asked. "Will he look
for Watteau's signature under the dirt?"

"Signature? He'd hardly depend on that. There
were two Watteaus; and Jean Antoine, the great one,
had three different ways of signing. Also, about the
easiest thing a faker does is forging the signature.
Of course most old painters didn't sign their pictures."

"I see!" Howard looked careworn. "They didn't
—just to make it harder."

"No, it was because they thought it would be so
easy," she told him. "Gilbert Stuart said he didn't
need to sign his pictures because they were signed all
over 'em. You see what he meant. You're pretty sure
of a Gilbert Stuart as soon as you see one, aren't
you?"

"I—I think so. I don't know why I am, though."

"How do you recognize a handwriting?" she
asked. "Or a voice on the telephone? Familiarity,
isn't it? Art experts have science and research besides; but of course even they can be mistaken sometimes. For instance, two Raeburn portraits that were
accepted and listed for years by Raeburn experts—
they've lately turned out to be Stuarts."

Howard rubbed the back of his head. "Sometimes
I think I see a little light; then I'm always more
mixed up than ever. Take Mr. Hollins's friend, for
instance—this Professor Egbert Watson: Would he
have known those two Stuarts weren't Raeburns?"

"Professor Watson? I doubt if he'd have passed
on them. He's not an authority on later Eighteenth
Century English painting, but on Seventeenth, and
his particular specialty's the earlier English portraits,
Holbein, through Mytens, Van Dyck and Lely to
Hogarth. He's top authority there."

"Oh, me!" Howard looked at her mournfully. "Georgina, I'm afraid you know everything. Not only about pictures but—"

They were interrupted. Two elderly women, prowlers among "antiques", came into the shop, and Georgina went to assist their pryings. Howard would have gone back to his catalogue; but the outer door, opening again, astonished him. For a moment he thought that as many as three possible clients were going to be present in Rumbin Galleries at the same time. Then, advancing, he perceived that the newcomer, a stooping and haggard man, came not to buy but to sell. He had brought with him a picture, a rather large one, insecurely covered by heavy brown paper.

"Ah—Professor Ensill, can I help you?" Howard said. "Mr. Rumbin's out of town. Can I—"

"No." Ensill looked at him drearily. "If he's out of town I'd better wait for her."

"Yes, you'd better," Howard said in simplest agreement, and was aware that hints of gin mingled in the air with the smell of Mr. Rumbin's preservative furniture polish.

The female adventurers departed; Georgina turned to Ensill, and, in response to her friendly greeting, he gave her a languid grey hand.

"When'll he be back?" he asked.

"Not for several days, I'm afraid."

"Several? That'll be too late. I wanted to show him—"

"It wouldn't have been of any use, Professor Ensill," she said compassionately. "He told me if you brought a picture in to tell you—"

"I know what he told you!" Ensill's husky and monotonous voice became a little louder. "He hadn't seen it, had he? Here, I'm going to show you—"

"Professor Ensill, there isn't the slightest—"

"How do you know?" he asked bitterly. "Here!" Carrying his picture laboriously, he went toward the rear of the shop. "Open up that room he calls his 'galleries', will you? I'm going to show it to you in a decent light, no matter what you say."

"Why, of course if you'd like to," Georgina said, and hurried before him. She opened the door of the room in which Mr. Rumbin showed paintings to his clients; Ensill passed in, removed the paper wrapping and placed his picture upon an easel. Howard Cattlet followed, glanced at the painting, then looked deferentially at Georgina and was surprised by the tense fixity with which she was already regarding it.

It was the half-length portrait of a serious fine gentleman, an obvious aristocrat—young and yet already deeply experienced, not only in high affairs but

in his own thinking. The face was scholarly and
sensitive, yet fearless; and the eyes seemed to with-
hold from the spectator a melancholy secret. Brown
hair, long and thick, descended upon his broad collar
of exquisite lace. His dark sleeves were slashed with a
dim white, and one of his lovingly painted delicate
hands held a rolled document; the other rested list-
lessly in his black velvet lap. Even under an old
varnish that had "bloomed" bluishly over most of the
picture, the paint showed itself to have been applied
suavely and cleanly in strokes that easily rhymed
with both the special modelings and the complete design. This technique wasn't definitely perceived by
young Howard Cattlet, though he was aware of per-
vading harmonies; but Georgina Horne instantly
understood that the work before her came from the
hand of a great Seventeenth Century master.

"I know that face," she said slowly. "It's Lucius
Cary, second Lord Falkland, finest hero of all King
Charles's Cavaliers. I've seen reproductions of portraits of him by Van Dyck and by Cornelius Johnson
—of course everybody must have wanted to paint
him. But the painter of this portrait I don't—I don't
quite—"

"Dobson," Ensill said with solemnity. "William
Dobson. That portrait was painted by William Dobson."

Color heightened in Georgina's cheeks. She stepped forward, closer to the picture, seemed about to kneel before it. "William Dobson." She spoke in a low voice. "Dobson! Yes; so it is. William Dobson!"

Her reverent utterance of a name but little known to Howard had a glamoring effect upon him; all at once the portrait seemed to him magnificent. It began to put a spell upon him, and his desire was to look at it in silence for a long time—with Georgina Horne. But the voice of Ensill intruded.

"Yes, I thought your seeing it'd make a difference. Not so often, what?"

"No. Not often," Georgina said. "I've made pilgrimages to every Dobson I could ever get near. This is—"

"Top!" the scout interrupted. "It's Dobson and Dobson at his top. What's Rumbin want? He's got to lay his hands on an 'Outstanding Master' for Hollins, hasn't he? Well, who's the greatest English master in the whole Seventeenth Century? William Dobson—with nobody near him. You might call Hilliard somebody; but Hilliard was only a miniature painter and so was Sam Cooper. Who's the first really important English painter that ever lived? William Dobson." He challenged Georgina lifelessly. "Deny it?"

"No, of course not."

"Hardly," Ensill said with dull satisfaction. "Then here's the greatest his race produced in a century. Can you say precisely the same for any other painter since Giotto, except maybe Velásquez and Goya and Raeburn and one or two others? Can you—"

Georgina interrupted him gently. "You don't have to convince me, Professor Ensill; I've been a Dobson enthusiast all my life. But unfortunately—"

"Don't begin unfortunatelying me!" Ensill said. "Here! I'll lay the cards on the table. This picture belonged to old man Ballard's housekeeper. When old Ballard blew up he kept it out of his auction and he gave it to her the day he died. Now she's passed out, too, and a niece of hers got her clothes and a couple of chairs and this picture. She showed it to me a week ago; and just this afternoon I got hold of an elegant painting of a watermelon, fish, and a bowl of oranges in a new gilt frame and I—"

"No!" Georgina cried. "You didn't—"

"Didn't I? She runs a boarding-house and thought she was clever; tickled to death working me for an even trade. Well, I need money; I want it right away. I'll name you a price you'll see how far I'll go for quick cash. Four thousand dollars. What do you say?"

Georgina was distressed. "Professor Ensill, I've already explained Mr. Rumbin's out of town. He left me two hundred dollars to run the shop with, and that's all."

"You could wire him, couldn't you?"

"It wouldn't be any use because he doesn't yet know himself how much money he'll need for the important picture he's gone to—"

"Oh, he's gone to buy?" Ensill's stoop increased. He moved toward the portrait; then stopped. "All right. Seems there's no argument. It's too late to show it to anybody else to-day and I'm too tired to carry it uptown, anyhow. I'll leave it here until to-morrow, if you don't mind. Lend me five dollars, will you?"

Georgina went to her desk; but, before she returned, Howard Cattlet had forestalled her and Ensill was shuffling out of the street door. She was cross. "What do you mean by it? Your salary's only half the size of mine."

"Yes," Howard said, and he added sorrowfully, under his breath, though she heard him, "That's the trouble!" Then, unaware that he had said anything possibly a little startling, he prepared to do some more furniture polishing; but the entrance of a messenger boy transfixed him. "Has he got the Watteau?" he asked, when the boy was gone and Georgina had read the telegram.

"No!" she said; and handed him the yellow paper. He read the words of anguish.

WINDOW NOONTIME NEIGHBORS CHILDREN HOME
LUNCH STOP ONE GLANCE PURELY HORRIBLE DIS-
GUSTING IMITATION EIGHTEEN SEVENTY STOP COUSIN
HIRED LAWYER LIBEL SUIT WHAT I CALLED HIM STOP
LOOKING FOR ME NOW SERVE PAPERS TRAINS ABSO-
LUTE BLACKMAIL STOP AIRPLANE ARRIVE GALLERIES
FOUR TOMORROW AFTERNOON STOP HOLD HIM DO
SOMETHING HOLD HIM

RUMBIN

Howard looked up, appalled; but Georgina's eyes
were sparkling. "How perfect!" she exclaimed.

"What, Georgina? To me things look about as
blue as they possibly could. I don't understand what
you're so excited and happy about."

"Don't you see?" she cried. "When Mr. Rumbin
gets here he'll find we have that magnificent portrait
of Lord Falkland waiting for him. It'll cost more
than he hoped to pay for the Watteau; but Mr. Hollins or any collector—even the dullest!—would jump
at such a picture. Let's go look at it again! Oh,
Howard, isn't it extraordinary?"

He agreed warmly that it was; but later, at home
in Hackertown, sat in puzzled reverie. Georgina,
worshiper of William Dobson, was captured by the
portrait, became entranced when she stood before
it and loved to look at it again and again. Yet she
was delighted with the prospect that Mr. Hollins

would buy it, though that meant she'd very likely never see it again. Mr. Rumbin, too, seemed really in love with one of his pictures sometimes and then delighted to part with it. In fact, the more he liked it himself the better pleased to sell it he seemed. What did these contradictions mean? Howard's reverie ended with his discovering the answer within himself; and that was one of the most important steps he took toward becoming really an Art Dealer's Assistant.

He'd caught from Georgina Horne something of her feeling for the Dobson portrait, knew it was a fine thing, a true work of art, even a masterpiece; the thought of it made a kind of glow within him, warming his imagination, and he, too, wished to look at the painting again and again. Yet he, too, was glad that it would be sold to Mr. Hollins—glad and proud. Here, then, was the secret; he was glad and proud because Rumbin Galleries, of which he was a part, had the handling of so splendid an object. In this and in his appreciation of the picture, he shared something, however distantly, with that long-dead artist who had painted it—and also sold it.

An art dealer's life, Howard perceived, could know rewards not financial. It was a life, too, of hazards, uncertainties and surprises; therefore fascinating with adventure. Moreover, though in his meditation he knew it not, these conclusions of his were about to be strikingly confirmed in regard to the hazards, uncertainties and surprises.

In the morning he and Georgina had a shock.

CHAPTER TWELVE

AT ABOUT TEN O'CLOCK Ensill came into Rumbin
Galleries for his picture and declined to leave it
there any longer.

Alarmed, neither Georgina nor Howard sniffed
the slightest trace of alcohol on the air about him;
they found they had to do with an Ensill in complete
sobriety, a creature harshly differing from the Ensill
of yesterday. Uninterested in the fact that Mr.
Rumbin, flying, was now but a few hours away, he
proved stone to persuasion, then became excitable—
even spiteful—in argument.

"Run for office!" he bade them. "Blah-blah might
get you elected. I'm giving this picture away for
quick money and I've practically got it. If I could
wait, wouldn't I claim a cut on whatever it sells for
to a collector?" He advanced toward the easel upon
which the painting rested. "Get me that paper I had
it wrapped up in, you!"

This "you" was addressed to Howard, whose immediate response was helplessly physical. He stepped between Ensill and the picture; then said sternly, "You listen to Miss Horne!"

"Listen to her?" Ensill laughed. "How much longer? I saw Max Enberzner an hour ago and will he always gamble on a pretty sure thing or won't he? I've got him so excited about this picture he's dropping cigarette ashes on his own clothes. I can get four thousand dollars by noon. How do I know Rumbin'll get here by four or that he'll take it if he does? Wait, your grandmother! Get me that wrapping paper."

Georgina looked desperate. "Professor Ensill, will you take two hundred dollars for an option until—"

"Option, no! I'm selling. If you won't get me that wrapping paper—"

"No!" she cried. "We've got to have it. We'll buy it ourselves!"

"Not with two hundred dollars you won't!"

"No," Georgina said. "I've got over nine hundred dollars in postal savings in the safe here and—"

Howard Cattlet, reddening, interrupted her. "I've got almost three hundred. It's in the bank and I've got a cheque-book in a table drawer in the stock room."

Georgina gave him a glance worth more than it cost him. "That makes twelve hundred," she said. "Twelve hundred down, Professor Ensill, and we'll pay the rest as soon—"

"Yes; so you say!" But Ensill had become reflective; his dull eye showed a gleam. "Look here," he said. "I'll tell you what I'll do. Rumbin's got a little Théodore Rousseau landscape; I know where I can sell it. You and this young fellow've got twelve hundred together and there's two hundred in the till. Get me that Rousseau landscape out of the stock room and—"

Georgina interrupted him. "But that picture's worth at least four thousand dollars itself and we couldn't—"

"Take it or leave it," Ensill said. "Hand me fourteen hundred dollars cash and the Rousseau landscape, and you get the Dobson. I mean right now immediately; but I'll give you five minutes."

"We—we've got to!" Georgina gasped, whereupon the facial expression of the scout became less disagreeable.

When details were completed and he had Georgina's postal certificates, Howard's cheque and Mr. Rumbin's bills in his pocket, and the wrapped Rousseau landscape under his arm, he was, indeed, almost genial. "I guess it's maybe just as well," he said, in departure. "Enberzner might have gone back on me, after all. You never know. By-by!"

"Well, we've done it!" Georgina exclaimed, as the door closed. "We're both bankrupt and Mr. Rumbin's lovely Rousseau's gone—but he wired me to 'Do something!' and he said I was to be in charge absolutely the same as himself." She paused, watching the stooping figure of the scout as it passed across the display window. Ensill was smiling faintly, entirely to himself; but Georgina understood that smile. "The old slicker! Worked it, didn't he?"

"Worked what, Georgina?"

"Exactly what I warned Mr. Hollins against so craftily!—how 'we dealers' scare clients about somebody else's snapping up a picture. Let him smile! We've got it and it's a grand thing and it saves the day for Mr. Rumbin. Now, thank heaven, we're ready for Mr. Hollins! I'll tell him so this instant."

Mr. Hollins's secretary informed Georgina, over the telephone, of a coincidence. He'd just been instructed to call Rumbin Galleries and say that Mr. Hollins wouldn't wait any longer. "But we've got it! We've got a great picture for him, just what he wants!" Georgina cried. "It's here! We're ready to show it to Mr. Hollins any time after four this very afternoon. That's why I'm calling. Please ask him—" There was a silence; but Howard saw her face grow bright again. Mr. Hollins would be at Rumbin Galleries at half past four.

In triumph this confident business woman was like a little girl. She put out a hand, "Howard! Let's go look at our divine Dobson again!"

Then, both radiant, they ran, hand in hand; but in the presence of the picture Georgina was sobered. "What's the matter?" Howard asked. "Don't you like it as much as you—"

"Yes—yes, of course I do." She went close to the portrait, moved back from it, went close again. "Of course it's Dobson," she said. "How could it be anything else? Look at those hands."

"The hands, Georgina?"

"Yes. A man named Morelli played hob with famous collections; showed a lot of pictures weren't by the special Old Masters claimed for 'em. Proved it mainly by fingers and ears, because nearly every early master painted certain details in his own typical way and always the same—particularly hands and ears, no matter *whose* hands and ears he was painting. Well, Dobson was a pupil of Van Dyck's and Van Dyck's influence shows in Dobson's painting. So there's the Van Dyck type of hand in this portrait, just as it should be."

"Then what made you—"

"Nothing, really," she said. "Just for a minute it

began to seem to me that I—well, that I missed something that ought to be in a Dobson portrait. There's a quality called 'temper'—it means the kind of man the painter himself really was. William Dobson was poetic and sensitive and refined and—"

"And what, Georgina?" her colleague asked anxiously, as she paused. "Aren't those things in this—"

"Yes, but— Well, look at a Frenchman's portrait of an American, for instance—doesn't the American always look at least a little bit French? Just for a moment it seemed to me I missed Dobson's Englishness. He was a rich colorist, too; loved Titian and—"

Howard protested. "But the color of this portrait's splendid, Georgina."

"Of course it is," she said. "It's quiet; but it's beautiful—yes, and English, too." She laughed. "Certainly it's Dobson! I'm such a Dobsonite, and we've been so excited—and dashing!—it's a perfectly natural reaction to get scared now and wonder if this portrait's really quite up to him. It is, though; so don't be frightened, Howard."

She was gay again; and the doubt had passed, not to return upon later reassuring visits to the portrait. Naturally there were other qualms, some of them severe, as the two awaited the arrival of Rumbin— of Rumbin and the impending more and more terrible Hollins holding in one Jovian hand gold and in the other the thunderbolt.

At half past three Georgina looked at Howard, clapped a hand to her pretty forehead and seemed to suffer. "Oh, dear, oh, dear, oh, dear—"

Howard was distressed. "Is there something wrong about me, Georgina? I mean, because you were looking at me and it seemed all at once to worry you terribly. Is my face—"

"No, your clothes!" she said. "You haven't got 'em on."

"What?"

"I mean that long-tailed black coat and the striped trousers Mr. Rumbin thinks you look so lovely in. You haven't got 'em on and Mr. Hollins is coming. Now of course there isn't time."

"Yes, there is." Howard strode to the stock room, and, within ten minutes, returned in his garments of state. "All right, Georgina?"

"Superb," she told him. "Now we've done everything we possibly can. All we can do is stand and wait and keep ourselves calm."

They stood and waited and didn't keep themselves calm.

"Anyhow," Georgina said tremulously, at five minutes of four, "anyhow, no matter what about Mr. Hollins, we're sure of one thing—when Mr.

Rumbin finds he owns such a Dobson he'll be wild with joy."

At least, Georgina was half right; she was wrong about only the joy. Mr. Rumbin arrived at twenty minutes after four, cured of flying ("Am I double dead from seasickness?" he asked) and, when led to the portrait and convinced that he owned it, he performed calisthenics, walked the floor and spoke in three foreign languages before he could get back to English.

"Seasickness!" he said, when he was calm enough, so to call it. "Lastly seasickness helped from ptomaine disease poisoning from a early breakfast bad fried oyster I swallered down and couldn't stop because I sees my second cousin and his shyster lawyer looking for me outside the restaurant window where I'm eating before good-by New Orleans! Firstly, it ain't a Watteau; nextly, it's hiding from bleckmail lawyers; lastly, it's seasickness from a airplane and oysters; and now it's what do I look like I own me a Dobson!"

"Dobson," pale Georgina echoed. "But Dobson's one of the greatest painters who ever—"

"You're telling me?" Rumbin shouted. "Tell somebody don't know it!"

"That's not consistent, sir," Howard ventured to say, incited by Georgina's tragic face. "If you admit yourself that Dobson was one of the greatest painters that ever—"

"Cattlet!" Rumbin shouted louder. "You're talking to me Dobson. Supposed to be a Art Dealer's Assistant, who oughts you to be talking?"

"Sir?"

"Kingsford J. Hollins!" Mr. Rumbin bellowed. "That's who you oughts to be talking; not Dobson. What's a art dealer's life, knowing pictures? It ain't; it's knowing human nature. What's the human nature of Kingsford J. Hollins? Cattlet, I'm asking you!"

"I don't know, sir."

"No, but I thought Georchie would," the dealer said in a choking voice. "Georchie she's so nuts on Dobson it socks her judgment clients. Listen, Georchie, the human nature of Hollins it's he wants pig names and you got for him one he don't know it exists."

"But he—he must!" she faltered. "Anybody who's begun to collect pictures—even just begun—"

"Georchie! Suppose Mr. Hollins just barely did heard of Dobson, does he want a name nobody has dinner with him gets impressed by? You could sell him a Albrecht Dürer, not a Hausbuch Meister. You could sell him a Lawrence, a Hoppner, a Turner, not a Girtin or a Bonington or a Lemuel Abbott he never hears about. You could sell him a

Fra Angelico; would he look at a Piero di Cosimo?
Rembrandt, Titian, Wan Dyck, Rubens, yes; but
not—"

"Please!" Georgina tried to interrupt his pas-
sionate volubility. "Please stand still just one instant,
Mr. Rumbin, and listen. Every sound writer on
English painting admits that Dobson—"

"Sound writers!" Mr. Rumbin cried. "Is Hollins
sound writers? No! He's a collecting commencer.
Can you sell him even wan der Weyden, even
Breughel? No! El Greco, wan Gogh, Gauguin he
ain't yet art-fash'nable enough for; can't stand the
pictures, he's too natchal-minded—maybe too
natchal-minded yet even for Goya. And now, when
he sees all I got for him's a Dobson—" Mr. Rumbin's voice cracked; he used falsetto. "Goes straight
to Morie's—French dealers gets him! Commences
Ingres; they sell him Monet, Manet, Renoir,
Cézanne—ends with Matisse, Picasso, Modigliani!
I'm ruined!"

"Please don't!" Georgina begged him piteously.
"You're always saying you're ruined, Mr. Rumbin;
but please, please don't now."

"No? Not even when lastly it's the *case?* Not
when what I oughts to had for Mr. Hollins is a
Stuart's Georche Washington and what I got's a
Dobson he walks out on me on?"

"But he couldn't, Mr. Rumbin; not if he looks at it! You haven't really looked at it yourself. You just began jumping and shouting, using your lungs not your eyes. You—"

"Eyes? I'm using my ears, Georchie. I'm hearing Hollins asking me 'Who's it by?' I'm hearing me choke trying not to say 'Dobson.' " Here Mr. Rumbin did glance again at the picture, sufferingly. "You say look at it, Georchie? What's the first thing I see? It's them Wan Dyck hands Dobson usual paints, so we couldn't even make it into a Peter Lely that Mr. Hollins anyhow must heard the name of, because Lely's hands is plumper; it ain't possible." Rumbin's voice rose, high and lamenting. "Oh, Georchie, Georchie—"

"Look out, sir!" Howard Cattlet, who had remained near the doorway, heard a sound and glanced out into the shop. "Mr. Rumbin, be careful! Mr. Hollins and another gentleman are just coming in."

CHAPTER THIRTEEN

"ANOTHER GENTLEMAN?" Mr. Rumbin, electrified, ran on tiptoe to the door, briefly exposed one eye, withdrew his head, then spoke in a vehement whisper. "My Lort, now Professor Egbert Watson he's got with him'll be hell selling him pictures if always *he* comes adwiser! . . . Georchie, stop crying, go wash your face, act like you're sneezing on the way! . . . Howie, where's that dumb aristocratic cold look you got natchal? Put it beck on your face; go quick tell Mr. Hollins you'll tell Mr. Rumbin he's here. Go, both! Handkerchief on the nose, Georchie! Quick!"

Georgina, crushed, pathetically sneezing, crossed the shop and went to a cubicle off the stock room, where she washed her humbled face. Immediately she wept again; then washed her face again, powdered tremblingly, and after that, trusting to a better self-control, returned to the shop. The indomitable actor, Rumbin, smiling brilliantly, was bowing the two visitors toward the doorway of the galleries wherein waited the fatal Dobson.

"No, gentlemen," he said. "I don't yet say which great Outstanding Master. I request, see the picture first; judge for yourselfs. Courteously walk in where's a masterpiece you can't say nothing but Ahs and Ohs, whoever looks at it."

"Ahs and Ohs, what?" Mr. Hollins was cold to the suggestion. "Me?"

Professor Egbert Watson was more encouraging. Anything but formidable in appearance, bald, stoutish and smiling, he said affably, "Nothing I like better than to Ah and Oh when there's the slightest excuse for it, Rumbin."

The three passed into the galleries; Howard Cattlet gave Georgina one last loyal glance and followed. Georgina, in stoic anguish, returned the glance, and then, unable to sit at her desk, stole to the open doorway and hovered there. Mr. Hollins and Professor Watson were standing before the portrait of Lord Falkland, upon which Howard Cattlet, at one side, turned the warming light of a tall reflecting lamp.

"Uniwersal!" Rumbin proclaimed with gusto. "Uniwersal's the appeal a such *chef d'œuvre's* got. In the highest connoisseurs it raises emotions, yet even in the most simplest child it—"

"Never mind the high pressure stuff, Rumbin," Mr. Hollins said inconsiderately. "Rather like it, myself, first shot. You haven't got any tablet on it. Who's it by?"

"By?" Mr. Rumbin repeated bravely. "Who's it by? Mr. Hollins, when I got a such masterpiece before me, always I first ask myself, 'Rumbin,' I say, 'Rumbin, what's it matter who's it by?' In my heart what's the answer do I hear? 'Simple it don't, Rumbin; it don't!'" Standing outside the spreading shaft of light from the reflector, he gave Professor Watson an acutely anxious glance from the side of an eye. The art expert was apparently spellbound. "Look at the Professor!" Mr. Rumbin exclaimed. "See how it excites him, Mr. Hollins, no matter who's it by."

"Interesting," Professor Watson said musingly. "You gentlemen no doubt recall that passage of Goldsmith's—when the Vicar of Wakefield bids his son go and fight for the king as his grandfather had fought before him. You remember what the Vicar said—'Go, my boy, and imitate him in all but his misfortunes, if it was a misfortune to die with Lord Falkland!'"

"Falkland?" Mr. Hollins asked coldly. "Who's he?"

"This is," Professor Watson said dryly, "Lucius Cary, second Viscount Falkland." Then he became benevolent, glanced at Howard approvingly. "The young gentleman knows, I fancy. Falkland, scholar, poet, Ben Jonson's patron and a great Cavalier hero, slain fighting for King Charles at Newbury. Falkland, whom Cowley called 'England's Falkland'; and do you remember, young man, what that other poet, Waller, wrote of Falkland?" The question was rhetorical; Dr. Egbert Watson didn't await a reply, but quoted sonorously:

> " '. . . . with what horror we
> Think on the blind events of war, and thee
> To fate exposing that all knowing breast
> Among the throng, as cheaply as the rest.' "

"It's putty," Mr. Rumbin said, swallowing anxiously at a little distance inside of his commending smile. "It's putty, and about poetry I often think to myself—"

Mr. Hollins cut him off. "I can read up on who the picture's of, myself," he said crossly. "What I want to know's who painted it?"

Mr. Rumbin said nothing, but breathed heavily.

Professor Watson stepped forward and scrutinized the whole surface of the painting as it glowed in the light. "Unmistakable. An interesting experience; very interesting indeed to renew my acquaintance with this picture."

"Renew?" Rumbin, staggered, was admirable. "Aha!" he exclaimed, as if in jovial triumph. "You see, Mr. Hollins? Professor Egbert Watson he already knows this great painting of mine. He loves—"

"Certainly I know it." Professor Watson, stooping, peered through his glasses at the left lower corner of the canvas. "Yes. Same tiny flake of paint off down here against the frame, showing the weave, exactly as when I last saw it. Dirtier and got a bloom but no restoration; practically perfect condition. I don't suppose Mr. Rumbin would mind saying where it turned up from."

"Frangkly speaking," Rumbin said, "frangkly, it reaches me through one of my agents from a private collector."

"I see." Professor Egbert Watson smiled intelligently. He turned to the client. "Mr. Hollins, I first saw that picture twenty-seven years ago in Wandour Castle, long before it was brought to New York and old Ballard bought it. I saw it again in Ballard's collection and had a good laugh at the old man—strictly to myself. He'd gone rather da-da in his head, got his pictures all mixed up and couldn't remember which was which. Told me solemnly this was a Dobson."

"Dobson?" Mr. Hollins said forbiddingly. "Never heard of him."

"No? A great painter, Mr. Hollins," the expert returned mildly. "His work's often mistaken for his master's. This Falkland portrait wasn't in the Ballard sale; I often wondered what he'd done with it. However, a well-known picture seldom disappears permanently nowadays; it usually turns up again like this."

"Well known?" Hollins asked quickly. "*How* well known?"

Professor Watson laughed cheerfully. "Well, I don't suppose I'll be increasing the price Mr. Rumbin has in mind; naturally he already knows at least as much about the picture as I do. It's recognized, Mr. Hollins, as the best of the three portraits of Lord Falkland he painted."

"He? Who, damn it?" Mr. Hollins spoke indignantly. "Best of the three *who* painted?"

"Why, Anton Van Dyck," Professor Watson said, surprised. "Anybody can see it's Van Dyck."

"Van Dyck?" The new collector's voice was slightly but perceptibly unsteady. "What! You say it's—it's Van Dyck?"

"Please permit!" Mr. Rumbin, who should have been stupefied, stepped superbly before Professor Watson and into the light; stood there commandingly—smiling and shaking his head reproachfully at his client. "For a such connoisseur like Mr. Kings-

ford J. Hollins, would me and all my art-staff and
agents be spending all this time and outstanding
sums exceptings for one the most outstanding well-
known paintings in uniwersal history? No, Mr.
Kingsford J. Hollins, you shouldn't thought it,
especial because of all my clients ain't I giving you
the first chance to acquire my great Wan Dyck from
Wandours Castles?"

Professor Egbert Watson, tactful, comprehended
that Mr. Rumbin and Mr. Hollins should be left
alone together. He turned to Howard Cattlet. "Ah
—perhaps I might be allowed to look over some of
the treasures in the other rooms, if this young gentleman doesn't mind showing them to me?"

This young gentleman didn't mind. With Professor Watson he returned to the shop, where his
gaze failed to find what it hoped for; Georgina had
retired to wash her face again, for she was weeping
again.

Professor Watson glanced twinklingly over his
shoulder at the closed door of the galleries. "Only
an excuse to let 'em go at it," he said. "I'm trotting
along. A matter of this importance'll naturally take
time to get settled. Hollins is lucky. Latter-day criti-
cism's been turning a little superior about Van Dyck's
second English period, but quite unwarrantably. This
portrait's entirely from the Master's own hand. I

rather suspect there may have been some luck in the matter for your boss, too—getting hold of such a picture." He looked inquisitively at the solemn young man; then laughed. "Don't worry. I'm not going to ask you how it happened. Good-by."

"No, sir," Howard said. "Thank you, Professor. Good-by." Then, turning, he saw Georgina, re-powdered, once more at her desk. "Georgina, Mr. Rumbin was marvelous! Could you see through the doorway how marvelous he was?"

Mr. Rumbin, himself, was at least equally appreciative. When Mr. Hollins had gone home wondering which he ought to feel—proud of owning a Van Dyck or heartbroken for his bank account— Mr. Rumbin was almost in awe of himself.

"Was you watching me close, Georchie and Howie?" he asked. "One hair's distance did they catched me letting my looks weaken? No! Oddawise where goes my client's confidence I know who painted my own picture as much as Professor Egbert Watson that wouldn't, exceptings for Wandours Castles? What a art dealer's face's lesson for you, Howie! Let it be wort' hundut times more to you than simple the outstanding money I got to hand you from going partnership with Georchie and me in Rumbin Galleries' great Kingsford J. Hollins Wan Dyck."

CHAPTER FOURTEEN

FOR THE YOUNG ASSISTANT here indeed was a windfall. Of course he and Georgina both protested;
though naturally they hoped that Mr. Rumbin would
remain firm in his appreciation of them and his
generous division of the spoils—and he did. Mr.
Hollins sent his cheque to Mr. Rumbin, full payment,
within the week, and the day after its receipt Mr.
Rumbin overcame the resistance of his employees.
Howard received, not as a bonus but as partner in
the special transaction just completed, something
more than twice the amount of his annual salary, and
his enthusiastic loyalty for an employer so scrupu-
lously fair-minded increased proportionately. He was
willing for Mr. Rumbin to be cross with him again
at any time the dealer felt that way.

In almost everybody's life there are times, usually
brief, when Fortune seems to have poured out her
cornucopia; but among the gold and fruit and flowers

and apples of silver there is always at least one spider. After childhood we're not intended to find flawless happiness in cornucopias. Georgina Horne also received a cheque for something better than double the amount of her annual salary, and that was Howard's spider. Not that he was mercenary; on the contrary, his trouble was a fear that he might appear so. She was still more than twice as rich as he was.

Meantime his education was continued. "Learning a dealer's business, Howie," Mr. Rumbin said to him, one day, in the shop, "for exemple, how would you hendle a case collectors' jealousy?"

"Sir? Collectors' what?"

"Jealousy, Howie. You know there's been pig art collections that wouldn't been near as pig exceptings they had nice jealousies making them pigger, don't you?"

"No, sir; I never heard of such a thing. I don't see how——"

"Wait." Mr. Rumbin placed the tip of a fore-finger on the end of his nose. "Listen. I show you by a objects lesson from what's inside yourself, Howie, because collectors' jealousy it's uniwersal, so some's got to be inside you too. Commence thinking about yourself. Are you?"

"Sir? Am I what?"

"Thinking about yourself," Mr. Rumbin said.

"For exemple, think about what feelings you had going on when you was maybe a little younger than now and had you a stamp collection. Natchly, when a little boy going to school you collected stamps of course and—"

"No, I didn't, sir. I never collected any stamps."

"No? What a feller! Howie, didn't you never collected anything in your life? Think beck."

Howard thought back. "Well—yes, I suppose in a way it might have been called a collection. Yes, I collected marbles."

"Marbles? You collected marbles, Howie?" Mr. Rumbin was astonished. "I didn't supposed you— You're sure you collected marbles, Howie?"

"Yes, sir; I did."

"You did?" Mr. Rumbin was not only surprised; he was deeply impressed. "Renaissance?"

"Sir?"

"I says was they Renaissance, Howie, them marbles?"

"Sir?"

Then, as the two stood looking at each other in a complete stalemate of misunderstandings, Georgina, who had been listening, thought it was time to explain them to each other. "Mr. Rumbin thinks you mean you collected sculptured marbles, possibly Renaissance," she said to Howard, and to Mr. Rumbin, "He means he collected little round marbles of the kind boys play games with, in the spring."

"Oh." A deferential expression that had come upon Mr. Rumbin's face changed to a look of relief, and he went on with the lesson. "Now think beck about yourself again, Howie. When you was collecting them kind of play-marbles, natchly you wanted to have more marbles, pigger ones, marbles that cost more, ones that was harder to get, and ones that nobody elst had any of, than the odda boys. Didn't you?"

"No, sir."

"What!" Mr. Rumbin cried. "Of course you did. You wanted to have the best marbles of any boy, the piggest, the most expensive, the marbles there was fewest of, the—"

"No, sir," Howard said, "I don't think I did."

"Listen!" Mr. Rumbin looked annoyed. "You ain't thinking. You—you—"

"Just a moment, Mr. Rumbin." Georgina interposed again. "I think I'd better explain. Mr. Cattlet'll never understand you if you make him an example, because he hasn't the kind of disposition you mean, Mr. Rumbin. Most people have, I'm afraid; but I've noticed that Mr. Cattlet seems to be lacking in that way, rather. When he was a little boy he'd have been delighted if all the other boys had as many marbles as he had, himself, and as big and as fine as his; and so, unless you find some other way of telling him about collectors' jealousy, he won't be able to understand you."

"Ain't he human?" Mr. Rumbin inquired, pained. "You ain't telling me Howie ain't human, are you, Georchie? What you think he bought himself that cutaway suit for he had when we first got him? What's the reason Orcas has bought his wife that new mink to go to the theatre with him for? I'm talking uniwersal elements, Georchie. Howie ain't no freak, is he? Howie ain't no luna—"

"Wait a minute, sir," Howard interrupted. "I think I can get at what you're after. I had a dog once, and I thought he was better than any other boy's dog, and I thought he was bigger and handsomer and stronger, and I wanted everybody else to think so, of course, and—"

"Aha!" Mr. Rumbin cried. "Didn't I told you, Georchie? . . . Now, Howie, listen. All you got to do it's to think suppose your dog had been a art collection, and that's the whole business."

"Sir?"

"Certainly. Suppose you're out walking with your dog, and you got a rope round his neck instead of a collar and he's got himself all dirty, and suppose some odda boy comes along with *his* dog that's nice and clean and got a putty collar on him—Well, firstly you'd buy your dog a nice new collar and then take him home and wash him up clean, wouldn't you?"

"Sir? No, sir, I don't believe so. My dog used to enjoy being dirty and I never cared much if he was, so I don't think—"

"Oh, my, my, my, my!" Mr. Rumbin wiped his forehead, and sat down. "Well, anyways, Howie, there *is* a such thing as collectors' jealousy, and if a dealer can create two clients that commences competing in the pictures they acquire, the dealer he's got a heppiness. You could understand that, couldn't you, Howie?"

"Yes, sir; certainly."

"Then why all the trouble?" Mr. Rumbin sighed. "Why didn't you say so in the first place?"

"You didn't ask me, sir."

"Oh, my, my, my, my!" Mr. Rumbin said again; but presently recovered his spirits, became brisker and took both Georgina and Howard into his confidence in regard to a matter he had much at heart. "If I can ever create Mr. Milton Wilby into a nice client, Georchie and Howie, it would be easy to push him and Mr. Hollins into collectors' jealousy. Them beings business partners makes it all the easier. Broddas-in-laws is good, too, when it heppens.

Sisters-in-laws would be best of all—look how sisters-in-laws gets about each odda's wrist watches, minks and all the luxury trades—but if one sister-in-law commences art collecting, the odda one won't. The trouble is, to get Mr. Milton Wilby commenced and then to commence him against Mr. Hollins, it needs Rumbin Galleries expands some to get holt the right choice of pictures. Since our Wandours Castles Mr. Kingsford J. Hollins Wan Dyck we're doing fine, Georchie and Howie—fine! But for expansion, what Rumbin Galleries needs right away most it's to get more reckanized from the odda dealers. I got a pig scheme in my head, Georchie and Howie, to put Rumbin Galleries in a high give-and-take position among the dealers." He chuckled. "You'll see, Georchie and Howie. Putty soon I tell you all about it."

"Not now?" Georgina asked. "You don't think you could tell us about it right now?"

"A few days," Mr. Rumbin said benignly. "Wait a few days. All I tell you now, I commence with F. Corr and Company."

"F. Corr and Company?" Georgina's grey eyes were bright. "You're going to try to open a connection with a great firm like F. Corr and Company, Mr. Rumbin?"

"Wait," he said again, smiling. "Rumbin Galleries

is getting to be a putty good firm itself, these days. I guess we can talk out putty strong to F. Corr and Company, Georchie. Rumbin of Rumbin Galleries, ain't he getting to be a putty important feller? Maybe no; maybe yes. Me, I think yes."

Mr. Rumbin thought yes, and, being a man who liked to have his appearance as well as his actions live up to his words, he decided to begin looking important. Continuously for several days he looked important, and then, one morning, looking more important than he'd ever looked before in his whole life, he went forth for the critical interview.

CHAPTER FIFTEEN

IMPORTANT Mr. Ferdinand Corr sat in an important Savary chair at his important Sheraton "Carlton House" desk and spoke plainly to the suddenly unimportant Mr. Rumbin—Mr. Ferdinand Corr's subject being none other than Mr. Rumbin's unimportance.

"Boiled down, Rumbin," Mr. Corr said, "my reaction to you is as follows: when you stand up here in my office, looking all dressed up and fat and sassy, you've got your nerve!"

Mr. Rumbin, who was indeed standing, not having been asked to do otherwise, looked all dressed up and fat but meek. "Sassy?" he said. "Why shouldn't I got my nerf? Ain't I doing a fine business?"

"For you—magnificent!" Mr. Corr laughed cruelly. "That's why you think you ought to be let in by old and important dealers. You want to play

145

with our auction group; you want to borrow and lend pictures on a percentage basis for sales—in a word, you want to be one of the boys. Were you ever on the membership committee of a good club, Rumbin? No, I see you weren't."

"Mind reading?" Mr. Rumbin asked. "Ain't a club got to have members? Oddawise is it a building for rent?"

"Not us, Rumbin," Mr. Corr returned. "Club members have to have qualifications. Briefly, we don't see any, and we know all about you, at that."

"All about me?" Mr. Rumbin's bright eyes widened. "You must be putty good; I don't, myself."

"No; that's why you're here," Mr. Corr said, and was pleased with his own repartee. "Rumbin, you amuse me. You wangled yourself that little place down on East Seventeenth Street, had the front to call it 'Rumbin Galleries', and you scrambled out of bankruptcy by making a few little sales to Mr. Kingsford J. Hollins. Hollins is your only client and now you're all puffed up because lately you sold him a Van Dyck for some real money. One client and one sale don't make you Somebody. No, Rumbin, we don't care to fish in your little puddle."

"Puttle?" Mr. Rumbin spoke suavely. "Your own business is so fine lately?"

"Not at all. Not over half a dozen pictures to museums; four or five to private collectors, twenty-five to fifty thousand each. Only one sale to Halbert —a historical Copley for the Halbert Collection. A dozen or so little things—five to fourteen thousand a piece. No, our business has been unusually slack, Rumbin."

"Slack?" Mr. Rumbin said, gratifyingly staggered. "Slack!"

"For us," Mr. Corr explained. "What looks big to the bump looks little to the mountain."

Mr. Rumbin misunderstood him, though not much. "Bum?" he said. "Now you're calling me a bum?"

"Bump, Rumbin. I was illustrating my meaning that what looks like a tree to the dwarf is only a weed to the giant—if you see what I mean, Rumbin."

"Me beings the bumps and weeds and dwarfses? Make it worst; call me a hopgrasser in them weeds. Does hopgrassers sell recorded Wan Dycks, answer please?"

"One Van Dyck, Rumbin—and you got hold of that purely by happenstance. A little bird told me."

"Named Ensill," Mr. Rumbin said. "Dirty old birt named Ensill. Picks up art information alleys, sells it ten dollars to Mr. Ferdinand Corr, then gets

himself ten dollars dirty drunk! Does spyings bought
from Ensill prove I ain't—"

"Don't flatter yourself." Mr. Corr looked annoyed. "Ensill threw that in about you for nothing,
on another matter. Be serious. Can you imagine my
ever being interested in any picture of yours, bor-
rowing it to show it to any client of mine? Ridiculous!
Then wouldn't we be silly to build you up by lending
you pictures of ours? My advice is to do yourself a
favor by not getting the idea you're a real art
dealer."

"Nobody at all—just only a bump and a hopgrasser?"

Mr. Ferdinand Corr laughed. "Let it go at just
only nobody at all!"

"So I'm treated by the great Mr. Ferdinand
Corr?" Mr. Rumbin said. "Yet once when me and
you was art assistants to old Palenberg and we was
friends and I called you 'Ferd'—"

"Call me anything you like," Mr. Corr interrupted, "just so it doesn't make you feel too comfortable."

Mr. Rumbin understood. "In odda worts, state
my business—I did and ain't got none—so get out!
Good-by, Mr. Ferdinand Corr." Walking proudly,
Mr. Rumbin departed.

Outdoors he gave the handsome façade of F.

Corr and Company a wistful glance, sighed heavily, and, turning southward, walked all the way down to Seventeenth Street, sighing again sometimes as he went. "Tried to be Somebody," he murmured. "No. Nobody at all. Always only a hopgrasser in them weeds."

His place of business, however, he found cheerful. His two employees were both busy. Georgina was tying up a package, and Howard Cattlet was showing a pair of silver candlesticks to a customer. The customer, moreover, was Mr. Milton Wilby.

"Mr. Milton Wilby, what a pleasure!" the dealer exclaimed. "Please tell me how's your partner, Mr. Hollins, and how's Mrs. Milton Wilby and all your family, Mr. Milton Wilby?"

"My wife? She's gone abroad with two of my granddaughters."

"Splendid!" Mr. Rumbin cried. "Shows the granddaughters all the picture galleries, all the pyootiful—"

"No, she won't. Catches cold in museums. Gone to attend a missionary conference in—"

"How nice!" Mr. Rumbin said blandly. "You seen Mr. Hollins's great Wan Dyck yet he acquires from Rumbin Galleries, Mr. Milton Wilby?"

"Seen it?" Mr. Wilby laughed gruffly. "How could anybody that knows Hollins help seeing it?

Can't go there to dinner without having to parade around over the whole place looking at his pictures and hearing him pretend not to brag about 'em! That Van Dyck, I'm sick and tired of it! What did you say those candlesticks were, Mr. Cattlet?"

The assistant wasn't permitted to answer. "Hundut eighty," Mr. Rumbin said. "Pyootiful old silver, clessic chasteness, hundut eighty. A such pair candlesticks Ferdinand Corr's it's six hundut the least. I ask only one question, Mr. Milton Wilby; it's do I send 'em your house this morning before lunch or do I send 'em this afternoon? Which?"

"Didn't say I'd take 'em, did I? All right, though. Send 'em along with the inkstand."

"Inkstend?" Mr. Rumbin for the first time seemed aware of the package, which Miss Horne had now completed. "Ah, he acquires too my pyootiful inkstend made from a early Seventeent' Century silver pomander; how I hate to lose it! Congratulations, Mr. Milton Wilby! Now we show you a few my great paintings and—"

"No," Mr. Wilby said crossly. "I'm not looking at any pictures, thanks. I've changed my mind entirely about buying a painting. Our Ducks on a Pond is quite good enough for me. I don't want to get like Hollins. Good day."

He departed with some brusqueness; but Mr.

Rumbin's secretary was elated. "Two splendid sales in half an hour!" she exclaimed. "Really, we're beginning to look up in the world."

"Up?" Mr. Rumbin's chin rested heavily on his collar. "No, Georchie, we been having the puff-head."

"Oh, dear!" Georgina understood, and drooped sympathetically. "Poor Mr. Rumbin! Then F. Corr and Company didn't—"

"No, it didn't," he said. "It got—it got kind of insulting at me, Georchie. Yes, I guess we had the puff-head, acting like we're selling to collectors like Halbert. We ain't; we're insecks. Bumps. Howie, you're supposed learning the art business. Of who am I speaking, Halbert?"

"Halbert, sir? I think I've heard the name but—"

"Thinks," Mr. Rumbin said. "Halbert probable doing the greatest art collecting in the worlt right now, Rumbin Galleries' assistant *thinks* he heard of him!"

"I'm sorry, sir."

"No, Howie, it's only your bad luck you're with me. Me, at your age I was assistant to a dealer, old Palenberg; he's so great he insults putty near everybody comes in his Galleries."

"Sir? But I shouldn't think insulting 'em would—"

"No, they think he's pigger for it," Mr. Rumbin

explained. "Insults 'em and smiles his insulting smile that's worst insulting than the insult. Once a gentleman says, 'Mr. Palenberg, I'm afraid it's wasting your time I come in so often to look at pictures.' Palenberg says, 'No, I only wish I had a dozen like you.' So the gentleman's surprised. 'That's nice,' he says, 'but since I never acquired no pictures of you I wonder you'd want a dozen like me coming in.' 'It's easy,' Palenberg says. 'I got couple hundut like you!'" Again Mr. Rumbin sighed, and loudly. "Ah, would it be sweet!"

"Sweet, sir? To offend everybody that—"

"Wouldn't it be a satisfaction to be pig enough, Howie?" Mr. Rumbin's eyes kindled; his gestures became eloquent. "I don't say you'd spend all your time insulting; but suppose Rumbin Galleries got maybe twenty splendid rooms you can't see anywheres nothing exceptings macknificent important pieces and macknificent important clients acquiring 'em!" The vision seemed to become real; no doubt for the moment the shop disappeared from Mr. Rumbin's eyes and twenty dazzling rooms took its place. "Howie, suppose who do I see stepping into a such Galleries? Not Mr. Milton Wilby for a couple insignificance candlesticks, no; suppose it's Mr. Halbert himself! Him we don't insult. So watch me. You're learning from me, Howie?"

"I hope so, sir."

"What do I do? First I bow nice." Mr. Rumbin smiled beamingly at the air before him, bowed grandly. " 'Ah, Mr. Halbert, you're feeling well, yes? I'm sorry, Mr. Halbert, not much to show. Your cless paintings, we got only a couple Vermeers out of the under fifty that's in the whole worlt. Out of the eight to maybe fifteen and anyways not possible forty Giorgiones, only one we got. Rembrandts, yes; Hals, yes; Veronese, Titian, Goya, yes. Reynolds, Gainsborough, Constable, English School, oh, yes, certainly. Tapestries maybe, Mr. Halbert? Well, one or two large Flemish—only one Cluny type, rather small—nothing over few hundut t'ousand dollars.' You're listening, Howie? Does it sound like a nightinsgale?"

"Sir? Yes indeed, sir."

Mr. Rumbin's exaltation increased. "Like nightinsgales singing from almond blossoms when it's moon's light in Tuscany! I say, 'Sculpture, Mr. Halbert—a few pieces Settignano, Mino da Fiesole, a Verrocchio bust, only one Donatello; got a ewer, Cellini, gold but not large. Glass, Mr. Halbert? Sixteent' Century English, only a few. Seventeent' Century, only one, but it's the Royal Oak goblet. Stiegel? Yes, certainly. Old welfets, embroideries? Couple Fourteent' Century copes, one or two Got'ic chasubles—

not expensive, runs ten t'ousand up. Enamels? A few Byzantine, some Limoges. *Île de France* Got'ic ivories—French Regency *petit point*—porcelains—carved crystal—Chinese ceramics, Chün ware Yüan Dynasty—Chinese art, T'ang, Sung, Ming—' "

Mr. Rumbin's naturally rich and deep voice had grown high-pitched; but it faltered and failed him—the mirage faded. Crumpling, he drooped into a chair and his ample chin sank again upon his winged collar. "Only a pipe's dream!" he said. "Only a pipe's dream from a art dealer they can call him a bump and a hopgrasser and he ain't outstanding enough to smack 'em for it!"

For the moment, intoxicated by luscious words, young Howard Cattlet, too, had seen Rumbin Galleries as Medici apartments brilliant with the loot of palaces, had seemed to stroll through aisles lined with masterpieces and to gaze upon walls where hung ineffable Renaissance blues and lemon-colored sunshine made of ancient paint. Pictures, ivories, bronzes, tapestries, porcelains, crystals and glass all whirled away, as the nightingale's song became a croak; and young Howard could only look at Georgina Horne in the hope of seeing something he liked even better. Looking at Georgina in this hope had grown to be a habit of his, indeed—naturally so, since sometimes her glance in return, through up-

and-down-moving eyelashes, was like the glint of a bluebird's wing in a thicket. Just now, however, her sympathetic attention was given entirely to her employer.

"What's it matter, Mr. Rumbin?" she asked. "If other people are doing better than we are, why, we're certainly doing well enough ourselves, aren't we?"

"Never mind, Georchie," he said. "You mean it nice; but I—I had kind of a beck-set this morning. I can't feel very good to-day." He got clumsily to his feet, walked slowly to the door of the room he called his galleries, paused there a moment and looked back over his drooping right shoulder. He made a pitiable effort to smile, failed, went into the galleries, closed the door, and remained in solitude.

CHAPTER SIXTEEN

Mr. FERDINAND CORR had been thorough. Mr.
Rumbin's mortification was painful to see throughout
the week; but on Monday morning a shabby person
shambled in from the street, and the pathetic mood
changed alarmingly. Mr. Rumbin's eyes bulged; he
made furious gestures.

"Snake-in-the-grass Ensill!" he cried. "Look at
the clothes you're wearing, too! Rolling in money
from my Rousseau and t'ousand dollars cash besides,
and fees from spy-work from Ferd Corr, you got to
roll also in a alley in pants and necktie I bought you
myself? Out o' my sight, dirty birt! Out!"

Ensill, habitually melancholy, looked absently at
a plump forefinger that pointed to the door. "Got
something," he said. "Flat again; played the market.
I want a little ready money and I know I can always
get it from you."

"Always? Never! You playing the market! Out!
Must I holler it louder?"

Ensill glanced toward Howard Cattlet and Miss Horne, who were at work in the rear of the shop. "Talk to you in private, Rumbin. Got a big thing."

Mr. Rumbin's forefinger ceased to point at the door, approached his nose and came to rest upon the end of it, denoting concentration. "Dirty birt, come!" he said, led the way to the stock room, let Ensill pass in, followed and closed the door.

He apologized for this somewhat slurring privacy later, when Ensill had gone. "Couldn't be nothing I wouldn't trust you with both, Georchie and Howie," he said. "But suppose some odda dealers finds out the secret Ensill sells me; Ensill says, 'Aha! Look who was listening!' Now he can't accuse you, and yet I tell you." Mr. Rumbin looked excited. "Howie, you're supposed studying art questions. What should be the importantest United States painting?"

"Sir?"

"I'm asking you, Howie! Who's how easy the United States greatest person? Next, who's the greatest United States painter? So if the greatest painter paints the greatest person's portrait, what's the importantest United States picture, Howie?"

"A—a portrait of George Washington by Gilbert Stuart, sir?"

"Boy's right!" Mr. Rumbin exclaimed. "Georchie, act incyclopaedia. How many Gilbert Stuart's portraits Washington in the worlt? From a hundut up?"

She laughed. "Not if you're careful. The best books on Stuart admit about ninety-seven. Of course other painters copied them by the dozen—Stuart's daughter Jane and Rembrandt Peale and Vanderlyn and Winstanley and—"

"You're telling me, Georchie? How many Stuart's Washingtons ain't I looked at over the mantelpiece with families hollering at me will I make Grandma out a liar because I says it might look kind of Washington but Gilbert Stuart no, a t'ousand times it ain't! How good on Stuart's Washingtons are you, Howie? Vaughan type, for exemple; what's it?"

"I'll try," Howard said. "Washington gave three sets of sittings to Gilbert Stuart. The replicas Stuart painted of the portrait he made during the first sittings are called the Vaughan type because of an engraving that was made of one of 'em owned by a man named Vaughan. Some experts say this Vaughan portrait was the original; but anyhow there are only twelve to fifteen Vaughan type portraits known to be by Stuart, and they're the most expensive."

"So? You could certain reckanize one of 'em yourself?"

"Well—I'd hate to have much depending on it, sir."

"How long you lived in Hackertown, New Chersey, Howie?"

"Sir? Why, all my life."

"You know a family their name's Apt'orn?"

"Family?" Howard said. "There's only Mrs. Apthorn and her daughter, Maisie. They're very dear friends of mine and of all my family, too."

"So? I hear these Apt'orns ain't so well off, Howie."

The assistant looked serious. "Worse than that, I'm afraid. These last few years I know my mother's often made excuses to send them a cake or a ham or something. Mrs. Apthorn's partly paralyzed, and Maisie's been—well, there's no word but angelic. They're lovely people."

"So." Mr. Rumbin paused in thought; then he went to the cubicle in the stock room, put on his overcoat, got his hat and returned to the shop. "Twenty minutes I'm gone to the benk," he said; and went forth, walking rapidly.

Howard, mystified, turned to Georgina Horne, who was at her desk. "I thought he was going to tell us about Ensill's secret, Georgina; but instead he—"

"He did tell us," Georgina interrupted. "He told us Ensill's discovered that your friends out at Hackertown, this invalid Mrs. Apthorn and her angelic daughter Maisie, own a Gilbert Stuart Vaughan type portrait of Washington and Mr. Rumbin's going out there this morning, with you, to buy it."

"What?" Howard's eyes widened. "I believe you're right! It does look like that." He became grave. "Yes, of course."

Georgina, bending over her work, spoke with seeming preoccupation. "Haven't you often seen the portrait—when you go to see Maisie?"

"No. It isn't in their living-room, at least. Of course they don't have anybody to lunch or dinner any more. It might be in their dining-room." He looked worried. "I don't believe either Mrs. Apthorn or Maisie'd have any idea at all of its value. What would it be worth, Georgina?"

"Any picture's worth what the owner can get for it, isn't it?"

"Yes, but—Georgina, do you suppose Mr. Rumbin would—"

She didn't look up. "Naturally he'd try to get it for as little as he possibly could, wouldn't he? That's his business."

"Yes, I know, but—" Howard was more and more disturbed. "This might get embarrassing," he said. "They're dear old friends and I wouldn't like to see—"

"Old?" Georgina's charming fair head continued to be bent close to her work. "You say Maisie, the daughter, is old, too?"

"No—only about twenty. Georgina, don't you see what a problem this might be for me? A Stuart Washington of the Vaughan type ought to bring— well, as much as ten thousand dollars, oughtn't it? Georgina, if Mr. Rumbin goes out there and gets it from them for perhaps a few hundred, why—why, it'd be—"

"Yes," Georgina said, turning her head to look at him coolly. "It would—especially if he takes you with him and you have to stand there looking on while he does it. Your friend Maisie might feel afterward that you ought to've made a fuss and stopped it, I'm afraid."

"Yes, and she'd have a right to, Georgina. On the other hand, I might still be walking the streets for a job if Mr. Rumbin hadn't taken me in. I've got to be loyal to him—and, as you say, it's his business to buy pictures for as little as he possibly can. Don't you see what a jam I might be in, Georgina?"

"Yes." She turned her gaze again to the papers upon her desk and murmured "Embarrassing" so un-interestedly that he was a little hurt as well as surprised.

"Well—" he said, and went blankly to some work

in the stock room. The loud voice of Rumbin summoned him forth.

"Hat and overcoat, Howie! Nice hired automobile's taking us riding to Hackertown. Might be we take a little money to them ladies you says is so poor." Mr. Rumbin laughed gayly. "Little as we can make it, natchly. Beck early afternoon, Georchie. Lively, Howie!"

"Yes, sir."

Georgina Horne didn't seem aware of the perturbed assistant as he passed her desk on his way through the shop.

"Simply begun to dislike me," he thought, in the car, and sat in brooding silence.

Mr. Rumbin became talkative when they were out of the city and coursing the Jersey flats. "Ensill! What a feller! Scratches like a hen art libraries, history books, old newspapers, courthouse records. Think he ever even seen this picture? He ain't. No; scratches up a Vaughan type portrait got willed to a young lady, name's Bissell, lived somewheres Westchester. Scratches all over Westchester; she's married, she's a widow, name's Apt'orn, Hackertown. Ensill scratches her a letter, has she got any old pictures, lentscapes maybe? She writes him she's got watercolors, painted herself, and a portrait Washington she used to belieft it was Stuart; but a friend that's a embroidery and art teacher that thinks she knows everything told her no, it's only a copy, because the only orichinal Stuart's Washington it's in the Boston Art Museum. What's that one, Howie?"

"Sir? It's the unfinished Athenaeum Washington, isn't it?"

"Boy's right!" Mr. Rumbin said approvingly. "So, because Stuart paints it from Georche Washington himself, the art embroidery lady tells Mrs. Apt'orn it's the only Stuart's Washington, instead the ninety-seven he certain painted." Mr. Rumbin laughed. "Crazy Ensill that had four, fife t'ousand dollars little while ago from thinking he sells you and Georchie a William Dobson, he's got not one cent. Brings me the letter for a hundut dollars down and fife per cent if I make a profit. We got the picture's history—Ensill turns over to me copies from all the papers—so all's needed's make sure it's the same got willed to her. She ain't a lady would run in a ringer on me, is she, Howie?"

"Mrs. Apthorn?" Howard was shocked. "Good heavens, no! They're—they're friends of mine, Mr. Rumbin."

"Yes; but still and yet," Mr. Rumbin said, "in a matter of pictures, there's friends hand you some awful astonishments. I'll know when I see it. Stuart done thin painting, pyootiful touches, clear flesh tints, clean fresh colors hundut years aftaworts. Putty often characteristic shadow from the nose, and one thing always—mouths' color delicate-like, so you don't look at it first more than other features. To a real Eye copies from Stuart looks like a baseball with lipstick rubbed on it trying to be a apple. For me, two glences, Howie!"

This wasn't boasting, the assistant discovered. In Hackertown Mr. Rumbin directed the driver to stop the car at a point about fifty yards distant from Mrs. Apthorn's house. "It's a expensive-looking car," he explained as they got out; and the reddening Howard could not but feel that his employer's expression was one of low cunning. "I'll tell you a vonderful use in my mind for this Stuart's Washington—vonderful! —after we get it, Howie."

Howard said nothing, and, when he and his employer had been admitted to the sad interior of the almost paintless "frame" house, he made the presentation of Mr. Rumbin huskily. Rumbin, courtly, bowed to the invalid lady, who reclined upon a green rep sofa; bowed again to her dark-eyed handsome daughter.

"A honor!" he said. "It's all owings to my young Head Assistant here he's friends with you, and also a letter Professor Ensill turns over to me about water-colors. We could courteously look at 'em, please?"

CHAPTER SEVENTEEN

Mrs. apthorn's wan face had become eager. "Maisie!"

"Yes!" the girl said breathlessly, and from a drawer in an Eastlake center-table brought forth a few watercolor paintings of flowers, mounted upon cardboard. She spread them upon the table, and Rumbin examined them benevolently.

"Flowers!" he said. "Flowers we love next to paintings, and here we got both—paintings and flowers, too! The letter says also there's a portrait —was it President of the United States, maybe John Quincies Adams?"

"No, it's Washington," Maisie Apthorn said. "It's in the dining-room. I'll bring it." She went to the door, and Howard, wishing to help, followed that far; but she stopped him there. "Don't bother; the picture's not heavy," she said, and might as well have told him openly that the dining-room table and the sideboard had been sold. She whispered to him, "Howard, you're an angel to bring him here!"

"I'm not!" he said desperately; but Maisie, hurrying down the hall, was unaware that he expressed anything except modesty.

She was back again in a moment; Howard took the picture from her and carried it to the light of a window, where Mr. Rumbin placed it upon a chair. "Orichinal frame," he said. "The picture not cleaned —maybe never since first painted."

"I'm sorry." Mrs. Apthorn spoke in tremulous apology. "But the lady who was here yesterday said she thought it was better we hadn't cleaned it."

"Lady?" Rumbin asked quickly. "Lady comes to see this portrait?"

It was Maisie who answered. "Yes, somebody we didn't know. She said she was motoring through to Philadelphia and just stopped in because she'd met a girl I went to school with who'd told her we owned a portrait of Washington and were willing to sell it."

"Name?" Rumbin asked. "Lady's name?"

"She didn't say," Maisie answered, "so of course we didn't ask her. She seemed to like the portrait— though she—she didn't make any offer. But—but—"

"But she did say she'd be back." Mrs. Apthorn's frail voice supplied the information appealingly; then her conscience compelled her to add, "Of course

we don't know that she'll buy it if she does. Until a
few years ago, when we were told it was only a
copy, we'd always believed in our family it was a
Gilbert Stuart, Mr. Rumbin."

"So?" he said. "You did?"

"Yes," she sighed. "Until the time came when we
thought of selling it."

"So?" Mr. Rumbin shook his head sympathetically. "Yes, it's always the way when it comes time
for selling. Looks good up to then; but selling, ah!
That's different."

"Mr. Rumbin, don't you think—" Howard Cattlet
began; but gave way to a fit of long and distressful
coughing. Finally he was able to control his utterance. "It looks like Gilbert Stuart to me, Mr. Rumbin." Howard coughed unhappily again. "Don't you
think—don't you—"

"Stuart? You got a bad cough, Howie," Mr.
Rumbin said, and paused to look not at the young
man but at Mrs. Apthorn. Then he returned his eyes
to the painting and meditated gravely. Howard, staring at him, grew conspicuously red and swallowed
nothing frequently. "Stuart?" Mr. Rumbin said, at
length, inquiringly. "Gilbert Stuart? You says your
family always did used to thought the picture was
painted by Gilbert Stuart?"

"Yes, we did; though even then I sometimes wondered why he hadn't put his name on it, because I know that of course artists always sign their pictures."

"Well—not always; not always, Mrs. Apt'orn. Sometimes mostly not." Mr. Rumbin turned the portrait upside down, studied it so for a time, turned it right side up, knelt before it, took from his waistcoat pocket a small magnifying glass, and, with its aid, frowningly examined the dulled surface. Then he put the glass back in his pocket, rose, and again stood in meditation.

Mrs. Apthorn, watching him, misinterpreted his gravity, and her slight patient sigh was just audible. "I see. You mustn't be disappointed, Maisie. I really didn't expect—"

"Didn't you?" Mr. Rumbin said, still grave. "It's a Gilbert Stuart's Vaughan type portrait Washington, good condition, no repainting. If you knew how to sell it, Mrs. Apt'orn, you could get a good deal more than I'll offer you for it. Maybe rather you let me do the selling for you on a commission basis? You can say. You might—"

Maisie Apthorn interrupted him sharply. "You just said you'd make an offer for it, didn't you?"

Rumbin took a billfold from his coat pocket. "I prowided myself some cash money," he said. "Always it looks more tempting. See." He went to the center-

"Until a Few Years Ago, We'd Always Believed It Was
a Gilbert Stuart, Mr. Rumbin"

table, placed clean new bills upon it, one by one, as if he were dealing from a pack of cards. "Seven hundut dollars," he said. "If you'd take it, my young Head Assistant here'd bust out coughing again and stop you; it's one reason I got him." He placed a cheque-book beside the bills on the table, and sat down. "The young lady gets me a pen, please? Altogedda we make it twelve."

"Twelve hundred?" The eyes of the invalid on the sofa were shining; her voice tried not to be incredulous. "You say you'll—you really mean you'll give us—"

"T'ousand," Rumbin explained. "Twelve t'ousand; it's a crime I'm doing you." He took a pen from the stunned Maisie, dipped it in the ink she'd brought with it, wrote his cheque for thirteen thousand three hundred dollars, waved it in the air, rose and carried it, and the bills with it, to Mrs. Apthorn. "Fourteen t'ousand I says, didn't I?" he asked.

She began to cry, and her daughter threw her arms about Howard Cattlet's neck and kissed him.

. . . "Nice girl," Mr. Rumbin said, in the car, to Howard. "Acts like she likes you." He looked affectionately at the portrait, which rested before them against the back of the driver's seat. "Georche Washington would done the same I done, Howie. Some people it's right you should steal their eyes' teeth, especial if they're grebbing for yours, like for exemple it might be Orcas. Odda cases, not always. Suppose this lady motoring stops beck from Philadelphia; they tell her Rumbin took it away for seven hundut dollars. I don't know who she is—maybe somebody important—squawks all over New York I'm a crook, robs sick widows and orphans, oughts to be sued! Could be damaging, Howie."

"Sir? You mean that's the reason you—"

"In a art business," Mr. Rumbin said, "when comes a oppatunity you can act complete a hog, you should a few times only give the temptation a half a kiss. Here's the use I told you I'd tell you for this picture, Howie. It's got to be sold to Mr. Milton Wilby."

"To Mr. Wilby, sir? Not to Mr. Hollins?"

"Wilby," Rumbin said, Napoleonic. "Mr. Hollins, he ain't got over it yet what he paid for my Wan Dyck. I show some people I'm a art dealer! Mr. Hollins has got Mr. Milton Wilby hating pictures so he can't stand even to see one. I sell my great Stuart's Vaughan type Washington to Mr. Milton Wilby!"

. . . The Napoleonic mood continued, was strong upon Mr. Rumbin at his Galleries while he delicately cleaned the picture with a quickly drying fluid of his own invention. His imperial temper was relaxed only as he briefly described to Georgina Horne the scene in Hackertown and the fondness of Howie's friend, Miss Maisie Apthorn.

"Got pyootiful loving eyes," Mr. Rumbin said. "Kisses him arms around right in front her mamma."

Howard, flustered, he knew not why, by a prompt sunny nod and smile of Georgina's, began an explanation of how long he'd known the Apthorns; but wasn't allowed to finish it. Mr. Rumbin gave him the portrait to carry and hurried with him to a taxicab Georgina had already called. She stood smiling and waving good luck to them from the doorway of the shop, as they departed; but nevertheless there was something about her that deepened a feeling the young man had that sometimes Mr. Rumbin talked too much.

. . . Mr. Rumbin, in Mr. Milton Wilby's library, showing the portrait, became more Talleyrand than Napoleon. He was supple, insinuating, brilliant. He confused Mr. Wilby's elderly intelligence with oral diplomacies; but, when he finally named his price, he seemed again to have talked at least that much too much.

"Thirty-seven thousand dollars!" Mr. Wilby exclaimed. "Take it out! Go waste your time somewhere else."

Mr. Rumbin straightway became seductive, mathematically. The last documented Vaughan type Washington sold had brought sixty thousand dollars; the only other now for sale was priced at one hundred and twenty thousand—averaging the two gave you ninety thousand; and therefore if Mr. Wilby took Rumbin Galleries' great Vaughan type Washington at thirty-seven thousand, Mr. Milton Wilby had virtually in his pocket a profit of fifty-three thousand dollars. Add how macknificent President Georche Washington would look upon the empty walnut paneling over the library fireplace, and what a madness would be Mr. Milton Wilby's not to acquire quick!

"Ah, what a spot!" the glowing dealer exclaimed. "What a library spot for a Washington! Leaf them Ducks in the parlor till I find you a fine spirichul lady portrait; but oh, for a such spot in a Milton Wilby library, what's ideeler than a Vaughan type Stuart's Washington! Mr. Milton Wilby, the picture belongs to you spirichul; I couldn't break my heart by taking it away. I wouldn't do you a such injustice."

Mr. Wilby weakened, but by no means all the way. "See here, Rumbin, I'm not buying any pictures. Take it away and if I change my mind I'll call you up. That's the best I'll say."

Mr. Rumbin, undampened, begged the privilege
of placing the portrait over the mantelpiece and leaving it there until Mr. Wilby changed his mind and
bought it. Mr. Wilby said he wasn't going to change
his mind; but consented to the trial. "Think it'll get
to working on me, do you, Rumbin? All right; let it
do its worst!"

"Bravo!" the dealer cried. "Almost congratulations, Mr. Milton Wilby!" Then, when Howard
Cattlet had hung the picture, Mr. Rumbin's gestures
seemed to repaint the august features of the Father
of our Country. "Majesty! See how the forehead's
painted. See the nose shadow. Typical! Ah, what a
nobleness! What a richness! Ah, how she speaks to
you, Mr. Milton Wilby, says, 'Here I am looking
at you and's fifty-t'ree t'ousand dollars asking to
walk in your pocket, besides. Could you send us
away?' "

"Yes, I could," Mr. Wilby returned. "You can
leave it here a couple of days, and I guess I'll be looking at it enough to please you—doctor's tied me in
the house this week—but there's no obligation on my
part, mind you!"

"No, no; none at all on you, Mr. Milton Wilby—
only on me that I wouldn't sell it to nobody elst, because after couple days how heppy's Georche Washington he finds this pyootiful new home with Mr.

Milton Wilby and family also when they come beck from Europe! So, now, Mr. Milton Wilby, we go beck to Rumbin Galleries where's all full with heppiness we placed a picture where it's heppy on account it makes the most heppiness!"

CHAPTER EIGHTEEN

RUMBIN GALLERIES wasn't so full with heppiness as he predicted. Returned there, Howard Cattlet became uncomfortable. Georgina's manner made him feel that she was somehow seeing him in a wrong light, and, just after closing time, he detained her for a moment on the sidewalk before he ran for his commuter's train to Hackertown.

"Good night, Georgina," he said. "Ah—of course you understand how it is in a little place like Hackertown, where all the young people grow up just like sisters and brothers and—"

She nodded and smiled. "Yes, of course. That makes it all the lovelier."

"Makes what all the—" he began; but she had already turned briskly away, and his train, in the other direction, wouldn't wait.

The next day she showed him a consistent cordiality. It gave him an uneasy feeling in his chest and

at the back of his neck, made him wish to tell her
some more about the young people of Hackertown
—how they were all like just one big friendly family
—but his lunch time came without his having found
an opportunity. When he returned from his cafeteria,
Georgina was busy looking over some etchings while
Mr. Rumbin talked loudly at the telephone.

"Certainly I'm well!" Mr. Rumbin was saying.
"How comes you're asking me if I am? Because
maybe I'm sick from standing up from not getting
inwited to sit down in your . . . Certainly I'm
always ready to do business, exceptings didn't you
told me yourself beings in them weeds I'm only a
bump, a hopgra— What? . . . Did I get holt of a
Stuart's Vaughan type? . . . Oh, you *know* I got
it? . . . Oh, you *want* it! You want it yourself? . . .
Your woice sounds—I says your woice sounds kind
of foxy excited, Mr. Ferdinand Corr! . . . No, I
won't. It's practical sold . . . Discuss it? No, I
wouldn't. Good-by."

Mr. Rumbin, stern, had just turned from the telephone when a tall young woman in brown tweeds
came into the shop. Her aspect was both scholarly
and fashionable, her manner decisive. "You're Mr.
Rumbin?" she said to the dealer. "I've just made a
mistake about you and I made a worse one day-
before-yesterday when I went on to Philadelphia

instead of seizing upon that Stuart Washington at
Mrs. Apthorn's instantly."

"Ah!" Rumbin bowed. "You're the lady."

"Yes, I am; and who'd have dreamed of such rot-
ten luck! They'd had that portrait in their musty old
house for years and years with nobody thinking of
buying it, and the very day after I get a look at it
you pop up, and I've missed the chance of a lifetime! I didn't take it first shot because I didn't want
to carry it to Philadelphia and back, and because I
couldn't see enough provenance."

"Plenty," Rumbin said. "Documented clear from
the first purchase by the family from Gilbert Stuart."

"You've got 'em? You've got all the records?"

Mr. Rumbin bowed smilingly. "Absolute!"

"Murder!" The tall young woman slapped her
brown-gloved hands together. "That does make it
worse!"

"What's the odda mistake?" Rumbin inquired.
"Please, the one about me?"

"I'd never heard of you," she said. "Mrs. Apthorn
told me you'd bought it, and I decided to find out
something about you first. My mistake was in making inquiries of another dealer, Mr. Ferdinand Corr.
I saw right away his only idea was to get in on it,
himself. He *hasn't*, has he—in the time it took me to
get down here from his place?"

"Tried." Mr. Rumbin's voice was soft. "Tried but ain't."

"Very well," she said. "I'd like to see the portrait again, please."

"No; I'm sorry. It's at a client's."

"What?" She spoke sharply. "Did he take an option?"

"Maybe not execkly a option but—"

"See here," she said. "We've been looking for a Vaughan type Washington at our price for two years. We set our own price for pictures because we know —and we don't change. I'm Evelyn Raines, secretary and curator for the Halbert Collection; Mr. Halbert's prepared to pay sixty thousand dollars for a properly recorded or documented Vaughan type in good condition. What have you to say?"

"Halbert!" At the moment that was all Mr. Rumbin had to say. "Halbert!"

"You know what it means for any dealer to place a picture in the Halbert Collection," Miss Raines said. "You'd better go and get it, hadn't you? I'll wait here."

Mr. Rumbin stared at Miss Raines; his mouth opened and closed twice while he still stared. "I'll get it!" he said. "Howie, bring my hat and overcoat; bring yours, too, like lightning!"

He was already on his way to the outer door.

Howard overtook him with the commanded apparel and finished helping him into his overcoat after they'd reached the sidewalk. Mr. Rumbin didn't pause to look for a taxi. "As quick walking to just off from Gramercy Park," he said. "It might be lucky you was a witness Mr. Milton Wilby didn't take no option, Howie."

"Sir?" Howard was troubled. "No, he didn't; but I—I'm afraid you gave him one, Mr. Rumbin."

"How could that be? Didn't take none, yet he's got one?"

"Yes, I'm afraid that was the understanding, sir— that you were to leave the picture there—two days was mentioned—while he made up his mind, and in the meantime he wasn't under any obligation to take the portrait; but you—"

"Me? I couldn't sell it to nobody elst because I gave him a option he didn't take? Is that legal?"

"I don't know, sir." Howard spoke nervously. "I'm afraid it's moral, though."

"Moral?" Mr. Rumbin seemed to ponder upon the word. "But I ask you where's a dealer passes up a colossal oppatunity such like we got now, I ask you, Howie?"

"Sir? I—I don't know—"

"No! Nobody elst knows! So all's needed I could silky speak to Mr. Milton Wilby absent-minded, say

I'm putty certain plenty art experts would agree it's probable Gilbert Stuart himself and ain't likely a copy from his daughter Jane. You think Mr. Wilby's going to acquire a picture when the dealer himself slips out a little doubt on it silky like that, Howie? Maybe I lose Mr. Milton Wilby; but it's only candlesticks sometimes he buys anyhow and fixes the legals and morals absolute." Mr. Rumbin's tone became triumphant. "We bring the picture beck with us, Howie."

"Yes, sir," Howard said in a blank voice. He hoped he wasn't priggish; but he felt that the nicest sense of honor demanded that Mr. Wilby's option should be respected and also that Mr. Wilby be informed of Miss Raines's offer. It was an unhappy Art Dealer's Assistant who accompanied his employer up the brown stone stoop and into the old-fashioned house near Gramercy Park.

Mr. Wilby sat in his library and listened absently to the silky explanation that Mr. Rumbin had brought his Head Assistant to make sure that the picture was hung with strong enough wire. "It's all right; I tested it myself," Mr. Wilby said, and looked up at the portrait thoughtfully. "I haven't made up my mind. Stuart was a great painter; but Hollins was in to see me last night and got me sick of art again."

"Sick?" Mr. Rumbin asked sympathetically. "Ah,

it's too bad! Mr. Hollins spoils the sale then, Mr. Milton Wilby? So now you're going to tell me I should right away take my picture down and carry it beck to—"

Mr. Wilby, not listening, interrupted peevishly. "I can get along with Hollins in business all right; but since he thinks he's gotten to be a picture collector I never saw a more self-important man in my life. Collector? You'd think he was Jem Halbert himself!"

"Halbert?" Mr. Rumbin, standing, looked down at Mr. Wilby concentratedly. "You understand Mr. Halbert he's now probable the greatest collector in the worlt, Mr. Milton Wilby?"

"Next to Hollins!" Mr. Wilby spoke with sarcasm. "Anyhow, Hollins tries to think he's in that class."

"No, Mr. Hollins knows better." The concentration in Mr. Rumbin's eyes increased as he looked down at Mr. Wilby, and so did another kind of concentration increase in the eyes of Howard Cattlet as he looked at his employer, much as he'd looked at him in Mrs. Apthorn's house, the day before. Mr. Rumbin seemed wholly unaware of this poignant gaze; what he said was therefore the more astounding. "Don't start coughing on me, Howie."

Howard gasped. "Sir?"

Mr. Rumbin didn't even glance at him. "Mr. Milton Wilby, you're going to tell me now this minute you'll take the portrait. Because why?"

"Yes," Mr. Wilby said, annoyed. "I'd like to hear because why!"

"Because when you own it, Mr. Hollins commences talking, all you got to say is, 'Yes, yes, you got some nice pictures, Mr. Hollins, very nice., Did you hear, Mr. Hollins, if Halbert's yet acquired a Vaughan type Washington after he was disappointed sick he couldn't get mine?' "

"What?"

"Certainly!" Rumbin was solemn. "Mr. Halbert wants right now to pay you twenty-t'ree t'ousand more than the t'irty-seven t'ousand dollars I gave you a free option on it for, no obligations exceptings on me. Mr. Halbert he's got to own this great Vaughan type Gilbert Stuart's Washington for sixty t'ousand dollars."

Mr. Wilby stared up at Rumbin; then rose and stood, confronting him. "You mean to tell me that Halbert—"

"Ask my Head Assistant here; he was a witness. You couldn't turn down a such profit just to keep a picture, could you, Mr. Milton Wilby? Halbert gets the portrait away from you at sixty t'ousand, don't he, Mr. Milton Wilby?"

From Mr. Wilby's aged eyes there came a hard

gleam unfamiliar except to people who'd seen him at moments of high financial crisis. "He does not!" he said angrily. "Halbert can go on looking for a Stuart Washington; he can't come in here and take this one off my wall! Maybe it'll dry up Hollins a while, too! I close my option and keep this picture."

Mr. Rumbin seized Mr. Wilby's hand and congratulated him vehemently.

. . . Outdoors, walking back empty-handed to the shop, the dealer was serious. "In a business concerning Georche Washington," he said to his confused apprentice, "you might *first* think nothing elst exceptings getting holt the adwantage, even if it's by silkiness; but when the crisis comes and you got to act, you should feel the influence of the great painting and behave as stricksly honorable as Georche Washington himself, like you just see me done. Some ways," Mr. Rumbin concluded serenely, "I'm like him, Howie."

"Sir?"

"Anodda thing," Mr. Rumbin said. "Did you watch how like lightning I sees I can turn Mr. Milton Wilby's art soreness on Hollins into collectors' jealousy?"

"Sir?"

"Listen hard, Howie. When you can talk a man

into he won't take twenty-t'ree t'ousand dollars profit
but keeps a picture instead, you got him made into a
collector. Can he stop acquiring pictures now he's got
a Stuart's Washington Halbert wanted, makes Hollins sick? Mr. Wilby don't know it yet; but I do. No,
he can't. So, bang! Rumbin Galleries got now two
ideel clients, each of 'em going to be ideeler and
ideeler because how collectors' jealousy is going to
work on 'em keeps Mr. Wilby and Mr. Hollins
struckling against each odda. What's also a pyootiful
point to it, Howie?"

"Sir?"

"Howie, it's whereby don't Mr. Wilby know in
his heart I could easy worked him out of his option
and grebbed the twenty-t'ree t'ousand myself? So
what odda dealer will he ever trust like me? Nobody. On the odda hand, we lose Halbert; but some
it consolations us you can't sell Mr. Halbert no pictures. He *buys* 'em. He's a picker. Now we got to tell
Miss Raines execkly the truth how Rumbin Galleries
is so honorable wouldn't dream taking no picture
away from a client that thought he held a option even
if he didn't. She's going to be excited."

Miss Raines, on the contrary, was cool, even icy.
She gave Mr. Rumbin her opinion of his perspicacity
as a dealer and she also told him why a great collector like Mr. Halbert had never until to-day heard

Mr. Rumbin Glanced at His Assistant

of Rumbin Galleries. She concluded, at the door, by prophesying that no subsequent news of this establishment would ever reach Mr. Halbert's ears, or her own.

She was severe; but rather promptly proved subject to change. She came into Rumbin Galleries the next afternoon, looking serious but affable, and made something like an apology to Mr. Rumbin in the presence of his two employees. "I'm afraid I was a little sharp yesterday," she said. "Probably you'll be able to overlook it, Mr. Rumbin, because, when I gave Mr. Halbert the details of my disappointment about the Stuart, he was disappointed, too, of course, but said he thought your scrupulousness was correct and rather unusual. He's asked me to say that if at any time you come across a picture of the quality he requires he'll be glad to hear from you. That's all; except that I've just been telling Mr. Ferdinand Corr what I thought of him for trying to muscle in yesterday. Good day."

She had been gone perhaps ten minutes when Mr. Ferdinand Corr called Mr. Rumbin on the telephone, and again Georgina and Howard heard half of a lively dialogue. "No, not to-day; I couldn't see you . . . Yes, might be; but it's yet more important to me I use my time to work on Halbert deals . . . Yes, it's true I turned down sixty t'ousand. Ain't a real

art dealer got odda clients besides Halbert? . . .
No, you could come see me some time next week maybe . . . I says next week, and maybe I let you sit
down whiles you're talking . . . No, no, don't get
discouraged, Ferd—maybe I decide yet I do some
fishing in your little puttle!"

Flushed with pleasure, Mr. Rumbin set down the
instrument and glanced with bright eyes at his assistant. "You see, Howie? Georche Washington he's
honorable about his little hetchet, gets to be President. You see, Howie?"

Not waiting for an answer, he began to sing his
favorite air, *Donna e Mobile,* and strolled with splendid casualness into the stock room behind the shop.

CHAPTER NINETEEN

HE HAD not quite closed the door behind him and could still be heard lightly singing. Georgina Horne was overpowered by a natural curiosity to know what he'd meant by speaking of George Washington's little hatchet and adding "You see, Howie?" As Mr. Rumbin seemed preoccupied with music, so to speak, there wasn't anybody she could ask about it except Howard; but she was just now upon peculiar terms with him, and, since his excursion to the house of the Apthorns, hadn't spoken to him except in response to remarks or questions of his, though she had continually maintained a facial expression of impersonal cordiality. However, her curiosity now became too much for her; she dropped the cordiality and looked indifferent, instead.

"Rather odd," she said. "I mean his talking about George Washington's hatchet and thinking you'd understand what he meant."

"But I did understand, Georgina." Howard spoke

eagerly, glad that she seemed willing, again, to engage in conversation with him. "He meant he's a good deal like George Washington."

"He meant he's what?"

"Like George Washington, Georgina. You see, he meant George Washington was always honest and honorable and so he got to be President, and Mr. Rumbin, leading the same kind of life—"

"He'll get to be President, too?" Georgina interrupted. "What nonsense!"

"No, no. Mr. Rumbin doesn't expect to be President, Georgina. To explain it I'll have to go back to the beginning. I—I know—" Howard paused, embarrassed; then went on, "I know you don't like my mentioning Mrs. Apthorn and Maisie and—"

"What!" Georgina laughed in a way that made him feel he wasn't doing very well. "Where on earth did you ever get such a frantic idea as that? Why in the world should I mind your mentioning anybody you care to?"

"Well, I—I only thought I seemed to have—I—" Howard stopped floundering, swallowed nothing and went back to his explanation. "I was only going to say that the other day he had a chance to cheat a—a widow with—with an only daughter—and he didn't do it. He behaved very handsomely, instead. Well, afterward he told me if he hadn't, he might have had a lot of trouble over it because maybe Miss Raines would have spread it round to his discredit. Then yesterday he was absolutely honorable with Mr. Wilby when it looked as if being that wasn't really good business, and afterward he told me he'd made the sacrifice because George Washington was honorable and besides he was going to gain a lot by it. And here to-day it seems he's gained even more! What he meant just now was I was supposed to see that being honorable like George Washington brought big profits in business; so that puts a pretty striking question before us, doesn't it?"

"What question?" Georgina asked coldly. "Before whom?"

"Before you and me, Georgina." Howard rubbed the back of his head. "I mean when—when Mr. Rumbin behaves so very honorably, ought we to think it's because he sees beforehand how well things are going to turn out or—or not? I mean, is it both? Or if he thought being strictly honorable *wouldn't* make things turn out so well, ought we to think he would still—"

"I'm sure I don't know." Georgina's curiosity about what Mr. Rumbin had meant was satisfied; she resumed her entirely impersonal manner and turned away from Howard to go to her desk.

"Wait just a moment, Georgina," he urged. "Now

—now we're talking again and everything seems all right, I do wish you'd please listen. In a small place like Hackertown people get to be neighbors and old family friends and it goes on for generations. You see, both the Cattlets and Apthorns were among the first settlers of Hackertown in the early Eighteenth Century, and their great-great grandparents and mine were friends, and so it's entirely natural that Maisie and—"

"Thirty-seven thousand dollars due April first," Georgina said absently. "This is March twenty-third, isn't it? Yes, of course it's the twenty-third."

"Thirty-seven thou—March twenty-third—What, Georgina?"

"Nothing." She had paused to hear him, but now turned away and went on again toward her desk. "Just something I hadn't entered in the books."

Howard, hurt, controlled an impulse to follow. "I beg your pardon."

"Not at all; not at all." Georgina, at the desk, turned over the leaves of a ledger. With a pencil crosswise in her mouth, she, too, hummed *Donna e Mobile*. In the stock room Mr. Rumbin began to sing more loudly his own translation from the Italian:

> "Ladies is changeable,
> Tra, la, la, la, lira—!"

" 'Changeable'!" the assistant said bitterly to himself, and, not even glancing again toward the musical desk, set about some work of his own. Misunderstood, he summoned his pride—or perhaps his pride summoned him—and for days his expression of impersonal cordiality was equal to Georgina's. He even reformed his habit of looking at her whenever it was possible; now he didn't look at her at all, except when a rigid interpretation of the rules of courtesy seemed to require it, and, when neither Mr. Rumbin nor a customer was present in the shop, the sound of voices was seldom heard there.

Mr. Rumbin, preoccupied with great plans, also became untalkative (for him) just at this time, and Rumbin Galleries, losing much of its previous air of geniality, was often almost a place of silence. A professional visitor, however, began to interrupt the quiet. Having come once, he came again, and yet again; and, when he came, his voice and Georgina's engaged in brisk and interested conversations. This professional visitor was an important young gentleman of precocious attainments; yet at first sight of him Mr. Rumbin's assistant loved him not, and, at every subsequent sight of him, loved him less.

Embittered, yet humble in spirit, Howard began to see no real future for himself as an Art Dealer's Assistant and was disposed to think he'd made a mistake, after all. True, in his first year out of college, he'd already done better financially than had any other of his classmates, so far as he knew; but that was due to the Van Dyck windfall. Such strokes of luck, like clear weather lightning, aren't known more than once or twice in a lifetime; and, by the advice of Howard's father, the money was already stowed away in government bonds, which, to a young person, made it the same as dead money. Pessimism took lodgings in Mr. Rumbin's assistant's diaphragm; he had little stomach for anything else, held a lower and lower opinion of his abilities, and several times was on the point of resigning from Rumbin Galleries. Nevertheless, winter had broken; the lilac leaves were tinily in bud at Hackertown, and even into the stonier air of Seventeenth Street spring flung little hints.

Georgina did more than hint of spring. In the shop, on a sunny April noon, she put on a new hat and a new grey coat. The hat, black touched with turquoise, was becoming to her fair head, and the coat was a dashing complement to her grey eyes. Howard looked at her glancingly and was sickened.

"I'll never know anything about art," he thought. "What's the good of my going on groping? Just groping round in the dust—that's all I'm doing!"

Usually slow-minded, he'd perceived in one flash of unpleasant light that Georgina wore the new hat and the new coat because she was lunching with her new friend, that wonderful young man Mr. Bruce Cherding, director of the Brookford Museum of the Fine Arts. Mr. Cherding, in fact, just at this moment arrived.

Watching them through the display window as they walked away, talking eagerly, Mr. Rumbin's assistant too easily saw how appropriate a companion for fair Georgina the distinguished dark young Mr. Cherding appeared to be.

Distinguished! Both Georgina and Mr. Rumbin had been heard to use that word in this connection. Howard himself was young and dark, but far, far from distinguished. More than ever aware of this, he sighed, turned his back to the display window and for a few moments stood looking wistfully about the shop.

His gaze passed over pictures mellowed to a "gallery brown"; caught fragile sparklings of fine old glass and cool shinings of silver on old mahogany sideboards. Almost a year, now, he'd worked here, every day (until lately) more fascinated; and yet— except just after the sales of the Van Dyck and the Stuart Washington—seldom free from apprehensions about the business itself as well as his position in it.

It had begun to seem to him that the business was a series of climbing adventures, attempts to ascend

a summitless mountain provided with plenty of preci-
pices but not with any secure resting places. When
one of these adventures failed, or seemed to be
failing, Mr. Rumbin slid moaning into the abyss;
then rose to undergo the nerve-strain of the next
effort to ascend. If it succeeded, he was lively for a
day; then began to show the strain of another at-
tempt to climb. Yet he was shrewd, experienced and
resourceful. Howard's feeling for him was an
affectionate, sometimes puzzled, sometimes dazzled
admiration, and he wondered why so masterly a man
hadn't yet been able to make his business into a
solid and settled permanency, not needing adventur-
ings to keep it alive.

Could it be, the young man asked the silent shop,
that most businesses were like this—if they lived and
grew? Then did they all depend for success—or even
for life—upon the courage and skill of the adven-
turer? Then what ought a young man in any alive
business—particularly in an art dealer's business—to
be learning in order to become distinguished? To use
daring directed by brains? Undoubtedly. Young
Howard Cattlet felt keenly but sadly that he'd like to
show Georgina Horne and Mr. Bruce Cherding (and
Mr. Rumbin, too, of course) that he possessed both
the daring and the brains—if he did. The trouble
was, he was pretty sure he didn't.

Neither was called for in the removal of that mysterious bluish mist called "bloom" from varnished paintings; but this was the routine task to which he now applied himself. In the stock room behind the shop he went at it glumly. Stout Mr. Rumbin, gloating visibly because of the elaborate French lunch he newly contained, and smoking a rich cigar, strolled into the stock room, a little later, and praised his assistant's skill.

"You've learned from me to disbloom good, Howie," he said. "The soft cloth damped light with my fluid and just gentle stroking. You show you know how, Howie."

"It's all I do know, sir."

"So?" Mr. Rumbin sat down, took pleasure from his cigar deliberately with three senses, taste, smell and sight. "You got troubles inside you, Howie?"

"I don't know anything about art," the young man said, continuing his work. "When I hear two people talking about art, they might as well be speaking in code—yes, and don't seem to care to be interrupted, either!"

"They don't?" Mr. Rumbin's bright eyes twinkled. "Howie, here's good news for you. There's just one thing a art dealer don't never need to worry about."

"Sir? What one thing?"

"Art," Mr. Rumbin said.

CHAPTER TWENTY

"WHAT?" Howard thought his hearing had failed him. "I beg your pardon, sir; I thought you said an art dealer—"

"Didn't need to know nothing about art," Mr. Rumbin interrupted placidly. "A art dealer's got to know about all the pictures ever got painted, all the sculptures ever got sculptured, all the *objets d'art* ever got febricated, all the collectors ever got born, all the dealers ever did dealings, all the kinds human natures ever got created, all the benks ever got talked into lendings, all the different kinds of smiles he can put on his face, all the face's expressions he can use admiring clients, and almost everything elst. All he don't need to know nothing about, it's art."

"But good heavens, Mr. Rumbin—"

"No, Howie. Listen. If your clothes don't fit you, anybody can tell it; if a auto don't run, everybody's got to admit it don't. On the odda hand, take a lady

I says she's good-looking, you says she ain't; could
I prove it to you? No; I could only get me and you
both sore because it's the same as art. What you
think about art it's your own business; keep it to
yourself, because if you tell it out loud you get somebody mad at you. Ain't it why when Mr. Bruce
Cherding comes in and him and Georchie talks art,
you get a expression like a waiter spills on you?
Ain't you noticed it on your face yourself, Howie?"

"On my face? No, sir," Howard said, surprised;
but added, "Maybe sometimes when they talk about
a painter I don't understand—van Gogh, for instance—"

"Wan Gogh it's a good case, Howie. Mr. Bruce
Cherding and Georchie they're art fash'nable, beings
now it's all wan Gogh. Wan Gogh writes a letter says
when he uses special reds and greens it means bad pas-
sions—and some looks at the picture and says yes,
they feels it and some says no, they don't. So they
argue, putty soon commences hollering and frequence
don't get over what they calls each odda. Quits
speaking because all they could do's holler it at each
odda again. Is that a art dealer's business, Howie?
No. What a art dealer's got to know about art, it's
to let his clients talk first so he can agree with 'em.
Besides listen, does Rumbin Galleries owns a wan
Gogh?"

"No, sir; but—"

"On the odda hand," Mr. Rumbin said, "if we did, all you got to worry about it's what's the nicest price we can get from who and if it's aut'entic from the Master not a copy or maybe a forchery. See, Howie?"

"Yes; but how much do I know about that? I've been studying the English School lately. Sir Joshua Reynolds copied a Rembrandt, showed the copy to the French painter, Carle Van Loo, who was certainly supposed to know, and Van Loo swore it was an original by Rembrandt. Then how can I ever hope—"

"It don't come in a minute," Mr. Rumbin said. "Take for example Mr. Halbert that's now doing the most important collecting in the worlt. Natchly when he commences the Halbert Collection he maybe had to made mistakes gets him sore; yet aftaworts didn't he early picked him up a Rogier wan der Weyden nine t'ousand dollars that's now wort' maybe two hundut t'ousand? Look didn't he also had the nerf to pay maybe four hundut t'ousand for a Jan wan Eyck ain't twice the size of a postal-card? Halbert ain't only a collector, he's a connoisseur. A connoisseur collector it's tough on a dealer, Howie."

"Sir? But I should think—"

"No," Mr. Rumbin said. "Simple a collector you

can help make up his mind for him. A connoisseur's
liable to make you feel what you're trying to sell him
you're a boob yourself to bought it. Mr. Halbert's
got now a Eye like a hawk's and a fox and a eagle's.
Oddawise would he have a collection makes any
dealer a pig man if Halbert acquires from him a picture? There, Howie; that's something you can worry
about. Ain't I scratching my hair bald, losing pounds
beef off my chest I'm so scared because he sends me
wort I can show a picture to him?"

"Scared, sir? I should think you'd be delighted."

Mr. Rumbin's French lunch no longer brightened
him; his relish of the cigar was gone. "No, Howie;
I'm scared serious. If I don't show him something
putty soon he forgets me; but any dealer shows one
single piece Mr. Halbert thinks is bum, he says he's a
time-waster, never won't even let Miss Raines, his
sec'tary, listen to that dealer on the telephone or
answer a letter. Mr. Halbert looks once, he don't
like, he's insulted, you're out." The dealer's stout
shoulders made an involuntary movement that would
have been a shiver if he'd been thinner. "Lately
didn't I had lines on seven pictures I could bought
or gone percentage on to show him? I'm scared out
of all of 'em. Now I got a line on anodda. Looks
good; but oh, Papa, am I shaking!"

"That reminds me, sir." The assistant had finished

his removal of "bloom" and he replaced the picture in its rack upon the wide shelf. "I happened to run into Miss Raines on the street yesterday and she said she'd show me the Halbert Collection at four this afternoon. Would you mind if I—"

"Fine, Howie! Maybe it's too much you take Miss Raines a bunch gardenias—could look like business flettery—but anyways keep listening to her like in wonder. Miss Raines she's got pig art influence on Mr. Halbert, don't forget, Howie." Mr. Rumbin again enjoyed his cigar, and, returning it to his lips with an intentionally graceful gesture, glanced at the small watch upon his large wrist. "Ah, that's good, too," he said. "Georchie and Mr. Bruce Cherding's spending a long, long time lunching. Nice, ain't it?"

"Nice, sir?"

"Why ain't it?" Mr. Rumbin asked, challenged by Howard's strong incredulity. "Ain't Mr. Cherding director Brookford Museum and don't Georchie know it's good we sell to museums?"

"Oh!" Howard said, and his gloom seemed suddenly lifted. "So that's all it is!"

"No, it ain't," Mr. Rumbin returned, too frank. "Ain't Mr. Cherding got looks like a prince and high critical art ideas and young to be director of a museum?"

"Brookford?" Howard's glumness was on him

again. "I motored to Brookford last Sunday, and I'm not up to primitives yet and don't understand modernists; but in the whole place I saw just one picture I'd go that far to see again. It made all the rest look flat to me—a half-length portrait by Sir Thomas Lawrence."

"Lawrence, no," Mr. Rumbin said, possessed by one idea. He shook his head. "A Lawrence I wouldn't dare show Mr. Halbert. Lawrences high critics nowadays says they're too glittery, too much alike and too much portrait flettery, Howie."

"Do they?" Howard looked obstinate. "That Lawrence isn't glittery; it's all character and life. Why, it even made me think of Frans Hals!"

Mr. Rumbin laughed. "So quick art-arguing with me, Howie, in spite I says that ain't our business?"

"No, sir; but—but either I'll never know anything at all about pictures or that Lawrence portrait at the Brookford Musuem is grand painting."

"Listen!" The dealer waved his cigar toward the open door that led into the shop, where a cheerful baritone voice could now be heard. "They're beck and he's doing the talking like usual; it's cute how sweet she listens." Mr. Rumbin rose and moved to the door. "Howie, let's go tell him what a fine splendid picture you find in his museum; it helps fletter him. Come on."

In the front part of the shop Georgina Horne was removing her grey gloves and listening appreciatively to Mr. Cherding, when the beaming Mr. Rumbin approached, followed nervously by his assistant. "Mr. Cherding, what a pleasure!" the dealer exclaimed. "Just now I'm hearing from my assistant, Mr. Cattlet here, what a fine museum you got. Tells me he sees there a such splendid portrait by Sir Thomas Lawrence. You're crazy about Mr. Cherding's Brookford Museum's Lawrence, ain't you, Howie!"

"I think it's a great portrait," Howard said. "It seems to me one of the finest—"

"Oh, that Lawrence!" Mr. Cherding laughed negligently. "Sorry I can't agree with you. Of course such a blot merely ruins a rather decent gallery."

"Blot?" Mr. Rumbin glanced unfavorably at the flushing face of his assistant. "Yes, natchly you're right, Mr. Cherding. Lawrences usual is too glossy."

"Not only glossy, Mr. Rumbin. While we were at lunch Miss Horne used precisely the word for Lawrence—tawdry."

Howard Cattlet looked at Georgina, who seemed pleased to be thus quoted. "Then may I inquire why you hang the picture, Mr. Cherding?" he asked, with a dogged air. "If it's only a blot, why do you—"

"Oh, dear me!" Mr. Cherding addressed himself gayly to Georgina. "This naive young gentleman doesn't seem to understand the rabbit's life led by some of us unfortunate museum directors. It's almost worse than being a college president. At Brookford luckily we're a perfectly happy family, though, except for one curse—an old lady who comes home from Europe every few years and threatens to change her will if the Museum doesn't do some special horrible thing she wants, so we always do it—temporarily! This time, about a month ago, she happened to remember that Lawrence portrait and missed it; so we had to bring it up from the cellar into which I'd managed to discard it. She sailed yesterday, and next time she comes home, if she remembers the Lawrence, it won't be there."

"Not even in the cellar?" Georgina asked approvingly.

"Not even in the cellar, Miss Horne. People still do buy Lawrences, it seems, and just now our purchasing fund hasn't a penny in it. Otherwise I might be talking to Mr. Rumbin about that School of Bruges Annunciation in the window yonder. May I take another look at it?" The question was merely courtesy; Mr. Cherding himself strode to the display window and lifted out the picture. "You were right, Miss Horne," he said, studying it keenly. "The

more I see of this panel the better I like it. Feeling for
organization some of these Flemish primitives had
—fine triangular relation here between the Angel
and the Madonna. Yes, it really deserves to be at
Brookford." He turned his handsome head to look
at Howard amusedly. "I'm sorry this young gentleman is only Mr. Rumbin's helper—since he admires
our Lawrence. If he were one of the firm, I'd offer an
even trade."

"You'd get it," the stung Howard said. "I'd trade
like a shot if I were Mr. Rumbin—yes, and wonder
why the Brookford Museum was crazy enough to do
such a thing!"

His tone was much more hostile than he realized;
Mr. Cherding's color heightened quickly and so did
Georgina's.

Mr. Rumbin himself took on a tinge of red, not
merely to harmonize himself with the three younger
people. "Cattlet!" he shouted, though even a low-
voiced use of the surname would have been token
enough of his indignation. "Cattlet, ain't we got no
more pictures needs disblooming instead your loafing,
putting on a such cross face's expression, poking in
on us your uncalled conversation?"

Howard said nothing. He turned about, strode
hotly back to the stock room and went straight to
the cubicle where he kept his hat and overcoat, his

*"You'd Get It," the Stung Howard Said. "I'd Trade Like
a Shot"*

janitorial overalls and the "cutaway suit". The re-
buke just suffered was all the more mortifying
because it came from an amiable and even long-
suffering employer; it would have been almost unbearable if administered in private. The injured
young man decided to resign actually, instead of just
thinking about it. He took down his coat of state, began to fold it; then paused. He could go back to the
job-hunting from which Mr. Rumbin had rescued
him; but where, except at Rumbin Galleries, could
he spend whole days—even if they were pretty
wretchedly silent ones—with Georgina Horne? He
stopped folding the coat, returned it to its hanger.

"No," he said. "If they want to get rid of me
they'll have to throw me out."

He went determinedly to the shelves of racks
where the pictures stood, brought forth another
that had "bloomed" and worked sorely upon it for
half an hour. Then Mr. Rumbin, walking heavily,
came into the stock room, went to the cubicle, got his
Homburg hat, pale grey gloves and pigskin-topped
Malacca cane. Again walking heavily, he returned
to the shop doorway.

"Cattlet," he said, pausing there, "how long am I
paying you a celery to be a assistant that assists me
beckworts? Cattlet, I'm telling you good-by!"

Howard was startled. "Sir?"

Mr. Rumbin's response was to turn his large back; then he marched out through the shop. The front door closed loudly after him, and his whole manner in this departure seemed very like that of an art dealer on his way to engage a new assistant.

CHAPTER TWENTY-ONE

HOWARD had painful sensations in his lower chest and upper stomach. He went out to the shop, where Georgina sat at her desk, working gravely. "Georgina, did he tell you— Is Mr. Rumbin going to drop me?"

She continued her work. "Don't you know what you did?"

"What I did? I—I may have spoken a little brusquely; but you heard Cherding keep calling me 'this young gentleman', didn't you, Georgina? He called me 'naive' too and—and—"

At that, she turned in her chair and faced him. "You don't yet realize what you did to a deal Mr. Rumbin and I were working on?"

"A deal, Georgina? But Cherding said himself their purchasing fund didn't have a penny in it, so how could—"

"Really! Did you ever hear of any client that didn't say that—especially a museum?"

"But, Georgina, I only—"

"You ruined it," she informed him. "Except for you, the Brookford Museum—that's really Mr. Cherding—would have bought our Flemish primitive. To establish his position as a dealer it's necessary for Mr. Rumbin to be represented in museums, and, what's more, the Brookford Museum was just about ready to pay a very fair price for that panel; they'd have paid in money, too—cash! Mr. Rumbin can't afford to have Mr. Cherding offended by treatment received at Rumbin Galleries; naturally he was forced to efface the impression your rudeness made. Besides that, Mr. Cherding laughed but he made excellent use of the argument that even Mr. Rumbin's assistant admitted that the Lawrence was worth more than our primitive. What could Mr. Rumbin do but accept Mr. Cherding's offer for an even trade? You lost Mr. Rumbin a really fine primitive in exchange for a Lawrence he doesn't want."

"I see," Howard said, and somehow kept his voice steady. "As an art dealer's assistant I'm a great help —to the customers. Two hours ago I was hoping for a chance to show brains in this business, Georgina— daring and brains. Mr. Rumbin told me good-by. Did he mean I'm fired?"

If she was mollified, perhaps even touched, she didn't let him see; she bent again to her work. "When it happens," she said, "I don't think Mr. Rumbin'll leave you in any doubt about it."

Howard returned to the stock room. "When it happens," he thought. *"When* it happens!"

The only question implied was one of time—and the time might be any time. "When it happens" was still cruelly repeating itself to him in Georgina's lovely voice, as he set forth, presently, for his promised view of the Halbert Collection, and the dismal phrase went on hammering him even after his entry into Mr. Halbert's astonishing house.

The splendid place made him feel worse. He realized that a year ago he wouldn't have perceived the differences between these quiet interiors and the expensive rooms in many other millionaires' houses or even the expensive rooms in a hotel for millionaires. For works of art he'd begun to have at least a little of what Mr. Rumbin called an Eye; and, when he saw such allied wares of his trade as furniture, tapestries, glass and porcelains, he was beginning to distinguish between what was treasure and what wasn't. Rumbin Galleries had given him something permanently valuable; he knew what he owed to Mr. Rumbin and to Georgina Horne, and now, if they cast him out, it seemed to him that he stood to lose everything. It was an anxious young man who followed the scholarly but attractive Miss Raines through the great rooms that sheltered the Halbert Collection.

He had no difficulty, however, in obeying Mr. Rumbin's instructions to listen to this young lady in wonder, as she showed him the Halbert Ghirlandajo, the Lorenzo Lotto, the four Titians, the Mantegna, the Benozzo Gozzoli, the tiny Jan van Eyck, the Rogier van der Weyden, the great Rubens Crucifixion, the Velásquez and the two famous Goyas. What Miss Raines knew about both the Masters and the paintings seemed to Howard everything that could be known. His own recent bits of education had only qualified him to be amazed; and, in the English Room, when she had spoken of what French art owed to Constable, had shown him Raeburn's long clean stroke and "square touch", Gainsborough's featherings, a miraculous handling of warm colors and cool tones by Sir Joshua, and had quoted Gainsborough's outcry upon Reynolds, "Damn the man, how various he is!" the visitor, forgetting his troubles for the moment, spoke out, though humbly.

"How on earth does one head ever hold all this, Miss Raines? I always feel that way with Mr. Rumbin and—and Miss Horne—but I'm afraid you make me even more so."

Miss Raines laughed. "That's how I feel with Mr. Halbert," she said, as they passed into the last of the rooms.

It was already occupied by a tall and thin, shy-looking elderly man seated contemplatively before a magnificent somber landscape by Rembrandt. He rose at once, as if to go out by the farther door; then, seeing that there was only one visitor, he thought better of it and remained. Oddly, instead of renewing his observation of the Rembrandt landscape, he stood facing an adjacent area of blank wall, looking at it fixedly.

"Detective?" Howard wondered. "Somebody to watch visitors? Then why doesn't he pretend to be looking at a picture instead of bare wall?"

To the elderly eccentric Miss Raines paid no attention other than to lower her voice somewhat as she told Howard that this was the Dutch Room and still incomplete. "You see there are twelve spaces for pictures and only ten filled," she said. "The plan is to open another room beyond this as soon as two more pictures are added in here."

"One, Miss Raines." The elderly man, again astonishing Howard, turned about suddenly and spoke with no shyness at all. "One. I've made up my mind to that this afternoon. We'll hang only one more picture in here. The blank space next to this Rembrandt we'll keep blank." He looked twinklingly at Howard. "How de do? Um—possibly one of the new crop of young curators?"

"I?" the awed Howard said. "No, Mr. Halbert, I—I'm from Rumbin Galleries, downtown. I—at least I'm assistant there. I mean I still am."

"Rumbin?" After a moment the great collector remembered. "Oh, yes; Rumbin. Enjoy your work? Yes, I see you do or you wouldn't be here." Mr. Halbert laughed abruptly. "Like to know why I've decided to leave that wall-space blank, young man? Because I want it to keep me reminded of my ignorance and my dishonesty."

"Sir?"

"That space is where I hung my first and worst mistake twenty years ago," the collector said: "—a picture I bought with many dollars and more rapture. Five years ago Professor Frank Prince and I together finally identified it as a copy after a lost original—nothing but a damned copy! What's worse, somebody'd forged the artist's signature, and that made the copy into a fake. That's what I'd rapturized over; so there's my ignorance. Here's my dishonesty; I hated the thing enough to destroy it, yet I sent it away to be sold without making any explanation. Only excuse is I was too upset to think. Now I'm trying to have the infernal thing traced so that it won't go on gulling people. Horrible story of a bad conscience, isn't it, young man?"

"Sir? I—well, I don't—"

"No?" Mr. Halbert stepped to the door, but paused there for a final quizzical moment. "Since you're on the picture-selling end you've already learned not to be troubled by such an article as a conscience? I see! By the way, tell Rumbin I still expect to hear from him. Good day."

Howard turned to Miss Raines, as the door closed. "Is he always as genial?"

"Heavens, no! I hope you'll never be present when somebody shows him what he thinks is a worthless picture. You'd better warn Mr. Rumbin to be careful."

Howard assured her that his employer was only too anxiously aware of the Halbertian peculiarities; nevertheless, he thought it his duty to deliver her warning. Mr. Rumbin wasn't in the Galleries the next morning; but, when the assistant returned from lunch, the portly dealer was engaged in serious conversation with Georgina. Howard approached them, whereupon they ominously ceased to speak and just looked at him. "It's going to happen now," he thought; but courageously repeated what Miss Raines had told him.

"Thank you, Cattlet," Mr. Rumbin said. "Beings

my bright assistant, of course you says quick beck,
'Oh, no, Miss Raines, Mr. Rumbin wouldn't need
to worry, on account he's already busy getting holt
a special pig masterpiece Mr. Halbert screams for
choy when he looks at.' You snaps that on her quick,
Cattlet—what?"

"Sir? I—no, sir."

"No, Cattlet? Maybe you was too busy enchoying
yourself looking at all them Lawrences Mr. Halbert's
got?"

"Sir? No, sir. Mr. Halbert hasn't got any Lawrence."

"What a astonishment!" Mr. Rumbin said, elabo-
rately sardonic. "Even Rumbin Galleries has now
got a Lawrence, Cattlet—the one you stuck us with,
Cattlet. There's a new School of Bruges panel at
Brookford Museum to-day, Cattlet, and in our stock
room we got a pyootiful Lawrence with a pyootiful
bloom on it—from Brookford Museum's cellar. Now
you're a such hot art dealer yourself you're pulling
off pig trades with museums, Cattlet, maybe it's too
much I ask from you a little disblooming on your
new Lawrence, Cattlet?"

"No, sir, I—I—" Howard gulped inaudibly,
looked from the intolerant eyes of Rumbin to the
averted face of Georgina; then, with eloquent noise-
lessness, almost on tiptoe, he went into the stock

room and began to remove the "bloom" from the Lawrence portrait.

When he had finished he stood before the picture broodingly.

The tablet at the base of the frame gave the name of the sitter, Edward Morris Esqre; and Mr. Morris had plainly enjoyed the experience of sitting to Sir Thomas Lawrence. The portrait, painted with visible ease, sweep and spontaneity, was that of a lively-minded, elegant young Beau of the Regency, seated in an unnoticeable chair. The head was turned partly away, in a three-quarters view; but the intelligent dark eyes glanced back at the spectator, and this glance, gayly satirical, was the first and last thing to detain him. The keen large nose, modeled superbly, partly shadowed a witty mouth done wittily with a few strokes of pigment; and the shadowed side of this mouth showed a just perceptibly lifted upper lip half smiling, as if the sitter responded humorously to a word from the painter, yet, for the painter's sake, took some care not to disturb the pose of the features. That, like the eyes, gave an incomparable look of life—or at least poor Howard thought so—and all the rest of the portrait was subsidiary.

The fine head of waved brown hair, the brownish mist of whisker before the ear, the luminous shadow on the white stock beneath the firm chin, the strip of yellow waistcoat, the superb brown coat descending into obscurity where the shadowed hands held loosely a dim manuscript, all were so suavely subordinated that only on second thought did the spectator become aware of them. Howard was fascinated by the six brass buttons on the breast of the brown coat; he understood that in the painter's studio these buttons must have twinkled brightly, arresting the eye; but in the portrait one had to look for them—yet they were there and it was a pleasure to find them and then to see how they were painted, each with one swirl of the brush and a touch or two.

"Do what you like to me," the simple Howard muttered, half aloud, "you can't tell me that isn't good painting!"

"Good painting, Cattlet?" Mr. Rumbin, suddenly coming in, had caught the last two words. "You yet can't stop talking Lawrence, Cattlet?"

"Well, I—Well, sir, I can't help believing this portrait is one of the—"

"So!" Mr. Rumbin's deep voice rose to hints of tenor. "Cattlet, how much can my insides stand you keep on talking, talking about a picture maybe some day I could sell four to six t'ousand dollars less than the one you made a present to Brookford Museum of, my important primitive wort' anyhow eighteen t'ousand dollars?" Mr. Rumbin got his hat, stick and gloves from the cubicle. "To Rumbin Galleries as a intelligence young business man you're wort' your weight in what, Cattlet?"

"Sir? You mean in something worthless?"

"I wouldn't go that high," Mr. Rumbin said. "Cattlet, good-by!" He struck the floor fiercely with the ferrule of his stick, and stalked out.

CHAPTER TWENTY-TWO

His ASSISTANT turned meekly to the portrait; but after he had again looked at it for some time his expression became obstinate and stayed that way while he tenderly gave the canvas a thin coat of mastic varnish. After that, still looking obstinate, he went into the shop. Georgina stood before a table upon which she was placing some miniatures.

"He's pretty sore at me, Georgina," Howard said. "He didn't deny the Lawrence was good painting, though."

"What? You're still going on——"

"Georgina, tell me this. Perhaps I oughtn't to ask you, because I know you're entirely off me ever since —ever since——"

"What is it you wish to ask me?"

"Well, it's this. Isn't there something you can learn to see is good painting almost as plainly as you can tell a three-base hit from a strike-out?"

"Nobody denies Lawrence knew how to put paint on canvas," she said. "What of it? There never was a great artist who didn't scorn his own popularity; but Lawrence let himself become merely a fashionable portrait painter turning out nothing but shallow and characterless pictures."

"But, Georgina, it seems to me there are some Lawrences almost no painter could beat. Couldn't it be that you and—and critics like Mr. Cherding, for instance—just got sore on Lawrence from seeing pictures he was too tired to do his best with? I mean, doesn't even the greatest racehorse have his off days and don't some of the people that lose on him then naturally get to telling it around he's no good at all?"

She made no reply; but with an impatient gesture pushed one of the miniatures aside.

"I see," Howard said. "You're just thinking I made a fool of myself because Cherding high-hatted me before you and—and I was jealous."

"No!" she cried. "I was thinking of something serious—that you're still talking about the Lawrence when you ought to be trying to make Mr. Rumbin forget it. Your—your position here—"

"I know, Georgina. I know I'm on the edge and—"

"So's Mr. Rumbin," she said. "He's on the edge of his nerves. You must keep remembering that."

"You mean he's on edge about my—"

"About selling a picture to Mr. Halbert! Or at least not showing him something that'll get him into one of his furies so Mr. Rumbin could never go near him again. If this turns out right, Rumbin Galleries really probably could move up into the Fifties at last, instead of worrying along down here where no client ever comes unless he's dragged. It's the turning point in Mr. Rumbin's career. Wouldn't you be under a strain if it were the turning point in yours?"

"Golly!" Howard said. "Isn't it?"

Again she didn't answer him; but this time she made no impatient gesture. Instead, with downcast eyes, she delicately wiped dust from the glass over one of the miniatures, and it seemed to Howard that a perturbed sympathy emanated from her—though of course he knew she despised him for liking Sir Thomas Lawrence.

The street door opened; their employer came in dramatically. Upon his large and plastic face there was a tensity, and, like an actor who completes a good entrance before speaking, he strode to Georgina's table; then halted abruptly.

"Georchie, it's Rumbin's Rubicon!" he said. "To-morrow afternoon I'm Chulius Caesar, commence swimming, come out Emperor or—or only little gas bubblings spits up to the top from where Rumbin's laying drownt!"

Georgina showed excitement. "To-morrow after-noon, Mr. Rumbin?"

"To-morrow afternoon four o'clock, Georchie. The picture's out the custom house to-day; I just seen it."

"It's the Rembrandt, Mr. Rumbin?"

"It's the Rembrandt," the dealer said solemnly. "What elst should I offer the greatest collector but the greatest Master? Fits in pyootiful because in Mr. Halbert's Dutch Room, Miss Raines tells me last week he's got there two blenk spaces and—"

"One, sir," Howard Cattlet interrupted timidly. "He did have two blank spaces; but one of them was where he used to have a picture that was an awful mistake and so he's decided to—"

"Cattlet!" Mr. Rumbin turned on him haggardly. "You're talking again, Cattlet?"

"Sir? I only thought I ought to mention—"

"Mention!" the exasperated dealer cried. "Cattlet, you can't speak t'ree worts I ain't scared you get my nerfs upset you nextly mention Sir Thomas Law-rence! Cattlet, it's come so I can't hear the sound your woice unless all I got inside my waist turns over twice on me on account what you done to me with that Lawrence! Cattlet, I ain't got time for my in-sides upside down, so quit speaking."

"Sir?"

"Don't!" Mr. Rumbin cried. "Don't say even 'sir'. Here's the piggest deal of my life and if I got to listen to you even once till it's over, Cattlet, I'm going to collepse down on the floor. Until to-morrow fife o'clock don't speak to me one single wort; don't speak at all, Cattlet. I ask you do you understand me? Don't answer out loud!"

The unfortunate young man bowed his head.

Mr. Rumbin groaned at him, "Good! Keep bowing for answers yes. Shake your head if it's no." He turned again to Georgina. "A such brochure comes with the painting, Georchie! Splendid experts' opinions it's a great Rembrandt. Brochures sometimes only shows how many smart people got fooled; but not when the picture speaks for itself like this one does. Orcas sends it to us to-morrow afternoon t'ree o'clock, Georchie."

"Orcas," Georgina said. "I can't help wishing Orcas weren't in it."

"On the odda hand, Georchie, can't be denied Orcas sometimes gets holt vonderful pieces. Look at the archaic Greek head he last year sold Berlin and the Geraerd David to the coast. Besides look, Orcas and the foreign syndicate that owns the Rembrandt with him stands me a pig percentage if I make the right sale immediate; it's good."

"Mr. Rumbin, Orcas doesn't know who you're—"

"Who I'm showing it to? Natchly not, Georchie. If he did, might try sneak to Mr. Halbert behind my beck, leaf me out. Orcas thinks I'm showing it to a prominence lady, and it's true, too, because I said so and ain't Miss Raines coming with Mr. Halbert to-morrow four o'clock? Beings you're now got to be kind of a friends with her, Georchie, you can sit with her and Mr. Halbert to look at the great picture and maybe work in some good whisperings to Miss Raines. You understand, Georchie?"

"Yes—I will if I can, Mr. Rumbin."

"Good." The dealer looked again at his assistant, not with pleasure. "Cattlet. To-morrow after your lunch time put them t'ree *Louis Quinze fauteuils* in the galleries in front the easel. Half past t'ree put on your cutaway and Escot tie. Odda instructions you get then, Cattlet. Understand me? Make signs yes or no, Cattlet!"

Again Howard plaintively bowed.

"Overalls, Cattlet!" Mr. Rumbin commanded promptly, upon that. "Must you stand there where I can see what you're still thinking? Don't I know what's in your mind—it's obstinance from Sir Thomas Lawrence? Doesn't no furniture needs polishing nor no windows washing, Cattlet?"

"Ye—" Howard began impulsively; but, upon a bellow, "Cattlet!" cut himself short and forthwith set about the semi-menial tasks that were a part of his duty.

They kept him busy for the rest of that afternoon and also for the whole of the next morning, during all of which time he said not a word to Mr. Rumbin and very little to Georgina. Returning from a late lunch, he placed the three *fauteuils* before the easel in the galleries; then, having dressed himself as Mr. Rumbin had instructed, he was brushing his hair when he heard Georgina's voice, in the stock room, outside the cubicle.

"Tremendous, Mr. Rumbin! It takes my breath every time I look at it!"

Howard came out of the cubicle. Georgina had gone back into the shop, and Mr. Rumbin with reverent care had just placed a picture upon a cushioned chair. The assistant had little more than a glance at the painting, caught but a brief impression of a grand tragic old woman in dark dress, white cap and white ruff, with a dim red rose on her breast, and all revealed in Rembrandtesque chiaroscuro.

"Eyes on me!" Mr. Rumbin exclaimed. "Cattlet, is it me or Rembrandt Van Rijn you gets your instructions from? Don't answer; listen! Go in the galleries, see all's right and stand there until after Mr. Halbert and Miss Raines and Georchie comes in, gets seated, I talk some and then give you the wort bring the picture. Then come beck here for it; but wait. Don't bring it quick into the galleries; make it t'ree minutes. T'ree minutes! Got it, Cattlet?"

"Ye—" Again Howard checked himself, and bowed; then, obeying the sweeping gesture of an imperious but trembling fat hand, he walked out of the stock room, across the shop and into the galleries. He made sure that the light of the reflector fell properly upon the easel, and after that stood waiting.

CHAPTER TWENTY-THREE

PRESENTLY he heard Mr. Rumbin, in the shop, calling to Georgina. "Georchie, get them pieces pressed glass off that shelf, hide 'em in a commode. That pig silver epergne, too. Antiques but not good enough—makes a bum impression on Mr. Halbert. We walk him through the shop quick's we can polite; but he's got a terrible Eye. Where's that carafe water, Georchie? Outside I'm wet, yet inside I'm dried up again like spilt on a hot stove. Does my woice sound like my stomach's feeling, Georchie? How much shaking can you see my hands doing?"

Her reply was inaudible to Howard; but a few moments later she came into the room where he waited and spoke to him anxiously. "He wants to know if you're sure you understand what you're to do."

"Yes, I am."

"He told me to repeat it," she said. "You see, he

wants to do the little he can to build up the right
mood in Mr. Halbert; we haven't let him, or Miss
Raines either, know anything about the picture—not
even that it's a Rembrandt. Mr. Rumbin wants to
lead up to a climax at the very last minute. That is,
after you've been sent for the picture, Mr. Rumbin
means to make a little talk ending with the surprise
announcement that he's offering Mr. Halbert a great
Rembrandt called The Old Woman With The Rose.
You must allow him three minutes for this before
you come back and set the picture on the easel.
Please, please don't make any mistake, Howard."

He looked at her wistfully. "Thank you for using
my name again when you speak to me, Georgina."

"What? Under the circumstances it's absolutely
necessary," she explained.

She returned to the shop, leaving him to comprehend three things: first, that Georgina wasn't ever
going to care to hear any more about the history of
Hackertown and the long friendship between the
Apthorn and Cattlet families; second, that when
tutor and pupil differ about art the pupil isn't for-
given in a day, especially when the tutor's opinions
are backed up by those of a distinguished young
museum director; third, that the pupil's intelligence
had again been unfavorably discussed.

"Think I'm so dumb they have to tell me every-

thing two or three times?" Much too plainly that
was what they thought.

Howard sighed; then stood at attention. Outside
in the shop, there was a light commotion; voices were
heard commingling, and then the group of four appeared near the doorway. Mr. Rumbin, stepping
aside, made a solemn bow, deeper than was convenient, while Miss Raines, Georgina and Mr. Halbert preceded him into the galleries. As they did so,
and were seating themselves before the vacant easel,
the resourceful dealer improved two hurried opportunities to wipe his brow, unnoticed, with a cambric
handkerchief. He wasn't helped much; he was moist
again by the time he reached the spot near the easel
where he'd decided to stand and formally address his
visitors.

"Mr. Halbert and also Miss Raines," he began, in
a voice that seemed adolescent, changing pitch in-
advertently. "Many pig honors has frequence been
pinned on Rumbin Galleries; but, frangkly speaking,
Mr. Halbert and also Miss Raines, to-day at last I
am feeling such deep feelings——"

"Oh, hello there," Mr. Halbert said, observing
Howard. "Remember you. You were at my house the
other day. Yes; assistant here, of course. I remember."

Mr. Rumbin persevered. "Frangkly speaking, Mr.

Halbert and also Miss Raines," he said, "to-day at last I am feeling such deep——"

"Remember what we were talking about?" Mr. Halbert asked, continuing to address himself affably to Howard. "That space I decided to leave blank?"

"Yes, Mr. Halbert."

"You might be interested," the great collector said. "Coincidence. Think I told you I've had people trying to trace that thing. Finally did; agent brought me definite news of it only two days ago—hardly an hour after I was talking to you about it. Seems it's come back to New York again. Agent says he's learned a shady dealer I never heard of's got hold of it; but thinks he can bring pressure on him presently so it won't cost me too much to get the damned thing burned up at last." Mr. Halbert turned inquiringly toward Rumbin. "Ever hear of a rather questionable dealer named Orcas, Mr. Rumbin?"

"Orcas?" Mr. Rumbin, possessed by stage fright and upset by the interruptions to his prepared speech of welcome, was disturbed by the name; but his impulse was to dispose of it hastily. "Orcas? I might heard o' the feller; but if I was you I wouldn't never have no dealings with him, Mr. Halbert." He coughed loudly at Georgina for silence—she was responding to something Miss Raines had been mur-

muring about the weather—and then hurriedly resumed his address. That is to say, he began it again.
"Mr. Halbert and also Miss Raines, many pig honors
has frequence been pinned—"

"What about this picture we're supposed to be
looking at?" Mr. Halbert asked. "Don't show me
any brochure first. Brochures are good enough if they
go with the right things; but anybody can make a
brochure as elaborate as you please, and some of 'em
only prove how many collectors, and perhaps even
experts, have gone wrong." He spoke peremptorily.
"Where is the picture? I'll see it at once, if you
please."

Mr. Rumbin wisely abandoned his address of welcome. "My Head Assistant brings the masterpiece
straight in front you, Mr. Halbert. Cattlet!" Howard, who had become pallid, was staring open-
mouthed at Mr. Halbert's aquiline profile and didn't
seem to hear until Mr. Rumbin indignantly spoke
louder. "Cattlet!"

"Sir?" The assistant recovered himself enough to
move. "Ye—yes, sir," he said in a strangled voice,
and walked dazedly out of the room.

The moment for Mr. Rumbin's climax had arrived,
and, though badly flustered, he tried to be equal to it.
"Mr. Halbert and also Miss Raines," he began.
"Not a wort I ain't yet says what masterpiece comes

now in front your gazes, knowing it's Mr. Halbert's wish a picture ain't boosted to him, and won't listen anyways if it is. So I wouldn't. On the odda hand, while the picture's on the way here and ain't come in yet, we got time I should simple make the announcement the Master's name which created this macknificent *chef d'œuvre d'art* and the title of the painting, because, frangkly speaking, in all the years I been a successful art dealer I ain't never before acquired no such a—"

"Yes, yes, Mr. Rumbin," the collector said, and turned conversationally to Georgina Horne. "Miss —um—Miss Horne, rather interesting what our young friend, the assistant, and I were just now speaking of. No doubt he thought me pretty eccentric the other day when I told him of my ignorance and dishonesty?"

"Him?" the confused Mr. Rumbin said hurriedly. "No, Cattlet's ignorant but ain't dishonest. Mr. Halbert and also Miss Raines, in all my years as a successful art dealer I ain't never—"

"Yes, yes, Mr. Rumbin!" Mr. Halbert said again, and Georgina, trembling, saw that the great collector began to be annoyed; he didn't intend to be talked to at all. The time had come to protect Mr. Rumbin from himself.

"What was your ignorance and dishonesty all

about, Mr. Halbert?" she asked. "Not about a work
of art, was it?"

"A filthy one!" he said with abrupt vehemence;
then laughed. "My first Rembrandt—one of those
grand, heart-wringing old women in cap and ruff. I
adored it for years, then was struck with hideous
doubt; finally ran it down with the help of Professor
Prince. The point is that I consciencelessly sent it
away to be sold without explanation, though I knew
it to be that most detestable thing, a wonderful copy
turned into a rascality by a forged signature. Probably it would delude the keenest eye now extant, for
a time at least. You see my wickedness, Miss Horne?"

Georgina looked at him with widening eyes. "A
Rembrandt? An old woman in a ruff and cap and—"

"Yes, one of those; but something's been added to
it since then, Miss Horne. It went to Europe and my
agent tells me some extremely shrewd person over
there must have recognized it—added a touch of
disguise so that it wouldn't easily be known as the
Rembrandt discarded from my collection. Stuck a
flower on the old woman! I learn that the picture now
bears the charming title, The Old Woman With The
Rose. Imagine Rembrandt doing that!" The collector
laughed angrily; then looked at his watch. "Has your
young man gone to sleep, Mr. Rumbin?"

Mr. Rumbin didn't reply. Utterly stricken, he could

only look at Georgina, who was already upon her feet. "I'll go see!" she said in a stifled voice, and fluttered toward the door. Disaster hung poised as she thus rushed to stop Howard Cattlet from entering the room.

Mr. Rumbin, whirling in space, had grotesque thoughts. The most practical one was that he could fall crashing to the floor, feigning sudden dreadful illness, and gasp heroically, "Come beck next week, Mr. Halbert and also Miss Raines. I ain't well enough to show you the picture to-day."

Georgina didn't reach the door.

Howard Cattlet, even paler than he'd been, entered the room carrying a picture. His expression was not that of a person who stubbornly risks everything upon a great stroke to establish the rightness of his opinions on art; no, his look was that of one who in fright performs a deed of daring directed by all the brains he has. These, in tumult, had been borne out of the room in Howard's head aware that the picture in all the world most abhorrent to the sensitive Halbert had lately arrived in New York consigned to the dealer Orcas. More, these same brains remembered that the eloquent vacancy in Mr. Halbert's Dutch Room was next to a Rembrandt.

Yesterday Mr. Rumbin had announced his crossing of the Rubicon; Howard Cattlet now crossed his own.

What he desperately set upon the easel before Mr. Halbert and Miss Raines was the portrait of Edward Morris, Esqre by Sir Thomas Lawrence.

There was an astounding silence. That is, it was a silence astounding to Howard, who had almost hopelessly prepared himself to whisper, "I'll explain later!" in response to an expected bellow from Mr. Rumbin.

Mr. Rumbin uttered no bellow, uttered nothing. He wiped his forehead, then the back of his neck, then the front of it, then his forehead again. Georgina, near the door, stood rigid. Mr. Halbert and Miss Raines, in their fine chairs, sat looking at the picture, and their expressions were those of persons occupied in scrutiny. It was Miss Raines who spoke first.

"I know this portrait," she said. "Edward Morris was a Regency wit and playwright, Mr. Halbert. It's the Brookford Museum Lawrence I once spoke to you about. You got it from Brookford, Mr. Rumbin?"

Mr. Rumbin, who so often made miraculous recoveries of his poise at a critical moment, was unable to rise to this one. "Yes—yes, ma'am—" was all he said.

"I hadn't any idea they'd let it go," Miss Raines murmured to Mr. Halbert.

"Seems they have," the collector said, not moving his gaze from the portrait. "I'm rather pleased with you, Mr. Rumbin, for not trying to knock my eye out with some terrific prodigy—a Bellini or a Rembrandt or a Hals, perhaps. Half of Lawrence's pictures I wouldn't look at, though it's always hard to beat his craftsmanship. When he painted character instead of an insipid prettiness he was Somebody! Rather got character into this one, don't you think, Miss Raines?"

"Yes, quite a little. Aliveness, too, Mr. Halbert."

"Yes, rather a happy aliveness," he said. "Been looking a long time for the right Lawrence for my English Room, Mr. Rumbin. Very nice. He hasn't even made the neck too long." Mr. Halbert rose abruptly and strode toward the door. "Well, Miss Raines, shall we be on our way?"

Upon that, Miss Raines rose, too; murmured polite words of parting and offered Georgina her hand. Rumbin spoke feebly.

"Mr. Halbert, you—you says you like my—my—my great Lawrence? You—"

The collector turned back to him. "Like it? All depends. I might like it if it's understood that I always fix my own price, yes or no. I think this ought to be twenty-two thousand dollars. Right?"

"Right!" whispered Mr. Rumbin.

All at once, Mr. Halbert looked excited, egregiously pleased; in spite of himself, his voice rang with triumph. "It's ours, Miss Raines! It's a great portrait. We'll hang it this afternoon. The assistant can bring it right out to my car. Doesn't need any wrapping. When I get a picture I want, I want it! Come along, please, Miss Raines!"

The group of four, Mr. Halbert, Miss Raines, Mr. Rumbin and Howard Cattlet, who carried Sir Thomas Lawrence's portrait of Edward Morris, Esqre, swept by Georgina Horne and passed on out through the shop and to the sidewalk. From inside the display window Georgina watched the final bowings of Mr. Rumbin as the collector's closed black car moved away.

Mr. Rumbin and Howard came back into the shop. Mr. Rumbin's face was wet but radiant as he opened wide his ponderous arms. Howard Cattlet, tremendously embraced, looked over his employer's fat round shoulder and beheld the eyes of Georgina Horne fixed upon himself with a strange new expression.

"Howie!" Mr. Rumbin shouted tearfully. "Howie, you're a art dealer!"

CHAPTER TWENTY-FOUR

HERE was another cornucopia; but there was still a spider among the apples of silver. People often wonder how it feels to be elected President of the United States; probably the successful candidate, receiving emotional congratulations in his library, has often suffered from a tight shoe or internal pressures requiring sodium bicarbonate. A great American, commander of the Republic's armies, ended the day of his most prodigious victory with the loss of all his teeth (the fault of his orderly) and knew little except distress until more could be procured. Howard Cattlet, embraced as a colleague and fellow of the academy of art dealers by a Rumbin grown great through the placing of an important painting in the Halbert Collection, was downcast because the strange new expression faded from the lovely grey eyes of Georgina Horne before he could decide what it meant.

He would have liked to ask her, but couldn't think

of just the right words for the inquiry. He knew that
if he asked, "What did you mean by it?" she in return would say, "What did I mean by what?" If he
then replied, "By the way you were looking at me
when I was looking at you over Mr. Rumbin's shoulder," he was certain that the result would be unsatis-
factory, even uncomfortable; yet he couldn't think
of a better way to set about the matter. Moreover,
she hadn't looked at him in that manner again; she'd
resumed the mien of a courteous mere acquaintance,
and two slight episodes increased her discomfiting
politeness to him.

Upon a morning not long after the sale of the
Lawrence, Mr. Cherding came into the shop, sweetly
appareled, and there was rhythmic correspondence
between a boutonnière of violets and a bluish handkerchief shown over the top of a breast pocket. He
was smiling, debonair, negligently confident; and
Howard, at work in the stock room and seeing him
through the open door, immediately had a chilled
stomach; waves of dislike passed over him. Mr.
Cherding and Georgina engaged in conversation near
the window for a time; then Mr. Cherding departed,
and Mr. Rumbin, who had been in the shop not far
from them, came out to the stock room, chuckling.

"Georchie's so loyal towards Rumbin Galleries
she don't waste her time," he said. "Is Brookford

Museum going to acquire any more Rumbin Galleries pictures right now or likely any odda time? No. Why not? Because Rumbin Galleries already placed a picture in Brookford Museum and don't needs to make the sacrifice no more to accept museum prices to get in that one, and she knows it. Wanted she'd eat lunch with him and aftaworts go look at a Modigliani portrait just new from Paris. Georchie's friendly with him; laughs and tells him she's tired of them long Modigliani portrait faces two inches wide on ostriches' necks what got painted when Modigliani's been drinking a little ether in his brandy. Ooh! Was Mr. Cherding art-mad at her! Bites him inside, like she tells me a mont' ago she's waiting to on account he's always too damn patronizing. Mr. Cherding, when you don't agrees with him he looks like you're one year old squeaking for the milk bottle, and even when you does agrees with him, he looks like he knows secrets about you that hands him a smile. Georchie tells him you placed the Lawrence in the Halbert Collection."

"Sir? You say Miss Horne told him *I* placed the Lawrence in the Halbert Collection?"

"Yes, Howie. It's true, too. Ain't it all owings to you I sends Old Woman With The Rose beck to that damn Orcas with a silky note Mr. Halbert's going to burn it for him?" Mr. Rumbin laughed happily.

"Georchie tells Mr. Cherding she's too busy to lunch and how Mr. Halbert grebbed the picture, nice price, and she thinks she's been making a mistake having such strong art opinions at her age, because young people often thinks they're thinking themselfs when they're only thinking what somebody elst told 'em or what they read somewheres maybe. So it's dangerous to think you're thinking yourself when you usual ain't until you're maybe forty, fifty, sixty years old. 'Don't you think so yourself, Mr. Cherding?' she says at him, and she laughs all putty, so friendly that his nose gets wider at its bottom, like he wants to say poohpooh! but he's too much a gentleman, so instead looks at his watch and says he's got a engachement with Dr. Vladimir Vekin that wrote the book on Sixt' Century Byzantine Mosaics. Goes off mad."

Howard, unduly delighted, too eagerly sought an opportunity to congratulate Georgina upon this change of mind—perhaps even change of heart. "Georgina, I think you did a splendid thing," he said, a few minutes after hearing the pleasant news. "There are a great many young people in this country need to be told that sort of thing."

"What sort of thing?"

"Why, the sort of thing Mr. Rumbin says you told Mr. Cherding, Georgina. He certainly needed it! Of all the cocksure—"

"What?" Georgina's eyes enlarged; it was a cold, cold stare she gave him. "What about yourself? You were pretty cocksure about the Lawrence, weren't you?"

"About the Lawrence?" he repeated, incredulous. "About the Lawr—"

"Certainly!" With that, leaving him completely dumfounded in his ignorance of what women are made of, she turned away and presently was more distantly polite than ever.

That was the first of the two episodes, and the second, a few days later, was less perplexing but much more unfortunate. Mr. Rumbin had gone home early; Georgina was finishing the balancing of her books, and Howard was pensively waiting to lock up the shop, when two sprightly young ladies, both pretty, came in breezily and kissed him. They were his sister, Mary, and Miss Maisie Apthorn.

When Maisie kissed him he gave the rear of the shop the look of a wounded dove. "I—I hope your mother's well," he said to the affectionate girl, faintly; then spoke more loudly. "I mean I hope your mother's as well as usual, because we're all so fond of her at our house. I've always been devoted to her, myself, and so have all our fam—"

"Good gracious, Maisie knows that!" his sister, Mary, exclaimed. "What's the matter with you?

We've been to a concert uptown and thought it'd be
fun to come down and see your place here and go
home on the same train with you. Maisie's coming to
dinner and you're going to take us to the Country
Club dance afterward. Oh, yes; you'll have to take
me, too, Howard—gooseberry or no gooseberry!
Now show us all over this funny place here—Maisie's
crazy to see it! Show us all over and tell us what you
do."

Howard unhappily showed them all over, and,
unavoidably passing near the desk with them, performed a slight ceremony in an embarrassed and embarrassing manner.

"Miss Horne," he said, as Georgina looked up
brightly. "Miss Horne—I mean Georgina—I mean
Miss Horne—this is my sister, Mary, from Hackertown where we live, and this is her friend—I mean
our friend—Miss Apthorn from Hackertown where
we live—I mean where she lives, too."

Mary laughed aloud. "Howard, what *is* the matter
with you! Is he always unnatural like this in the shop,
Miss Horne?"

"No." Georgina shook her head sunnily. "Only on
great occasions."

"But this isn't—" Howard began. "It isn't a—I
mean it's—"

"You must be sure and show Miss Apthorn the

stock room," Georgina said. "You'll be interested in that, Miss Apthorn, because that's where he is most of the time. Both your sister and Miss Apthorn'll be interested in the stock room, Mr. Cattlet."

Smiling pleasantly, she was at her work again, and Howard, sighing, said, "Well—well, this is the way to the stock room."

He showed Maisie and Mary the stock room and the galleries, put two or three pictures on the easel for them; and then, when Mary said it was time to be on the way to their train, they passed out through the shop, and he almost wished Mr. Rumbin hadn't bought the Apthorn Stuart Washington. Maisie had always been fond of Howard; but since the purchase of the great painting, a transaction she persisted in attributing solely to him, her gratitude had become an almost passionate devotion.

"Isn't he darling!" she asked Georgina, who had completed her work and walked with them to the outer door. Maisie walked with her hand fondly on Howard's arm. "It must be wonderful for you to work with him every day, Miss Horne. Don't you and Mr. Rumbin adore him?"

Georgina was laughing but noncommittal. "I'm sure you all do at Hackertown, Miss Apthorn."

They reached the sidewalk. Maisie and Mary waited till Howard locked the door, and Georgina,

nodding and murmuring good nights, went upon her
way. Howard had a feeling that she heard the half-
suppressed exclamations that followed her, "What
a lovely girl!" "Isn't she charming!" but that she
didn't care what Maisie and Mary—or anybody else
—thought of her.

She made no reference to the visitors, the next
day; but her formality had increased. Unquestionably
it had increased, and Howard once more became
despondent about himself and the possibilities of a
career for any Art Dealer's Assistant. Mr. Rumbin,
as a contrast, was never more optimistic. Ransacking
shops, haunting auctions, dealing with other dealers,
he'd laid hands upon an early Copley portrait, a portrait by Blackburn and one by the elusive Feke; had
sold all three to Mr. Milton Wilby, and there was no
longer any doubt that Mr. Wilby had become a collector of early American pictures. Quite as certainly
the partners, Mr. Kingsford J. Hollins and Mr. Milton Wilby, had been suavely innoculated with the
virus of that expensive disease, collectors' jealousy.
Probably Mr. Rumbin wouldn't have been able to
sell the Feke to Mr. Wilby if Mr. Hollins hadn't
talked patronizingly about art to his partner half an
hour before Mr. Wilby's appointment to see the
picture.

Having purchased the Feke, Mr. Wilby was so

patronizing, in his turn, that Rumbin Galleries easily disposed of a Flemish primitive, a Joos van Cleef, Saint Jerome, to Mr. Hollins, who wouldn't have been able to bear the picture except for Mr. Rumbin's telling him how much more distinguishedly naive it was than a Feke.

Mr. Hollins remained the great, the "ideel" client, first in the hearts of Rumbin Galleries, and did so well in that capacity that before he went abroad with his family, at midsummer, Mr. Rumbin had at last settled upon the move to Fifty-seventh Street as a reality not far distant. Mr. Milton Wilby also went abroad, at the end of July; business was slack, almost at a standstill, and Mr. Rumbin spent a great deal of time with real estate agents and investigating vacancies in uptown buildings.

Both Mr. Hollins and Mr. Milton Wilby returned with the earliest autumn and, before September was over, Mr. Rumbin announced to his two employees that he was ready to cast the die.

"Rumbin Galleries moves uptown next mont' in the middle," he told them, upon a happy morning. "I been nine times over them galleries that's wacant on Fifty-sixt' Street, Georchie and Howie. It's a place ideel! Pig rooms, pyootiful picture gallery, and I'm going to hire a second assistant under you, Howie, and also a porter that does your janitor work, so you

can live almost pure in your cutaway. Ain't you both
tickled laughing, Georchie and Howie, answer me,
please?"

At this bidding, Georgina did laugh, and Howard
Cattlet, looking at her, obediently laughed, too; but
with reservations.

"Ain't you heppy, Howie?" Mr. Rumbin said.
"You're laughing like machinery sounds."

"Sir? Yes, sir. I was just thinking of something I
had on my mind I thought you'd like to know, Mr.
Rumbin."

"On your mind, I'd like to know, Howie? So what
could it be?"

"Something you did, sir." Howard glanced again
uneasily at Georgina; nowadays he could never tell
how she was going to take anything. "It's about the
Apthorn family you bought the Stuart Washington
from. I mean it's about Mrs. Apthorn's daughter."

"The daughter? Aha!" Mr. Rumbin cried. "The
putty one that kisses you arms around?"

"She's always been just the same as my sister,"
Howard said hurriedly. "My Uncle Rupert helped
to invest the money you paid them. They bought
stocks just at the lowest and they've been going up so
splendidly that everything's different for them.
Maisie's just got engaged to my cousin, Rupert
Cattlet, Second, and he's found a job and they an-

nounced it last night at a little dinner party. I thought you'd be pleased to hear it, sir. I certainly was, myself."

"So?" Mr. Rumbin laughed. "Pleased when now maybe your cousin, Rupert Second, don't never any more let her get kissing you arms around; yet you says you're pleased, Howie?"

"I certainly am!"

The young man spoke with conviction. He wasn't certain; but he thought that Georgina, in the most covert manner, looked pleased, too. He was almost sure she did look that way, and for a moment he was breathless. Then he remembered that her salary was still double his own and that her Van Dyck windfall still made her more than twice as rich as he was.

"Howie, ain't you listening?" Mr. Rumbin asked. "Why the brains wanderings foolish smiles when I'm talking about moving up to Fifty-sixt' Street?"

CHAPTER TWENTY-FIVE

"Sir?"

"Fifty-sixt' Street!" Mr. Rumbin repeated. "Celeries might get raised, too. Couldn't I get you laughing some about them celeries, Georchie and Howie?"

Again Georgina laughed, and Howard tried to laugh. He'd be glad to have his salary raised, of course; but he foresaw that Georgina's would continue to be double his own, and how could any self-respecting young man ask a girl to begin being engaged to him under such circumstances?

"Laugh louder, Howie," Mr. Rumbin said, and his bright eyes twinkled. "Don't he oughts to, Georchie? Ain't it Howie's cutaway suit and that aristocratic dumb look he's got's always gone so good on clients? Ain't he Rumbin Galleries' Mascot? Wasn't it execkly when I firstly picked him for assistant that I catched my ideel client, Georchie?"

"Exactly then," she answered, with grey eyes, sud-

denly kind, upon the blushing assistant. "The luck
he's brought's stayed with us, too, so now we have
other ideal clients besides Mr. Hollins."

"Ah, but Mr. Hollins," the dealer exclaimed, "he's
yet always the ideelest! Mr. Milton Wilby he's next;
but's a long distance between 'em and sometimes I got
pig doubts I could sell any more to Mr. Milton Wilby
exceptings Mr. Hollins would keep him upset acquiring new ones." Mr. Rumbin abruptly checked himself. "Oh, how I am talking! What a mistake! I'm
ashamed!"

"Ashamed,   Mr.   Rumbin?"   Georgina   asked,
puzzled.

"It's the wort 'sell'," the dealer explained. "We
don't use that wort no more, Georchie and Howie,
exceptings in private among ourselfs, and even then
we oughts to use the odda, so's to get used to it, unless talking too fast or excited. You know what I
mean, Howie?"

"No, sir."

"Uptown dealers like we're going to be oughts
never to say 'sell', Howie. From now on, commence
practising, and me, too, I got to learn it. After now
we don't say we sold such-or-such a picture to Mr.
Hollins. We say we placed it. We say we placed it in
Mr. Hollins's collection or, simple, we say we placed
such-or-such a picture in a permanent collection.

Somebody comes in, asks, 'Where's that nice School of Clouet used to be in Rumbin Galleries?' We answer dignified, 'We've had the honor to place it in a permanent collection.' You see, Howie?"

"Yes, sir."

"Also, Howie, whenever heppens a possibility to silky slide it in, we should say something about the great picture we placed in the famous Halbert Collection, or maybe the famous picture Rumbin Galleries placed in the great Halbert Collection, maybe saying it both ways; yet always remembering we should speak of placing in the famous Hollins Collection or the great Hollins Collection whenever talking to anybody knows Mr. Hollins and would maybe tell him they heard Rumbin Galleries speaking of his great famous collection. Always think how to please Mr. Hollins. Take from Rumbin Galleries Mr. Kingsford J. Hollins and would we be moving up to Fifty-sixt' Street? Might be we wouldn't. Where is there any feature to Mr. Hollins that ain't ideel?"

"He gets pretty cross sometimes," Georgina suggested. "His temper—"

"Cross?" Mr. Rumbin waved this objection away. "Crossness in a client gives a dealer his piggest chances to prove if he's a real talker or just only a mouth-noiser. Crossness don't comes between a client and no outstanding dealer. Think, Georchie, who's

the worst comes between a art dealer and his clients?
Is it clients' temper? No, it's their wifes. Does Mrs.
Hollins? No, she don't, owings to her beings kind
of a spoilt flutter-head lady she wouldn't have sense
enough to even if she'd oughts to, which it ain't, him
beings too wealt'y he don't needs it. So look, Georchie, Mrs. Hollins for a client's wife she's ideel, too.
On tops that, Georchie, think how I got him teached
to trust me."

"Yes, and he certainly ought to, Mr. Rumbin," the
loyal Georgina said. "He hasn't any Eye for art at all
himself and you've entirely formed his collection.
You've sold him—I mean you've placed some pretty
sound and splendid pictures in the Hollins Collection."

"Yes, and I'll place some more!" Mr. Rumbin
said. "Don't never forget Mr. Kingsford J. Hollins
he's Rumbin Galleries' beckbone and eyes' apples,
Georchie. Ain't I studied his human nature so good I
can tell whenever he's ready to acquire anodda picture, no matter how broke he swears me he is? Ain't
I seen that art-acquiring look commencing on him
again only last week, and wasn't I 'phoning him
yesterday putty soon I'm showing him a new great
painting? Any time now he'll be calling up trying to
sound like he don't want no more pictures but fretful asks when."

"Maybe he's already asked," Georgina said. "There's a letter from him in the morning's mail; it's on the desk."

"Aha!" the pleased dealer cried, went to the desk, found the letter and opened it eagerly. At once, however, he lost his enthusiasm; the first sentence in Mr. Hollins's missive didn't lead at all in the direction expected. "Kindly do me a favor" was this first sentence. Mr. Rumbin looked bleak, murmured, "Oh, my!" and handed the letter to Georgina. "It don't commence right," he said. "Read it to me, Georchie, and use your woice nice to make it sound as good's it can."

" 'Kindly do me a favor,' " Georgina read aloud, in agreeable tones. " 'No doubt you have heard of the Strout-Webster collection of Old Masters formed by E. P. Strout, deceased, the noted connoisseur. His daughter, Mrs. Strout-Webster, the present owner, is a widow and a valued relative of my wife's. The collection has always seemed to me most remarkable and talking it over with me lately, Mrs. Strout-Webster mentioned that she'd like to have a real expert's opinion upon its present-day artistic value. I told her I knew you would be delighted to inspect the paintings and give her your opinion. As my friend Dr. Egbert Watson is abroad indefinitely I know of no one whose judgment would be more trustworthy than yours. If convenient, I wish you would run out to Mrs. Strout-Webster's house at Old Eastfield to-morrow afternoon, arriving about three, and oblige her as I have indicated. I shall appreciate this service on her behalf. She will be expecting you if you will kindly telephone my secretary confirming the appointment.' "

Mr. Rumbin spoke resignedly. "Well, telephone yes, I'm all delighted, I'll go. Did ever you heard of the Strout-Webster Collection, Georchie?"

"No, not of the collection. I've often heard of Mrs. Strout-Webster, though—wealth, charities and fashionableness."

The dealer frowned. "Natchly I got to chump for choy to do on Mr. Hollins a favor; yet reporting about pictures and collections pure for friendship, it's a kind of foolish waste of time." He sighed. "Anyways, I take Howie along with me, passes the time talking, Howie and me, in the automobile I got to hire. Takes couple hours to this Old Eastsfields, don't it, Howie?"

"Yes, at least, sir," the assistant said, not displeased. He knew that Mr. Rumbin would do all the talking, but liked listening to him and was in a cheerful mood the next day when they set forth upon their excursion, after an early lunch. Mr. Rumbin was less buoyant.

"E. P. Strout," he said meditatively, when they were out of the city. "Last night I asks Ferdinand Corr did he ever knows this E. P. Strout—'noted connoisseur', the letter calls him. Ferd says no, he never acquired nothing from F. Corr and Company nor nowheres elst he hears of. Anything important sold in New York last twenty years, I'd know it, myself; but till the letter I ain't heard the name. Looks to me, Howie, we're going to see a old-fashion' collection finished maybe twenty t'irty years ago—maybe longer."

"You think a collection that old-fashioned probably wouldn't be a very good one, Mr. Rumbin?"

"Can't tell, Howie; might be all the better. On the odda hand, likely might be artists used to been popalar that critics been chumping hot on, so prices dropped and now collectors that reads art fashions goes light on 'em—scared gets highbrow laughed at. Cabanel, Bouguereau, Jean Léon Gérome, Meissonier, Schreyer, Henner, Jules Breton, Alma Tadema, Leighton—even Greuze, Guido Reni, even Murillo. Plenty oddas gone out o' fashion, too. Maybe pops beck in again some day, you can't tell; but if they do a art dealer's got to know when, Howie."

The young man whistled briefly. "What an art dealer has to know! It's always going to be too much for me, sir."

"No, Howie; you got to." Mr. Rumbin's eyes glowed; he was upon a favorite theme. "Now I got you commenced learning, I make you into a art dealer if it wears your whole head's hair off, little of mine too! After the first thing a art dealer's got to know, which's human nature for hendling clients, nextly it's all periods, all styles from all nations' architectures, paintings, sculptures, tapestries, needleworks, embroideries, welfets, brocades, glass, porcelains, ceramics, ivories, enamels, rugs, furniture, armor, leather, gold, silver, pewter, bronze, brass, copper, iron and plenty oddas."

"Is that all?" Howard asked.

"No. Also all nations' histories, costumes and ornaments, because for exemple, suppose you see a Wenetian Fifteent' Century portrait of a lady sitting in a dress that's French from maybe a hundut years later, could you now get stuck with a such picture, Howie?"

"I don't think so, sir. That'd be fairly easy; but I'd probably feel like asking somebody else for his opinion, too."

"Oh, yes, certainly," Mr. Rumbin admitted. "Special subjects even a art dealer, like a collector or a museum, he frequence gets help from a expert, I don't say no; yet even then look what can heppen— like what did to the piggest Nineteent' Century critic-expert with the Velásquez for the great public gallery in London, for exemple."

"The expert made a mistake, Mr. Rumbin?"

"Yes, Howie—him beings intellexual scholar macknificent; writes grand, was putty near king art critic of the worlt. Public gallery acquires a new Velásquez —it's a lentscape beckground, human figures in the foreground. The pig expert says he likes the human figures in the foreground, typical Velásquez; the lentscape beckground ain't so good, somebody elst might painted it. Then, after he says so and everybody's talking how much he knows and what a Eye he's got, slips out a horrible secret that before he seen it the picture's cleaned and ironed, and the hot iron accidental took all them human figures practical clean out, so the foreground's wacant and the cleaner's scared thinkless. But he's got a friend that paints vonderful on china, so he private gets him to paint foreground figures beck in well's he can. He must done putty good, too, because them china-painter's-figures was what the great expert says he reckanizes as typical by the Master, Velásquez. You see what can heppen to the highest; it's frequence kind o' ticklish, Howie."

"Ticklish, Mr. Rumbin? Sometimes it seems to me that about so many old pictures there's such confusion and uncertainty and sometimes even trickery that—"

"Might be, Howie; yet look, ain't them execkly what sprinkles the fescination on any business? Look again, it usual ain't so hard to learn to know a honest picture from a crooked one and to reckanize a honest picture that's good painting, and whenever you get holt a honest picture that's good painted and brains in it, you got something, no matter if experts quarrels who painted it. Furdamore, experts ain't quarreling about something 't ain't no good. More besides, from every great Master that ain't too terrible early there's a certain number his works, usual most of 'em, complete settled, can't be doubted by nobody, safe like mountains."

"I know, sir." Howard shook his head. "I suppose I get confused for a very simple reason."

"Dumbness, no," Mr. Rumbin said kindly. "Your face shows you got more modesty than you got dumbness, if a person looks at you careful, Howie. Right to-day when you're seeing Mrs. Strout-Webster's collection, I bet you're going to surprise yourself how much you know in a couple glences at most the pictures. I bet you two dollars serious you surprise yourself, Howie. Take it?"

CHAPTER TWENTY-SIX

HOWARD DECLINED on the ground that if two glances
at any of the paintings proved he knew anything at
all he'd surprise himself, and he was wise not to make
the wager. When the hired car, rolling upon crushed
stone, had crossed the forepart of Mrs. Strout-
Webster's landscaped estate, and the two visitors had
been conducted by Mrs. Strout-Webster herself to
the wing of her big house containing the "Art Gallery", Howard began to surprise himself at the very
entrance to that series of oblong, sky-lighted apartments.

Mrs. Strout-Webster, fifty, pale-eyed, fluffy and
vivacious, gave the impression of having been resur-
faced with great care by a modish woman-servant,
though massage and cosmetics hadn't removed from
her face lines and contours betokening a changeful
temper. She was more than gracious to the two gentlemen from Rumbin Galleries, however, and, as she

led the way with Mr. Rumbin into the first gallery,
praising his sweetness, her voice seemed to Howard
much like that of a retired coloratura soprano still
practising trills.

"So sweet of you, Mr. Rumbin!" she cried, over
and over. "Really, it's the sweetest thing. Indeed, indeed it is! So sweet of you!"

A few feet behind them, Howard paused impulsively in the wide doorway. Before him, at the
other end of the long room, was another such doorway, open, and the vista of two farther galleries. His
first impression was of a richly warm spaciousness
and of light pleasantly reflected from parquetry
floors and the glossy marble tops of big gilt tables;
but almost simultaneously a curious disquiet came
upon him. He was aware of the paintings only in
their mass, so to speak; but the experience was somewhat as if an inviting doorway brought him an un-
inviting odor. He disliked seeing paintings hung
above other paintings, as here many of them were,
and he had a prejudice against elaborate frames,
especially against frames not carved but heavily
loaded with gilded plaster in baroque shapings. These
objections of his had nothing to do with the true
beauty or value of works of art, he knew, and
were not what halted him. In fact, he wasn't
sure what did, and, after the one queer moment,

came into the room and began to look about him.

Mrs. Strout-Webster was continuing to be effusive over Mr. Rumbin. "No, I simply couldn't tell you how sweet it is of you, you kind man! Simply the sweetest thing I ever knew anybody to do! Of course, though, a man who knows art from A to Z as you do, Mr. Rumbin, can't help taking pleasure in the master-pieces that such a connoisseur as my father brought together here. You knew him, Mr. Rumbin?"

"Only by of course repatation," the courtly Rumbin answered, "him beings a such noted connoisseur, Mrs. Strout-Webster. Natchly E. P. Strout it's a name I wouldn't hardly belonged to the art-world myself, knowing A to Z like you says and beings a friend of Mr. Kingsford J. Hollins, placing the best of Rumbin Galleries' great famous masterpieces frequence in the famous great Hollins Collection, if I didn't heard it by now. I would loved to knowed your papa, E. P. Strout, Mrs. Strout-Webster."

"Ah, you'd have worshiped him, Mr. Rumbin! A man of your taste—oh, yes, Mr. Hollins simply raves about you!"

"I like him, too," Mr. Rumbin said. "I like him beck as much as he does me. More! Mr. Hollins is the same to me as if he was my uncle and my nephew or my aunt or anything up from a cousin. How much I like Mr. Hollins I can't say to his face, it's em-

barrassing; it could only be from odda people I says
it to's telling him."

"I'll be sure to," Mrs. Strout-Webster returned
graciously, and seemed to feel that preliminary
courtesies were now sufficient. "Shall we give the
collection a little attention? I'm only going to point
out one or two of the very greatest treasures. I
simply must know what you think of the Raphael."

Mr. Rumbin's expression was of a courteous per-
plexity. "Raphael? I—I beg your pardon, Mrs.
Strout-Webster, I—Where—"

"Why, straight before you!" she cried, and
pointed to a small painting in a brilliant, heavy
frame. "Really, isn't it a sensation—such a wonderful little Raphael, Mr. Rumbin?"

Mr. Rumbin stared at the picture—a diminutive,
sweet-faced Madonna, feebly modeled, in robes of
red and harsh blue, and hard in outline against
chalky clouds and a milkily turquoise sky. A slight
convulsion passed over his face, beginning at the top
of his forehead, just below the hair, and descending
as far as the second section of his double chin. This
plastic alteration was involuntary; he corrected it,
apparently by a powerful inflation of his chest.

"Vonderful!" he said in a husky voice.

Mrs. Strout-Webster was delighted. "I knew of
course you'd say so, Mr. Rumbin; but it is such a

comfort to hear it from someone Mr. Hollins says is
the authority! Now I'm going to absolutely dum-
found you. What do you suppose my father paid for
that divine little Raphael?"

"Frangkly speaking, I couldn't guess, Mrs. Strout-
Webster."

"Well, I won't give you the exact figure," she said
triumphantly; "but I'll tell you this much confi-
dentially, Mr. Rumbin—it was under five thousand
dollars! Of course the picture's small; but think of
it—a Raphael at that price!"

"You don't tell me, Mrs. Strout-Webster. Again
vonderful!"

"Wasn't it!" she exclaimed. "And only think what
it's worth now!"

"Yes," Mr. Rumbin said, even more huskily.
"Think what it's wort' now! My!"

"You see," Mrs. Strout-Webster explained, "my
father understood his opportunities. He picked up
these priceless things at auctions and from dealers in
all sorts of odd places that ordinary tourists never
know about. Besides, you see, he got hold of them
long before people began to appreciate these great
artists."

"He did? Mirackalous!"

"I knew you'd think so!" the gratified lady cried.
"Now tell me what you think of the Correggio.

Don't you agree with me it's really a gem, the Correggio, Mr. Rumbin?"

"Correggio?" With an air of cunning, Mr. Rumbin pointed at a large canvas opulent with imperfectly foreshortened mythological personages intermingled with a marble balustrade. "Aha, yonder! Aha, the Correggio!"

Mrs. Strout-Webster looked up at him in marveling admiration. "Mr. Rumbin, I never saw anything like you in all my life! To be able to walk into a gallery and pick out all the artists, exactly who painted which pictures, the way you're doing—well, it simply shows! The Correggio's really my favorite. Tell me if you don't think it's as fine a Correggio as you ever saw."

Mr. Rumbin smiled upon her almost tenderly. "Frangkly speaking, Mrs. Strout-Webster," he said, "a such Correggio I ain't often seen before, and if Correggio would come to life he would be excited himself."

Mrs. Strout-Webster clapped her plump little hands, applauding. "You say the cleverest things, Mr. Rumbin, and I can't tell you what your enthusiasm means to me." She gave his sleeve a coquettish pat with brightly ringed fingers. "Now I'm not going to be your cicerone any longer; I just wanted to see the impression my collection was going to make on you, and now I know. You and your assistant can go over it more thoroughly without me chattering at you, so now I'll just run away until tea time when I'm going to have a delightful little surprise for you." She fluttered to the doorway they'd entered, called back gayly, *"Wiedersehen,* you kind man!" and went lightly away, down the marble-floored corridor.

Howard Cattlet spoke in a hushed voice. "Mr. Rumbin, you said I'd surprise myself, and I'm doing it. To me both those pictures look like—well, like just a prettified kind of gaudy painting, and if anybody but you had said they were authentic Raphael and—"

"I didn't, Howie. I didn't said so."

"What? You mean I've guessed right and Raphael and Correggio no more painted 'em than I did?"

"Maybe not even as much as you, Howie."

"But, Mr. Rumbin, I heard you tell Mrs. Strout-Webster—"

"I don't tell no lies," Mr. Rumbin said. "All I done, I double-talked her."

"Sir? You what?"

"I double-talked her," Mr. Rumbin explained, surprised that Howard hadn't understood. "I double-talked her, meanings I tell the truth but in a such nice way she thinks I means something elst she likes

*"Mr. Rumbin, I Never Saw Anything Like You in All
My Life! To Be Able to Pick Out All the Artists—"*

better. I says the Raphael's vonderful, and it is; it
oughts to astonish anybody, Raphael especial. I don't
tell no recklar lies; it's all so. I says if Correggio sees
that Correggio he'd be excited, and *ooh!* wouldn't
he?"

Howard was aghast. "Yes; but she thought you
meant—"

"Can't help it," Mr. Rumbin said. "Double-
talking's more a art dealer's got to know, Howie.
Important more. We ain't here appraising for a sale.
You could call it a wisit putty near pure social. In
social politeness a dealer's got to keep himself
popalar like anybody elst—even more. A dealer's
popalarity—"

"I know," Howard protested. "But, Mr. Rumbin,
when pictures aren't what they—"

"Howie, can you go inwited in people's houses
and when they ask you, 'What you think of my nice
picture Papa bought me?' can you tell 'em? You
can't say it no more than if they show you their
little boy can you tell 'em, 'My, how snub-nose he is!
Think he's genuine?' "

"But see here!" Howard was greatly disturbed.
"Why, then—then all you're going to do's praise
this collection, no matter what?"

Mr. Rumbin remained calm. "Don't I must? Suppose I speak up harsh and tell Mrs. Strout-Webster,

'No, you ain't got no Correggio, no Raphael,' what
heppens, Howie? Her face you can see under the
powder she's a lady flies off the hendle quick. Tell
her no Raphael, no Correggio, she cusses me bleck
and blue to Mr. Hollins, gets him upset, even maybe
he don't trust me no more, owings to he's got no Eye
himself and always belieft her papa a pig connoisseur
wouldn't been no such sucker. All Mr. Hollins wants
it's us to come out here do Mrs. Strout-Webster a
pleasure. Am I going to blow up like a wolcano
spoiling innocence willages? No, it's no harm she
goes on beliefing she owns Raphaels and Correggios."

"Well—I—" Howard looked about the room.
"But see some of these others, Mr. Rumbin. They
don't exactly seem to be—"

"No, maybe they don't, Howie. What her papa
pays for the Raphael it tells the story what he pays
for the oddas. Them pig tablets on the frames, look,
you can read the artists' names half across the gallery, like they're yelling at you, 'Listen, I'm Velásquez, I'm Rembrandt, I'm Rubens, I'm Tintoretto,
don't you call me a liar!' "

"I would—with this one anyhow, I think,"
Howard said, stepping closer to a murky portrait
tableted TITIAN. "Did Tiziano Vecelli usually
place a man's ear a full inch too high?"

"Usual not, Howie. Also didn't paint noses' high lights in zinc white, neither," Mr. Rumbin returned. "Some people does picks up treasures for nothing; but mostly they're like Professor Egbert Watson, trained from schooldays, and goes hunting t'ousands times for once they shoots the bell. Old E. P. Strout you can see he buys anything that's got a grand label if it's cheap enough. Ain't it a human nature, Howie?"

"Human nature!" the assistant exclaimed. "Is it? If somebody on a back street had offered that old man half a million dollars worth of diamonds for under five thousand, wouldn't he have had him arrested?"

"Diamonds yes, maybe, Howie; but not works of art. In all the worlt what's the easiest thing to think about yourself?"

"Sir?"

"That you're the smartest," Mr. Rumbin explained. "Old E. P. Strout he knows he don't know diamonds. Well, he don't know works of art neither; but he don't know he don't, because putty near anybody in the worlt thinks they knows whether a picture's a good picture or a bad picture, even if sometimes they're scared to speak it right out. E. P. Strout hands himself a pig time, beliefs he picks up bargains odda people ain't smart enough to find.

Also when he thinks he buys a Raphael for probable couple t'ousand dollars, maybe in Naples, he secret thinks the feller sells it's laughable dumb or elst maybe stole it from some foreigner that oughts to been stole from. To old E. P. Strout and plenty odda people it looks just as much a Raphael as Raphaels do that's in the Uffizi, and anyhow the label says so. Comes home, sticks it up in his gallery, and most his wisitors gets bored when they looks at the pictures and if some sees the difference natchly they don't says it."

"So probably he never knew." Frowning, Howard was moving from picture to picture. "And his daughter'll never know, either, Mr. Rumbin?"

"What for should she?" the dealer inquired, with plaintive sarcasm. "Just to get her mad? Also to get Mr. Hollins sore on Rumbin Galleries on account he has to apologize to her he got me out here?"

Howard waved a hand toward the walls about them. "But wouldn't Mr. Hollins himself know at least that these pictures—"

"No, he wouldn't. He don't. He's a collector can enchoy a picture after you tell him how or it's a pig name artist proved aut'entic; but he's innocence as a robin if you don't tell him. My Lort! How easy I could sold him pictures no better'n these, myself, exceptings I'd cut my t'roat before I'd hendle 'em. No,

Howie, when we sees Mrs. Strout-Webster again, tea's time, you got to get off that face's expression, make all smiles."

"Smiles? How can anybody smile when—"

"Well, I let you keep your face honest whiles we're here alone, Howie; I don't ask too much."

CHAPTER TWENTY-SEVEN

MR. RUMBIN, like his assistant, was now examining
the pictures, one after the other. Sometimes he
sighed, sometimes he muttered, as if hopefully.
"Well, anyways here ain't a bad copy." Once he
groaned, "Wan Dyck I seen insulted plenty; but
never like this." Then, when he and Howard had
passed together into the second gallery, he halted in
satiric amazement. "Look! Here we're in the Louvre,
Howie! See them tablets—Claude de Lorraine,
Poussin, Watteau, Boucher, Nattier, Fragonard,
David, Ingres, Delacroix, Corot. Oh, a such Corot!
Him too I never seen insulted worst."

"What about this Millet?" Howard asked. "It
was in the newspapers that Millet's grandson's been
painting fake Millets lately in Paris; but the French
government wouldn't prosecute him because he was
only selling them to Americans. Maybe this one—"

"No, Howie." Mr. Rumbin looked at the Millet.

"This Millet ain't by no grandson of Millet's. For a Millet like this you got to go outside the family."

He made a tour of the room, now and then puffing out his breath in audible discontent; then he said, "Let's see what's beyond; might be nicer." But after they'd entered the third gallery, the slight hope died. "No, here it's the English School, and one, two, t'ree—yes, four!—four Turners not by Turner. T'ree Reynoldses that ain't even Beecheys or Coteses. Hogart'—oh, what a Hogart'! My, my! How many old pictures like these is there yet in the worlt, Howie?"

"How many?" Pleased to be asked, Howard could only suggest a speculative answer. "Who knows? How many thousands and thousands of painters have been copying and imitating Old Masters ever since the Sixteenth Century? Then, reading old books, you come across items like one in Farington's diary, for instance. In Eighteen hundred and three he said some hard-headed bankers loaned a hundred and twenty-five thousand dollars on a collection of Old Masters brought from Vienna to London for exhibition—a thousand pictures. The President of the Royal Academy, Lawrence, told Farington there was scarcely an original in the whole thousand, and he valued them at an average of ten dollars a piece. A lot of those very pictures are certainly still somewhere, and there must have been a good many such exhibitions since then, mustn't there, Mr. Rumbin?"

"Before then, too," the dealer said, and further tested his pupil. "What you think of this Gainsborough lentscape, Howie?"

"Gainsborough?" The assistant approached the painting, looked at it, and laughed. "Gainsborough died in Seventeen eighty-eight, and here are foreground figures in clothes of the daguerreotype period. I believe it's the worst—"

"No, Howie," his employer said. "The Gainsborough's a nicer Gainsborough than this Kneller is Kneller. When Kneller was good he was splendid; but when Kneller was bad it's awful hard to find worst painting. Yet Mr. E. P. Strout he done it. It must took talent; but he finds him a Kneller that's worst than the worst Kneller ever done, himself."

"What do you suppose these things cost him?" Howard asked curiously. "I mean altogether, Mr. Rumbin?"

"Well, I shoot a guess, Howie. Old E. P. Strout, connoisseuring where them odda tourists doesn't goes, I speckalate he sticks himself altogedda maybe t'irty forty t'ousand dollars—maybe more."

"And what's it really worth, Mr. Rumbin? I mean all of it."

"Millions—if it's aut'entic, Howie. But beings it
ain't, put it up at auction and there's decorators and
architects fixing up flats they could use a number
over mantelpieces. There's some nice decorative pictures, some putty good old copies, too. At auction
the whole collection brings as high as t'ree, four
t'ousand dollars, maybe a little more, maybe some
less. In my life's time I seen some important boob
collections; but old E. P. Strout from me he gets the
medal. It's kind of a night's mare."

"Yes," Howard said gloomily. "Yet if I'd seen it
myself a year and a half ago, before you took me in,
Mr. Rumbin, I wouldn't have known the difference
between this and—"

"All smiles, Howie!" Mr. Rumbin interrupted in
a whisper.

A man-servant, approaching, summoned them to
tea, and Mr. Rumbin, hastily renewing the usual
courtliness of his mien, followed this messenger out
through the galleries, along the corridor and to the
doorway of a goldenly upholstered drawing-room.
Howard, accompanying him, was surprised to be-
hold therein not only their hostess and two other
middle-aged ladies, one of whom was Mrs. Hollins,
but the well-known figure, dry face and cold eye-
glasses of Kingsford J. Hollins himself.

Mrs. Strout-Webster, leaving the others near a

tea table, came forward, met Mr. Rumbin half way and seized both of his hands. "I know you're exhausted!" she cried. "They tell me you great art people simply wear yourselves out with emotions when you're looking at Old Masters. Mr. and Mrs. Hollins are my surprise for you. Wasn't it lovely of them to join us? And this is my dear, dear next door neighbor, Mrs. George Williams. Do sit down and rest your poor selves. Fleming, give Mr. Rumbin and Mr. Um what they want. There!"

Mr. Rumbin, beaming caressively, accepted a brocaded chair, a long glass and a delicate sandwich. Howard sat down beside Mrs. George Williams and was given tea by the hostess, who had returned to her seat at the table. "I've just been saying how delightfully excited you were over the Raphael and the Correggio," she said. "I mean when you stood there gasping out 'Wonderful! Wonderful!' over and over, Mr. Rumbin. Now that you've been through the whole collection, *you* must tell us the rest. What's your verdict?"

"Ah, Mrs. Strout-Webster!" Mr. Rumbin, though seated, bowed to her gallantly. "It ain't needed. You know already!"

"Of course I do!" Mrs. Strout-Webster cried. "That doesn't keep us from wanting to hear it from you, though, Mr. Rumbin. Did you or didn't you find the whole collection, every single bit of it, just as wonderful as you told me it was at first?"

"Execkly, Mrs. Strout-Webster," the double-talking Rumbin said benignly. "It's all of it just execkly as vonderful as I says firstly. Absolute, the collection's vonderful all over!"

Mrs. Strout-Webster and her friend Mrs. Williams uttered cries of pleasure. Mrs. Hollins, equally pleased, patted Mrs. Strout-Webster's hand and spoke with the air of being herself an authority. "Unique is the word I've always employed for Gertie's art gallery—unique. Wouldn't you call it unique, Mr. Rumbin?"

"Unique?" Mr. Rumbin's private definition of this faded pretty lady as "kind of a spoilt flutter-head" was far from interfering with his outward profound deference. "Ah, Mrs. Kingsford J. Hollins, it's you always says it the elegantest execkly! Unique is right." Remembering her favorite combination of colors, he tried for two birds with one stone. "Look for exemple, Mrs. Hollins, Rumbin Galleries last week acquires from England two slim Adam chairs you ain't yet seen, covered with pyootiful old rose and ivory *petit point* that's unique in their own cless for a boudoir and couldn't be uniquer. On the odda hand, in a different cless Mrs. Strout-Webster's collection it's unique, too."

Mr. Hollins wasn't as interested in this rather puzzling comparison as his wife was. "Let's don't get to talking about chairs," he said with some sharpness. "Keep to the collection, please, Rumbin. We'd like to know, for instance, how many private collections in the United States you'd rate as high as this one."

Mr. Rumbin seemed to cogitate, while his assistant, watching him, became red. "Mr. Kingsford J. Hollins," the dealer said slowly, as if with a scrupulous accuracy, "in the United States I seen many private collections; but in the whole Nort' America and Europe I ain't never seen as much as six like this one."

"Bravo! Bravo!" It was Mrs. Strout-Webster, flushed with triumph, who thus applauded. "Now, you kind man, will you answer just one more question? I hope you won't think it's a terribly vulgar one, though it's certainly very human. Don't you really think, Mr. Rumbin, that such a collection must be worth at least two hundred and fifty thousand dollars?"

Mr. Rumbin peered deep into his glass of iced refreshment. "Quotter million," he said reflectively. "Quotter million dollars? The whole collection?" Then he looked up and shook a rallying fat forefinger at his hostess. "Aha, Mrs. Strout-Webster, *you* ain't going to sell your papa's E. P. Strout connoisseur collection for no quotter million dollars. Not you! I'm too smart to think so."

Again the three ladies made a happy commotion. Mr. Rumbin's popularity was complete. Amazed by his easy and confident knowledge, Mrs. Strout-Webster, Mrs. Hollins and Mrs. George Williams exclaimed almost as loudly over his modesty.

"No, no; it ain't nothing but a Eye and a life's time's experience," he protested. "Give you the same, and you, beings smarter because ladies, you'd probable know even more than me!"

He was still insisting upon this point when he and his assistant rose to go; then, however, while taking his leave, he squeezed in a little business. "Don't forget them rose and ivory chairs," he whispered to Mrs. Hollins, and also contrived an unctuous word aside with her husband. "I hope you're pleased, Mr. Hollins, I done you to-day this little favor. At Rumbin Galleries to-morrow I got a pyootiful important surprise I could show you."

Mr. Hollins made no response; but Mrs. Strout-Webster was already at Rumbin's elbow, bubbling grateful tributes, and, a few minutes later, in the hired car, the dealer added a little to these, himself. "I done excellence, Howie," he said. "Practical sells them chairs to Mrs. Hollins, you'll see, and also slips in working up Mr. Hollins on the new picture I got picked for him. Such a hit I makes on them ladies helps nice on him! Now you see, Howie, no harm's done, only good, and oh, what a hollering mess would it been putting on the collection couple bleck eyes!"

Howard Cattlet was engaged in serious thoughts. "Mr. Rumbin," he said, "you don't suppose Mrs. Strout-Webster's thinking of selling her collection, do you?"

"Sell? No, she's rich. She just wants to get prouder of it. What makes you a such foolish question?"

"I hope it's foolish, sir," Howard said. "While we were milling round in there, getting out, Mrs. Williams was telling me how pleased she was for her friend's sake that you had given such a tremendous opinion of the pictures, and then she pouted and went on, 'Oh, I do wish Gertie'd present the collection to Old Eastfield to found an art museum, instead'!"

"Instead? Instead what, Howie?"

"That's just it, sir. She didn't say; but—but it seems to me she might have meant instead of selling."

"Selling?" Mr. Rumbin laughed. "No, no, Howie. When people's worming themselves out good-by from tea, ladies speaks lots extra words don't mean nothing, they don't know they says 'em. Anyways, when she says 'instead' she probable means instead keeping. No, Howie, we come through nice, all's good."

Mr. Rumbin was serene. He remained so for the rest of the drive, and he arrived at Rumbin Galleries the next morning at ten o'clock in the same comfortable mood. He brought with him in a taxicab the picture he designed as the next item for the Hollins Collection, carried it to the stock room himself, then returned into the shop, smiling and rubbing his hands cheerfully.

"Howie tells you how nice we done yesterday, Georchie?" he inquired of his secretary. "Tells you what good double-talking we done at Mrs. Strout-Webster's?"

"Yes," Georgina said thoughtfully. "He rather thinks, though, that she wants to sell her collection."

"Again, Howie?" Rumbin glanced at the preoccupied face of the assistant and showed some impatience. "Obstinance, Howie? Just because the lady-friend says 'instead'? Sell it? How could she? Who to? Who's that dumb? Nobody! So quit thinking foolish, Howie, and right away set them two Adam chairs nice decorative in front the Georchian mantelpiece. Mr. Hollins I don't expect till late this afternoon on his way from the office; but Mrs. Hollins putty certain comes in this morning, on account she knows the *petit point* on them chairs is rose and ivory. Tell Mrs. Hollins you got rose and ivory she don't never disappoint you, Georchie. Hand the little fat boy ice cream sprinkled from strawberries, will he eat it?"

CHAPTER TWENTY-EIGHT

ALMOST PUNCTUALLY Mrs. Hollins confirmed his diagnosis. Twenty minutes hadn't passed when the dealer rushed out to the sidewalk, helped her from her car and brought her volubly into the shop. The ideal client's wife's face was sprightly over an adornment of sables and orchids. She nodded graciously to Georgina and Howard, and immediately was charmed with the Adam pieces.

"You're very sly, Mr. Rumbin," she said, archly interrupting a discourse of his favorable to the chairs. "Sometimes I almost suspect you of buying things to aim at me because you think I'll fall for anything that's rose and ivory. I'll take them, though. Send them up to-morrow, please."

"Ah, Mrs. Kingsford J. Hollins, what a pleasure them chairs from now puts in your life and Mr. Hollins's!" Mr. Rumbin became softly insinuating.

"Speaking of Mr. Hollins, Mrs. Hollins, if he comes home to lunch courteously remind him I told him yesterday Rumbin Galleries got a pyootiful new masterpiece if he stops in this afternoon."

Mrs. Hollins looked self-conscious, also embarrassed, also secretly triumphant. "Well—I hardly think so, Mr. Rumbin." Then she seemed to change the subject rather abruptly. "You were so nice at Cousin Gertie's yesterday afternoon, Mr. Rumbin; we all appreciate it. You see, we felt that was the only way to get your unbiased opinion of her collection and—and settle the right price for it and—"

"Price?" Mr. Rumbin, agitated, had a dismal inspiration. "Unbiased? You wouldn't mean she worked my unbiased opinions by not telling me she's—she's selling?"

"Well—maybe a little like that," this somewhat irresponsible lady admitted. "I mean Mr. Hollins and Cousin Gertie and I all thought that'd be the best way. You see, Cousin Gertie's planning to go and live in California from now on—so of course if she could find somebody to take her art gallery off her hands and—"

"Off her hands? Somebody? Somebody *who,* Mrs. Hollins?"

"Well—" To cover her increased embarrassment Mrs. Hollins employed a rush of words. "I do think

it'd be lovely for people to have a complete collection like that, and everything all settled, instead
of pictures being collected one by one and keeping
the apartment stirred up all the time finding places
for new ones and moving everything all around
and—"

"Ooh, my!" Rumbin uttered a plaintive outcry.
"Please, Mrs. Hollins! I'm excited. Speak slow, Mrs.
Hollins. You're telling me—"

"No, no," she said hurriedly. "I really mustn't tell
you anything about it. Of course Mr. Hollins'll have
to let you know, himself, some day." Escaping from
Rumbin's unbearable eyes and her own too great
impulsiveness, she went hastily to the door; but, with
her hand on the latch, she paused to be archly con-
soling. "Mr. Hollins is a very shrewd man, Mr.
Rumbin; but don't you worry. *I'll* still be your customer anyhow—especially if you find me some more
chairs like these. Good day, Mr. Rumbin."

For once Mr. Rumbin didn't accompany her to
her car, being completely unable. With his hands
behind him he was feeling for something upon which
to sink; they found a love-seat, which creaked dan-
gerously as it received his weight.

Mr. Rumbin's two distressed helpers had often
known him to be in deep depression; but even in
those dark days when actual bankruptcy had hovered,

he was not like this. They had never seen him in a collapse so pathetic.

He spoke faintly. "Only little whiles ago I asks Howie who's so dumb enough buys the Strout-Webster collection. I got the answer. Mr. Hollins buys it—for a quotter million dollars. We lose him permanent. His wife says he's a very shrewd man."

"But you must go straight to him!" Georgina cried. "You must explain the whole thing, and, if he's already done it, you must insist on his canceling—"

"Canceling? On what grounds, Georchie? On the grounds he's so shrewd he's crazy? On the grounds I never says at Mrs. Strout-Webster's what him and her and Mrs. Hollins and Mrs. Georche Williams would all go in court and swear up and down I says it? What a worlt!" The unhappy man uttered moans, some of them coherent. "Asks me do a favor on a lady, tells me nothing so he gets my unbiased opinions —and look what he got! And for Rumbin Galleries no Fifty-sixt' Street now; we stays. Who done this to me, Georchie and Howie? Me! Makes me feel better I done it to myself?"

They tried to inflate him. "But you couldn't help it, Mr. Rumbin," Georgina said. "Mr. Hollins didn't give you a chance—no, nor himself, either!"

"No, the poor boob!" Thus in anguish Mr. Rumbin at last defined his ideal client. It seemed to do him a little good; he was able to raise his head. "Get him on the wire, Georchie," he said heavily. "Maybe by the time he answers, my lecks is strong enough to walk me far's the desk. Call me when."

"Yes, Mr. Rumbin," Georgina said; but when she called to him from the desk in the rear of the shop, a few moments later, it was not to summon him. "Mr. Hollins isn't in his offices, Mr. Rumbin; he's just gone out to the country and won't be back to-day."

"To the country, Georchie? *Ooh!* Not to Old Eastsfields?"

"I don't know, Mr. Rumbin. I asked where; but they said he didn't say."

"It's Old Eastsfields!" Suddenly the great bulk of the dealer heaved and undulated; desperately he got himself upon his feet. "It's to Old Eastsfields and he's just started. Georchie!" he cried. "Get me Mrs. Strout-Webster at Old Eastsfields quick's a cat, Georchie!"

"Mr. Rumbin!" Howard Cattlet exclaimed. "You'll tell her the truth? You'll tell her she mustn't—"

The dealer, his head up, was already striding toward the desk where Georgina was busy with the telephone. "I do what I can," he said.

Howard was enthusiastic. "Oh, I must say I think

this is splendid, Mr. Rumbin, and by far the best way to stop it—telling her the truth. If she's at all a conscientious woman it's the only possible—"

"Don't talk to me, Howie. My brains's commenced working like somebody under water that can't swim commences thinking can he learn his nose not to breathe so he won't drown and can act like a fish? Don't it needs silence when you're thinking how to safe your life and business and—"

"I've got the house," Georgina reported excitedly. "They're giving me the extension to her own room." Then she jumped up to let Rumbin sit at the desk. "Here she is," she whispered.

Rumbin seated himself, said, "Mrs. Strout-Webster?" in a dulcet voice, and his whole manner changed. He bowed, apparently to the desk; his rotund face wreathed itself in deferential smiles; his eyes were honeyed and his voice grew sweeter and sweeter. The two anxious listeners, primed for a heroic exposition of terrible truth, hung upon his every word; but hung with more and more amazement. What they heard didn't resemble what they expected.

"Mrs. Strout-Webster, it's Mr. Rumbin . . . Yesterday I was so excited enchoying myself in the vonderful collection I forgot to tell you such pictures like yours shouldn't get dusted with no cloths, no ordinary dusters—leafs scratches, so you should use just the softest feather duster. So excuse me calling up; but I thought I oughts . . . Oh, then I'm heppy you're pleased I'm doing so, Mrs. Strout-Webster . . . Yes, you want to ask me . . . Yes, I still think to-day the collection's just as unique's I says yesterday . . . Yes, more so, because thinking about it all night I wakes me up this morning thinking it's more uniquer than even I says to you yesterday . . . Yes, like you says, Mrs. Strout-Webster, them pyootiful pictures stays in the mind. So I think maybe two hundut fifty t'ousand—what, Mrs. Strout-Webster? . . . Listen serious, I'll tell you. Serious, Mrs. Strout-Webster, what you think your papa, that great connoisseur Mr. E. P. Strout, would says to you if now in heaven he hears you're talking his collection it's wort' only as little as two hundut fifty t'ousand dollars? What's a quotter million for Raphaels, Correggios, Titians, Tintorettos, Mrs. Strout-Webster, when only kind of lately just one single Raphael sells for probable over a million? . . . Thank you, Mrs. Strout-Webster. Frangkly speaking, again I'm heppy you're pleased I called up about dusting the pictures. Remember, only the softest feather duster . . . Yes, you're sweet, too, Mrs. Strout-Webster. Good-by."

He replaced the telephonic instrument decisively,

and rose, his manner again altered. His look was stern and inscrutable, as Georgina Horne waved incredulous open hands at him.

"Mr. Rumbin!" she cried. "I do honestly believe you've gone stark crazy!"

"Might be," he responded coldly. "Later we sees. Firstly, I'm anyways going eat me a pig lunch at Feydeau's."

Maintaining this new inscrutability, he went forth, walking determinedly, and, when he returned, toward three o'clock, he may have been aware that his arrival interrupted a helplessly prolonged discussion of him; but he deigned to offer no explanation of either his thoughts or his conduct. His mien was that of an iron statesman who pursues a course far above the comprehension of the multitude and holds to it though the populace snarls and his friends despair. He spoke upon routine matters only, and his high and rigid manner was still with him when Mr. Hollins's well-known automobile, covered with dust, stopped before the door, and Mr. Kingsford J. Hollins himself, looking disgusted, got out and strode into the shop.

"Rumbin," he said, "where's this picture you've been talking so much about? I'll take a look at it."

CHAPTER TWENTY-NINE

MR. RUMBIN betrayed no emotion. He bowed with reserve, turned to his assistant and said calmly, "Mr. Cattlet, put my new great painting upon the easel and get the reflector on it proper."

Then, with dignity, he led the way to the galleries. Mr. Hollins followed, and from the stock room Howard Cattlet brought a lovely Eighteenth Century English landscape. He placed it on the easel, and Mr. Hollins looked at the tablet.

"Richard Wilson? I've read something about him; but I forget. It's a nice-looking picture; but who was he?"

"Precursor," Mr. Rumbin quoted in a dispassionate voice. "Great precursor of all the English lentscape painters. Represented in all important museums and—"

"Never mind; I didn't ask for an oration!" Mr. Hollins, suddenly unable to contain an unreasonable indignation, turned upon Rumbin angrily. "I've had about plenty of your picture boosting these last two days! As if you hadn't done enough yesterday, sitting there clinking ice and guzzling liquor and gushing over Gertie Strout-Webster's collection! Do you know what it could have cost me? Then, on top of that, here you had to go and call her up again this morning and—"

"Excuse," Mr. Rumbin interrupted frigidly. "Natchly I done so, beings that you writes me I should do you a favor showing interest and politeness on Mrs. Strout-Webster's collection. Could I knowed it wouldn't please you I called her up on account scratches she should use a soft feather duster?"

"All right, all right!" the great patron exclaimed. "But see here, Rumbin! All I wanted was to get a plain statement of your unbiased judgment. I never dreamed you'd go slopping over the way you did about pictures you weren't selling, yourself!"

"Mr. Kingsford J. Hollins!" Mr. Rumbin's reproachful dignity became visibly noble. "It commences looking like you ain't been treating me execkly frangkly. Suspicions come my opinion was secret to settle if you acquires the collection, me beings deceived into talking like a childs all innocence in the dark. Could I be right in a such suspicions, Mr. Kingsford J. Hollins?"

"Well, you might be," the millionaire admitted, perhaps a little abashed for the moment. "It was the best way I could think of to—"

"What, Mr. Hollins? You didn't know me no better than to think I wouldn't leaned over beckworts to speak high of the collection because me beings too honorable to show I'm jealous in case your wife's maybe talked you into buying it, on account Mrs. Strout-Webster beings her Cousin Gertie and Mrs. Hollins don't like furniture getting moved around when pictures comes in one by one?"

"I don't question your motive's being honorable," the millionaire said irascibly. "But look what happened! Gertie Strout-Webster'd agreed that if you said her collection was worth as much as two hundred and fifty thousand dollars she'd turn it over to me at that figure. Yesterday afternoon, after your boosting, she was shifty about it; but, before Mrs. Hollins and I left, it was all set again—and then, when I went out there this noon to get it down on paper and signed, she went straight back on her word. Said her Raphael alone was worth more than two hundred and fifty thousand. Said she was practically giving me the collection. Said if I didn't raise the figure to three hundred and fifty thousand, at the very lowest, she knew her father in heaven would never forgive her and she'd rather present the collec-

tion to the town of Old Eastfield for a memorial
museum!"

"Fine Arts Museum?" Mr. Rumbin asked, with
an inimitably sly appearance of naiveté. "You think
that's better than costing you t'ree hundut fifty
t'ousand dollars to stop it, Mr. Hollins?"

This subtlety was lost upon the angry client. "Let
her build her old memorial! I walked out on her like
a shot, and it's a lesson to me never to try to do
business with a woman again or to pull off a deal in
pictures with an amateur. I called up my wife and
told her, and she's as sore on Gertie Strout-Webster
as I am. No, sir, no matter how fine a collection you
claim it is, Rumbin, I'm through with it! Now tell
me in plain words who was this Richard Wilson and
what you think this picture'd add to my collection."

Mr. Rumbin, suffused, told him. Mr. Hollins
crossly bought the picture, and departed.

Returned from bowing Mr. Hollins's car away
from the curb, Mr. Rumbin received congratulations,
embraced Georgina paternally and winked at
Howard over her shoulder. "Pig day! Georchie's a
nice girl, Howie!" he said embarrassingly, as he re-
leased her. "You like her, too, don't you, Howie?"
Not awaiting a reply, he changed the subject. "What
art dealer lesson works into your brains from all

Mr. Hollins Crossly Departed

these troubles Rumbin Galleries been having on account old E. P. Strout building him up a collection
that's now going to be Old Eastsfield's Memorial
Art Museum, Howie?"

"Lesson, sir?" Howard pondered. "I suppose—I
suppose perhaps it ought to teach me that if ever I'm
called upon for an opinion about anybody's pictures
it would be better to forget about tactfulness and just
straightforwardly say what I honestly think about—"

"No!" Mr. Rumbin was disappointed in him.
"That ain't the lesson. Look and listen, Howie.
Suppose we walks in to tea and liquors and ice and
cigars at Mrs. Strout-Webster's, and I'm eating her
gooses' liver sandwiches like I was, and she asks me
ain't it wort' quotter million dollars like she done,
should I says it ain't wort' quotter million hairs from
sick rabbits, it's a bum collection? No, because there's
everybody mad, and Mr. Hollins—answer me what
Mr. Hollins thinks about it, Howie? Answer me
that."

"He ought to have been grateful," Howard said.
"If you'd given him your opinion that the collection
wasn't worth anything, he ought to have been grateful that you'd saved him from throwing away two
hundred and fifty thousand dollars for nothing."

"Wouldn't," Mr. Rumbin returned promptly. "If
I act like that, all Mr. Hollins remembers is I

showed him up for a know-nothing about pictures
and a sucker all ready to sock himself quotter million
dollars for nothing, so he hates the sight of me! If he
acquires any more pictures he goes to some odda
dealer because he don't want never again to look at
my face, and don't want my face never again to look
at his. You get the lesson, Howie?"

"Well, sir, I don't know. I—"

"You don't? Again look and listen, Howie. Here
firstly I *did* safed Mr. Hollins from throwing away
quotter million dollars, and nextly safed him again
from knowing I safed him from it, because if he
knowed it he'd be mad at me just the same. So it's
got to be a secret. Look, too, how much good I done
Old Eastsfields, creating for the place a Fine Arts
Museum, because now she's got to build Old Eastsfields a building to put the pictures in and—"

"Wait a minute, sir," Howard interrupted.
"There's another thing puzzles me. If Mrs. Strout-
Webster builds this art gallery and puts her awful
pictures in it, with probably a director and a curator
or two in the outfit, why, the whole thing's a sham,
isn't it? Somebody'd be sure to expose—"

"Expose, no!" Mr. Rumbin laughed. "Old Eastsfields gets the pictures and the building and probable
a endowment, too. So it keeps the building, while the
endowment gradual buys some more pictures, nice

ones, and putty soon the director slides them E. P.
Strout pictures down cellar or maybe slips 'em into
auctions. It all works out good and's all owings to
how double-talking I protected Rumbin Galleries'
ideel client. You get the lesson yet, Howie?"

"Sir? Well, I—I—"

"Take it easy, Howie. Comes, but comes slow."
He put a hand upon his assistant's shoulder, winked
over that shoulder at Georgina. "All the better
you're Rumbin Galleries' Mascot just the same because it comes slow. You like him, too, don't you,
Georchie?" Again not awaiting a reply, Mr. Rumbin
continued, "Yes, she likes you too, and I like you,
and you like us, and on account next mont' in the
middle we're all t'ree going to move uptown into
New Rumbin Galleries on Fifty-sixt' Street I inwite
you, Georchie and Howie, to a little dinner half
past seven o'clock this evening at Feydeau's. Howie,
could you escort Georchie to this little dinner just
for the t'ree of us?"

"Yes, Mr. Rumbin," Georgina said. "Howard'll
bring me."

Howard was startled. This was the first time
Georgina'd ever used his first name in the presence
of Mr. Rumbin; but that wasn't the astonishing element in what she said. There were two causes for
breathlessness: one was her quietly taking it upon

herself to reply to Mr. Rumbin and the other was a difference in the quality of her voice. Strangely, this difference of tone, almost unbelievable to the ears of Howard Cattlet, seemed to be completely inaudible to Mr. Rumbin.

"Good," he said calmly. "Feydeau's seven-t'irty." Humming *Donna e Mobile,* he got his Homburg hat, his pearl-grey gloves and his pigskin-topped stick, and, having stopped for a moment to speak privately to Georgina at the desk, went forth to sign the lease for the New Rumbin Galleries on East Fifty-sixth Street.

It was closing time, and Georgina was putting the desk in order. "Georgina—" Howard said. "Georgina—"

"Yes?" Soft color was upon her cheeks and her grey eyes were kind—perhaps a heavenly bit more than kind. "Yes, Howard?"

Once more he remembered the abyss between their salaries. "Georgina, I—I'd better come for you about a quarter after seven, hadn't I?"

"Yes." She laughed feebly, as if at herself, and closed the lid of the desk with a slight bang. "About."

. . . The little dinner at Feydeau's was by candle-light. The candles had amber-colored silk shades, and

glowed softly upon the warm benignity of Mr. Rumbin, the gravity of Howard Cattlet and the ornamental loveliness of Georgina, who had received and wore
two bouquets; one of gardenias from Mr. Rumbin
and one of violets from her colleague in the shop. The
three ate caviar just in from Russia; they ate boneless
terrapin from Philadelphia; they ate snails lately
from France; they ate English sole, artichokes, a
salad dedicated to Mr. Rumbin by Feydeau himself,
mixed cheeses, mixed ices and mixed fruits. Mr.
Rumbin, strangely delighted to have all these, and
three types of wine, inside him, added coffee to them
with gusto and drew bravely upon his exotic long
cigar.

"So at last comes it's a new life Rumbin Galleries
is now going into," he said, beamingly serious. "From
now on we look beck on the little place in Seventeent'
Street like we wonder we could ever enchoyed ourselfs there; yet sometimes might be we'd miss the
little shop. You think maybe so, Georchie and
Howie?"

"Yes," Georgina said, and her eyes were wistful.
"We'll miss it sometimes, Mr. Rumbin—maybe we'll
even wish ourselves back there."

"No, no, Georchie. Missing but not wishing ourselfs beck. We had good luck there, and plenty excitement; but now on Fifty-sixt' Street ain't it going

to be more so? Why? Because now we got the experience that learns us how to keep excitements turning into good luck. Ain't that what pushes a art dealer up in the worlt? My, what a pyootiful business! Ain't it?"

"Yes, it is, Mr. Rumbin," Georgina responded. "I don't see how anybody that's once been in it could ever bear to be in anything else."

"No?" Mr. Rumbin laughed. "Howie he's just sitting. Don't speaks a wort."

"Sir? No, I—I was just thinking. I mean I'm not sure I *am* in the business, because I don't yet feel I'll ever know enough to—"

"No?" Mr. Rumbin's fat laughter continued. "That ain't all you're thinking, Howie. I know the rest of what you're thinking and I'll speak to you about it private by-and-by."

"Sir? I only—"

"No, let it go till by-and-by, Howie." Through the thin smoke of his cigar Mr. Rumbin looked at the young man indulgently. "Wait and I fix it for you. Now this minute I'm talking about your not knowing enough. Well, who does? Nobody. Nobody can't know enough. Ain't I frequence says to you that's what puts the glam—What's this wort?—glamishness. That's what puts the glamishness about it, Howie. Who could know all art from when it commences up to now? Besides, what is it, anyhow?"

"Art, sir? What's art? You told me yourself that's something an art dealer doesn't need to know, Mr. Rumbin."

"No, he don't; but he can speckalate about it, Howie. So, well, what is it? What's art from the time some feller's got hairs growing all over him but no clothing scratches a picture on a piece of bone up to now when some odda feller's got him a fency suit and paints a nice watch hanging doubled over the edge of a table like it's made of soft candy? It's a art dealer's business to hendle art; but art ain't no business. Art's the only thing that people make that ain't a business. Anything elst they make—shoes, automobiles, telescopes, lawyers' books, cough medicine, breakfast rolls, saddles for sitting on horses— making it's a business. So art's something you can't say what, exceptings making it ain't no business and it's the only thing in the uniwerse that making it ain't. Ain't it so?"

His listeners, impressed, considered this thought; but Georgina found an objection. "What about architecture, Mr. Rumbin? It's one of the Fine Arts, and architects make buildings. That's a business, isn't it?"

Mr. Rumbin wouldn't admit it. "No, it's a builder builds the buildings. The art a architect's got inside him, it's like poetry and painting; he would make it in his mind, or drawings maybe, whether it was ever going to get builded into a building or not. Just the same like the poet's going to write it whether it gets printed or not. No, still I'm right; art's the only thing that people make that ain't a business. You see it, Howie?"

"I'm not sure, sir; because artists certainly sell their—"

"Sells it, yes, maybe; but sells it no or yes, he anyways makes it, even if sometimes he only makes it in his mind. Can't help it. Why can't he help it? On account he'd be unheppy if he didn't. So it must be he makes it to get heppiness whiles he's making it. Look at all great paintings even if they're sad ones, and ain't it so? No matter about what comes when the artist finishes 'em, he got away from unheppiness whiles he was painting 'em. Look at Rembrandt, a sad old man painting some odda sad old man, both of 'em poor and maybe coughing, got beckaches. Wasn't Rembrandt saying to himself, 'Pyootiful! Pyootiful how the light smiles along that wrinkle from this poor old feller's eye, and pyootiful how I just slid that light onto the canvas!' So anyways even if nobody can't say what elst art is, it's got

heppiness in it. So then, after all, Howie, what's a
art dealer's business?"

"Sir? Well, you've told me again and again it's
knowing human nature, in the first place, and—"

"Phooey! Phooey!" the exalted Rumbin exclaimed. "Phooey on all what I told you! Forget it.
Commence over, Howie, because ain't I just proved
a art dealer's business is selling heppiness? Art ain't
heppiness, I don't says so; but it's in it. Or why
would people build pig stone museums for centuries
and where would there be any collectors? Would
they do it to make themselfs feel bad? No, it's a art
dealer's business to place heppiness in permanent
collections at the nicest profit he can. The artist
makes the heppiness, and the dealer spreads it over
the worlt to the people that's got abilities enough to
enchoy it. So, then, what's the history of art-
heppiness?"

"Sir?"

"Look and listen; I'll tell you," Mr. Rumbin said,
and, in his own way, he did.

He returned to his savage happily absorbed in
scratching upon a piece of bone; spoke of Crô-
Magnon pleasure in cave murals, of the delight that
must have been felt by the earliest Mediterranean
carvers in stone, by Egyptian and Chinese and Greek
sculptors and painters. He dwelled upon Byzantine

enamelers and their joy in baking miraculous pastes upon gold; his unctuous voice lingered fondly upon the Gothic sculptors, and ivory and wood carvers, and workers in stained glass. He was eloquent upon the joy of the great Venetian colorists in their painting, and insisted that the more serious Florentines had an even profounder pleasure in their work.

Thus, after dilating long upon the Seventeenth Century Dutch artists, merriest of all at their easels —for how could Frans Hals with four strokes of a brush have flicked living laughter upon canvas and not been merry!—Mr. Rumbin skimmed lightly over the Eighteenth Century, English and French, and came to rest, so to speak, upon the verbal jocosities of Whistler. Georgina and Howard, willingly convinced, agreed that it was an art dealer's business to spread happiness over the world, and, becomingly flushed with this agreeable conviction, Georgina went to the ladies' coat-room for her wrap.

"Now I tell you what a whiles ago I says you was thinking, and spread a little more heppiness, Howie," Mr. Rumbin said, as they waited in the small lobby for Georgina. "At New Rumbin Galleries middle next mont' your celery is raised execkly one hundut per cent; it's doubled." Then, as Howard began to try to thank him, the dealer waved gratitude aside. "No, no; it only makes your celery the same as

Georchie's is up to now. Tell her about it whiles
you're on the way taking her home, Howie."

Georgina joined them; they went out to the street,
and Mr. Rumbin stepped into a taxicab. "Couldn't I
take you both?" he asked, before he closed the door.
"Wouldn't you like——"

"No, it isn't far," Georgina said. "I think I'd
rather walk, if Howard doesn't mind."

"He don't," Mr. Rumbin assured her, laughed
and added, as farewell, "Don't forget to tell her
about the celery, Howie!" Then, as he was borne
away, they saw his bright eyes twinkling at them
through the glass of the window.

. . . "He meant my salary," Howard explained.
He and Georgina had turned from the lighted door-
way of Feydeau's and begun to walk slowly toward
Georgina's apartment.

"Yes, Howard, I understood. I didn't think he
meant the celery we had for dinner."

Howard was cast down. "You're laughing at me,
of course, as usual."

"No, I'm not," she said, and he saw that she
wasn't; yet he remained gloomy.

"Georgina, what Mr. Rumbin meant was that he's
just told me he's raising my salary so that after we
move uptown it'll be the same as yours has been

until now. Of course he's raised yours, too, corre-spondingly; so I suppose we might congratulate each other."

"No," she said gently. "Just before Mr. Rumbin left the shop this afternoon he told me he wasn't going to raise mine."

"What?"

"Yes. So, you see, you can't congratulate me; but of course I can congratulate you. So I do."

"Oh!" Howard said. "Oh!" For some moments, as they walked along together, he was deeply thoughtful; then, moving even more slowly, he was sad no longer but breathless. Georgina's profile, be-side his shoulder, was noncommittal but of an un-earthly loveliness in the Rembrandt chiaroscuro of a New York side street at night. "Georgina, are you— are you disappointed? Georgina, are you sorry he didn't raise your salary?"

"No."

"Georgina—" Howard said. "Georgina, I've waited a—a long time to—to ask you if you think you ever could—ever could—"

"Yes, I ever could," she said. "You're right about it's having been a long time, Howard."

. . . Mr. Rumbin, enclosed, moving in noisy traffic on Seventh Avenue, was also becomingly in chiaroscuro, as vari-colored oblongs of light swept across him, shaped by the windows of his taxicab. He lighted another cigar, drew upon it, and, in high content with himself and with life and business, murmured a single word. "Heppiness!"

He did not dwell upon this word, however. Already his mind was busy with Mr. Kingsford J. Hollins and Mr. Milton Wilby.

Lightning Source UK Ltd.
Milton Keynes UK
UKOW04f1938071113

220657UK00001B/29/P